有限公司
g Ltd.

管理人英語

4週養成計劃！

28項管理精要＋全面提升英語力

由【辦公室管理】、【組織行為】、【處理管理】等...5大管理主題，
延伸出 28 件管理個案、28 種經驗分享和 28 個管理小偏方，
4 週就能速成管理人英語！

資深 **CFO** 執筆＋全書 **中英左右對照**
成為管理階層憑藉的是 **努力＋能力**
【欲】成為專業管理人憑藉的是更全方位的 **領導能力＋英語力**

📖 由28【例】個案
迅速掌握28項關鍵英語 力

> 面對各式情境~
> 更能運用自如

> 處理各種職場疑難~
> 更能知彼知己、立於不敗

📖 由28個經驗與分享
迅速融入職場 百態

📖 由 個管理小偏方
迅速駕馭管理 眉角

> 面臨管理課題~
> 更能深得人心

WEEK 03
WEEK 02
WEEK 01
WEEK 04

黃啟銘◎著

作 者 序

『管理來自工作中，學習就在生活上。』從實務的工作當中，體會到管理上的技巧和精神，用貼近生活的實例，練習著朗朗上口的英文詞句，沒有深奧難解的理論，不用艱澀繞口的詞彙，自然輕鬆地學習英文，深入淺出的體驗管理，這就是本書希望和所有管理人分享的目標。

本書選材自二十八個管理上的實例，是筆者多年來實務管理工作上所接觸到，最真實的場景，相信許多管理人也會有類似的經歷和體驗。透過淺顯生動的情境對白，讀者不單可以練習到生活化的英文，以及所衍生的詞句運用；更可以從實例中咀嚼到一些管理上的概念和技巧，和管理人本身的經驗相呼應，或有所學習。

在每個單元之後，筆者就和該實例相關管理上的議題，提供一些個人的經驗和分享；最後也已該議題所引用的管理理論、知識或專有名詞，提供給讀者進一步的參考。期許本書能做為管理人實務而好用的英文學習手札。

黃啟銘

編 者 序

　　管理是門高深的學問，在各個層面上也考驗著學習者對人、事和物的拿捏，也非短時間就能速成。《管理學四週英語養成計畫》以個案、經驗分享和管理人小偏方為主體，在理論和實務上做了更多的結合。作者在個案中鮮明的描繪出各個角色與管理者之間的互動和多樣化的相處方式，體現出更逼真的管理內容。在經驗分享中像是辦公室手則等，更提供讀者許多實用資訊。而管理小偏方中更包含許多管理人必備小常識，能在管理上更為駕輕就熟而有更好的拿捏。

倍斯特編輯群

目　次

Section I.　Office Administration

Section II. Organizational Behavior

Section III.　Processing Management

Section IV. Leadership

Section V. Special issues in Management

Section 1

Office Administration

1-1 Don't Smoke in the Office
別在辦公室內抽菸

 Conversation 情境對話

Jennifer **frowned** sitting in front of the computer, while Amanda, next to Jennifer, uncomfortably cover the nose and mouth by hand. The office **filled with** a faint smoky flavor

珍妮佛坐在電腦前面皺起了眉頭，而旁邊的阿曼達難過的用手遮住了口鼻；辦公室裡隱約瀰漫著一股煙味。

They **couldn't stand** finally, and went to the manager's office **furiously**. A minute later, the manager went to the reception area of the office.

兩人終於受不了了，氣沖沖的跑到經理室內。不到一分鐘後，經理走向了辦公室的會客區。

Robert was **livid**: "The air here seems not so good. What's going on? "	經理面有難色的說：「這邊的空氣似乎不太好，到底怎麼回事？」
Alex **puzzled** and asked: "Really? Our central air conditioning works very smoothly."	亞歷不解的問著：「會嗎？空調的運作很順暢啊！」

George put out the cigarette in hand **implicitly**, indicated to others, and then said: "Just a little bit of smoke, and will be **dissipated** very soon. It should be okay! "

喬治偷偷地熄掉手上的菸,再用手示意著其他人;然後他接著說:「就一點點菸味啦,很快就會散掉的,應該還好啦!」

And then all others there **put out** the cigarettes **reluctantly**.

其他人也不情願地將手上的菸熄掉了。

Robert: "Didn't you see the 'no smoking' mark that **puts up** in the wall of office? The company regulation had been prescribed that no smoking in the office, isn't it? "

經理:「你們沒看到辦公室牆上貼著『禁止吸菸』的標示嗎?公司早就規定不要在辦公室內抽菸的,不是嗎?」

George: "You know that, Rob. When the **craving** comes, we just customary lit a cigarette to smoke. This is a help in our thinking and a boost that will make our conservation more harmonious.

喬治:「經理,你是知道:當菸癮來的時候,就習慣性的點起了菸來抽,這可以幫助我們思考,也能幫助我們的談話更融洽。」

Robert: "But, have you ever think of that this will affect the health of other people, who have to endure the stench taste you made? Many of our colleagues have complained to me."

經理:「但是,你們就不會想到這會影響到其他人健康,還必須要忍受你們所給予的惡臭味道嗎?已經有好多同事在跟我抱怨了。」

Alex **muttered**: "But just a cigarette strike. Are there so serious? "

亞歷喃喃自語的說：「就抽根菸罷！有這麼嚴重嗎？」

Robert pretend **stern**: "Or, why don't you do this? You all go together into the small meeting room, **shut** the door **down,** and smoke after work today. No one can leave only after he has been continuously smoking of five cigarettes."

經理假裝很嚴肅的說：「不然這樣吧！今天下班後，你們就一起到小會議室裡抽菸，把門關上，每個人得連續抽完五根香菸後才能離開。」

These guys all revealed fear and **embarrassment**, and were scared speechless.

一群人臉上露出了驚恐和尷尬，都嚇得說不出話來。

Robert: "I believe that respect for others is a basic courtesy, especially when we're working partners. **Do unto others, do not impose on others**. So, don't smoke in the office anymore. "

經理：「我相信尊重別人，是種基本的禮貌，何況大家都是工作的夥伴；己所不欲、勿施於人，以後別在辦公室裡抽菸了。」

Vocabulary 字彙解析

■ **frown** *n., vi., vt.* 皺眉、愁眉苦臉

〔同義詞：**scowl, glower, glare**〕

He **frowned** as he reread the letter.

She **frowned** at him defiantly

■ **furiously** *adv.* 憤怒地、狂暴地

〔同義詞：**angry, indignant**〕

She worked **furiously** to build up the business.

He became **furiously** angry.

■ **livid** *adj.* 鐵青的、激怒的

〔同義詞：**angry, ashen, purplish**〕

He was **livid** at being left out.

I slopped the stuff on the **livid** timbers of our bench.

■ **puzzled** *adj. vt.* 困惑的、迷茫的

〔同義詞：**confused, perplexed**〕

The questioners were met with **puzzled** looks.

One remark he made **puzzled** me.

■ **implicitly** *adv.* 暗中的、含蓄的、絕對的

〔同義詞：**utterly, tacitly, absolutely**〕

She **implicitly** suggested that he was responsible for the error.

He trusted Sarah **implicitly**.

■ **dissipate** *vi., vt.* 消散、浪費、放蕩

〔同義詞：**scatter, squander, fritter away**〕

The cloud of smoke **dissipated**.

He had **dissipated** his entire fortune.

■ **reluctant**   *radj.*   勉強的、不情願、捨不得

〔同義詞：**unwilling, disinclined, unenthusiastic**〕

She seemed **reluctant** to discuss the matter.

The rural community was **reluctant** to abandon the old ways.

■ **craving**   *n.*   欲望、意願

〔同義詞：**desire, longing, yearning**〕

It's a **craving** to work in the dirt with your bare hands.

Miranda felt a wistful **craving** for the old days.

■ **mutter**   *vt., vi.*   喃喃而語、低語、抱怨

〔同義詞：**mumble, murmur, complain**〕

He **muttered** something under his breath.

Nina **muttered** an excuse and hurried away.

■ **stern**   *adj.*   嚴肅的、嚴厲的

〔同義詞：**serious, solemn, severe**〕

A smile transformed his **stern** face.

My father was very **stern**.

■ **embarrassment**   *n.*   窘困、羞愧、尷尬

〔同義詞：**mortification, humiliation, shame**〕

I turned red with **embarrassment**.

They suffered the **embarrassment** of losing in the opening

Phrase in sentence 片語和句型解析

■ **fill with** 充滿、瀰漫

〔同義詞：**make full, fill up, penetrate**〕

I filled up the bottle with water.

The shrapnel had filled with his head and chest.

■ **cannot stand** 受不了、不堪

〔同義詞：**cannot bear, be unequal to**〕

It seemed that we cannot stand such pain.

He couldn't stand even a tray of brimming glasses.

■ **put out** 熄掉、撲滅

〔同義詞：**extinguish, exterminate, stamp out**〕

Since his first full season in 1997, he leads center fielders in putouts and assists.

Firemen were soaking everything to put out the blaze.

■ **put up** 張貼、搭建、設置

〔同義詞：**post, set up, install**〕

A curt notice had been put up on the door.

We're planning to put up a new shower.

■ **shut down** 關閉、關門

〔同義詞：**close up, shutdown, closed door**〕

The temporary shutdowns will affect 8,000 workers.

Many hospitals now face very high possibility of shutting down.

Do unto others, do not impose on others：己所不欲、勿施於人

∞ Practice in Management

Interpersonal relationships refer to the social relationship of interdependent and interrelation among the interaction of social groups. In the workplace, they include the relationships between employers and employees, leaders and subordinates, colleagues, and even friends. Interpersonal relationships have a significant impact not only on the emotion, life, and work of individual, but also on the organizational climate, communication, operation, and efficiency.

In the workplace, for some people, often the deviant behavior and disrespect to others either verbally or non-verbally are attributed to the habits and self-awareness, such as office smoking, littering, exposure, frivolous language and actions, and etc. Most of these behaviors may be just mild or occasional, but they would make others uncomfortable and stressful. Many companies then had set up their "office code" in order to facilitate the management.

More serious deviant behaviors in office are **workplace bullying** and **sexual harassment**. Such situations are usually vague, but negative and will seriously affect the overall management of the organization and harmony. Managers must have a complete and careful control measure. Whenever such an incident occurs, it needs to be decisively handled to avoid great damage.

經驗與分享

人際關係是指社會人群中因交往而構成的相互依存和相互聯繫的社會關係；在職場上，包括了僱傭關係、領導與被領導關係、同事，甚至是朋友關係等。人際關係對每個人的情緒、生活、工作都有很大的影響，甚至對組織氣氛、溝通、運作、與效率均有極大的影響。

在工作場合裡，經常有些人，會因著自我的習慣和認知，出現一些偏差、或不尊重別人的行為或言語，例如辦公室內吸菸、亂丟垃圾、暴露、輕挑的語言和動作等，雖然大部分都是輕微或偶發的，卻會帶給別人得不舒服和困擾，因此許多公司也會訂定其『辦公室守則』，以利管理。

在辦公室裡較為嚴重的偏差行為，當屬**職場霸凌**與**性騷擾**了：這類的情況經常是較為模糊，但卻是負面不良、而會嚴重影響整體組織的管理與和諧，管理者必須在事先有完備而謹慎的防制措施，每當事件發生時，要果斷的處理，以免造成更大的破壞。

Tips in Management

Workplace bullying

Workplace bullying, refers to individuals or groups who react to colleagues or subordinates unreasonably in the workplace, and this includes verbal, nonverbal, physical, and psychological acts of abuse or humiliation. Generally, the types of workplace bullying can be classified as:

Threats of professional status

Including belittle the views of the parties, professional humiliation in public, blaming the parties for lack of effort, and the use of disciplinary procedures for intimidate or punish.

Threats of personal status

Including the destruction of personal credit, destructive innuendo and sarcasm, making inappropriate jokes targeting, ongoing teasing, name calling, insults, intimidation, and threats.

Isolation

Including preventing the opportunity of visitation, the physical or social isolation, and conceal the necessary information.

Excessive fatigue

Including unnecessary stress, impossible deadlines, and unnecessary interference.

Unstable management

Including non-recognition of good work, assignments meaningless, shirkers, repeatedly reminded mistakes, fail in goals setting, and modifying team goals without notice to the parties.

管理小偏方

職場霸凌

職場霸凌，泛指在工作場所裡，個人或團體對於同事或是下屬進行不合理的霸凌行為。包含言語、非言語、身體、心理上的虐待或羞辱。一般職場霸凌的型態如下：

專業地位的威脅：

包括貶低當事人的意見，公開進行專業上屈辱，指責當事人缺乏努力，恐嚇使用紀律或懲處程序。

個人地位的威脅：

包括破壞個人信用，破壞性的影射和諷刺，進行不適當的笑話目標，持續的戲弄、對罵、侮辱、恐嚇、威脅。

隔離：

包括阻止訪問的機會，身體或社會隔離，隱瞞必要的信息。

疲勞轟炸：

包括不必要的壓力，不可能達成的最後期限，不必要的干擾。

不穩定的管理：

包括不承認良好的工作，毫無意義的任務分配，卸責，反覆提醒失誤， 設定目標失敗，更動團隊目標而卻瞞著當事人。

1-2 Repeated Lateness
總是遲到

 Conversation 情境對話

It's almost nine thirty. Jenny stepped hurriedly into the office, and then **rushed** to her seat in panic, so that she wasn't even aware that the manager's passing by. Then, the assistant Daphne, just appeared unexpectedly in the office after Jenny.

時鐘都快走到九點半了；這時珍妮才匆匆忙忙地踏進了辦公室，慌張得趕往自己的坐位方向去，連經理擦身而過了都沒察覺到。但沒想到，跟在珍妮的後頭，助理戴芬妮這時才出現在辦公室裡。

Robert felt annoyed about these situations, and talked to both Jenny and Daphne in that afternoon.

羅柏對於這情況感到有些苦惱，當天午後就把珍妮和戴芬妮找了過來。

Robert: "I know you two were very late to work today, and always late during this period of time. Such a situation is not so good. Are there any problems for you two?"

經理：「我知道今天兩位很晚才進到辦公室來，而且這陣子似乎經常性的遲到，這情況可不太好，是否有什麼困難嗎？」

Jenny **blushed** with shame: "I'm really sorry, Robert. I knew this might cause your trouble. I did try to come to work on time, but..."

珍妮羞愧的漲紅著臉説：「實在很抱歉，羅柏，我知道這會帶給你困擾。我也想盡可能準時上班，但是……」

Robert: "I could understand that you had been **dedicated** on job. But, **after all**, the issue of your regular lateness is needed to be **confronted with** and solved."

經理：「珍妮，我了解妳在工作表現上，一直都是很盡心盡力的，但妳經常遲到的情況，總是要正視和解決的。」

Jenny: "My family and I moved to the remote countryside a while ago. I've got to catch the earliest bus everyday, to be at work on time. I do value my work a lot, but just don't know what to do."

珍妮説：「前一陣子我家搬到較偏僻的鄉間，每天必須要趕上最早的巴士，才能準時到辦公室來；我是很珍惜現在的工作，但不知道怎麼辦才好？」

Robert: "Oh, I see! Some other colleagues seem to have similar problems. **So be it**, I'll try to discuss with the executives regarding this issue. It might be applied in a way like 'flexible working hours' to solve this problem. But the basic **premise** is that it can't affect the regular operation of our organization."

經理：「喔，原來如此，有些同仁似乎也有類似的困擾！這樣吧，我再跟公司討論這個議題，或許是用『彈性上班時間』之類的方式，來解決這個困擾，但前提是，不能影響到公司業務的推動的。」

Meanwhile, Daphne looked impatient and said: "Excuse me, Robert. Could I please leave early today?"

這時戴芬妮神情有些急躁地說：「不好意思，羅柏，我今天可不可以早點離開辦公室呢？」

Robert said with an unpleasant countenance: "Daphne, you've not only shown up late regularly, but also requested for an early leave. I can't feel that you do care about this job. So, what's your situation?"

聽到這話，經理臉色有些不悅的說：「戴芬妮，妳不但經常遲到，還要要求早退，我似乎感覺不到妳是很在乎這份工作的；那妳的情況又是怎麼了？」

Daphne felt sad and **innocent**: "I'm sorry, but I did not mean to. It's because that I study in the night college, and need to **go off** work from office on time to catch the class there. The courses are so late and I sometimes just can't wake up in time, that's why..."

戴芬妮哀怨又無辜的說：「非常抱歉，但我不是故意的；因為我晚上在大學夜間部上課，所以必須要準時下班才能趕得上學校的課；且每天課上到很晚，有時候早上都爬不起來，所以……」

Robert: "But your work has been affected. I think, maybe you need to make a choice between work and class."

經理：「但妳的工作已經受到影響了，我想或許妳必須在工作和學業上，做一個選擇！」

Daphne was anxious and almost **cried out**: "I can't quit my class suddenly. But I also like my colleagues here, and it's very happy to work here. What I got to do?"

戴芬妮急得快哭了出來，說：「現在我不能突然放棄課業，但是我也很喜歡這裡的同事，能在這裡工作是很快樂的事！這該怎麼辦？」

Robert frowned and **distressed**: "It's really a problem. It might be workable **only if you** changed the hiring status as a part-time **dispatch**, and then re-adjust your job title and work hours. But I have to discuss with the executives, too."

經理眉頭深鎖，面有難色的說：「這可就是個難題了；除非是重新調整妳的職稱和工作時間，改以兼職派遣的方式聘用，或許還可行，但這我也要一併和公司方面討論一下吧！」

Vocabulary 字彙解析

rush *vi., n.* 趕緊、急忙行事、衝鋒

〔同義詞：**hurry, dash, pressed for time**〕
Jason rushed after her.
He rushed to the stronghold.

blushing *adj.* 靦腆的、臉紅的

〔同義詞：**bashful, embarrassed, ashamed**〕
Don't be blushful about telling folks how you feel.
I was pretty blushing at school.

dedicated *adj.* 專心的、忠心的

〔同義詞：**honest and just, upright, devoted**〕
He was a dedicated husband.
This hospital has a team of dedicated doctors.

premise *vt., vi., n.* 前提、預述

〔同義詞：**precondition, presupposition**〕
If the premise were true, then the conclusion must be true.
The reforms were premised on our findings.

innocent *adj.* 無辜的、合法的

〔同義詞：**childlike, affirmed, allowable**〕
His action is proved as the arbitrary execution of an innocent man.
She speaks with an innocent directness.

distressed *adj.* 苦惱的、哀傷的、窘困的

〔同義詞：**vexed, grieved, awkward**〕
I was distressed at the news of his death.
I didn't mean to distress you.

dispatch *vt., vi., n.* 調度、派遣

〔同義詞：**despatch, manage. send**〕

He dispatched messages back to base.
Congress dispatched the task to the agency.

Phrase in sentence 片語和句型解析

▪ look over 查看、翻閱

〔同義詞：**examine, browse, turn over**〕
The doctor looked over me and said I might need a caesarean.
He stopped to look over a sporting goods store.

▪ after all 畢竟、終究

〔同義詞：**eventually, actually, at last**〕
The largest firms may after all become unstoppable.
After all he arrived to join us.

▪ so be it 就這樣吧、只好如此

〔同義詞：**so be, that's all**〕
We have no other choice, so be it!
So be it, that's the final conclusion.

▪ go off 離開、跑掉、中斷

〔同義詞：**depart, run away, become unavailable**〕
He went off as hard as he could lick.
Just as the operation was going on the lights went off.

▪ cry out 喊叫、嚎叫

〔同義詞：**shout, outcry, howl, yell**〕
She cried out only for joy.
Mom took Anna away, cried her out for her bad behavior.

▪ only if 才、除非

〔同義詞：**unless, only when, only in the case that**〕
Only if you have a photographic memory, repetition is vital.
Saturday is not the day only if I got my hair done.

Practice in Management

Employees' **lateness** and **leave early**, for managers, are usually trivial but troublesome, and this situation can be easily disregarded or ignored at the very beginning. However, without a better control system, and then over time, the order and discipline of the office will be affected, resulting a common atmosphere of idleness and indifference. Furthermore, this will result in the overall low morale and productivity.

Cases of the regular lateness (or leave early) of employees, need for a special concern are the key to understand the problems and particular causes and figure out the solutions and improvements timely. Sometimes, regular lateness for work might be caused by the particularly reasons, and even a very common phenomenon. Managers need to explore the arrangement of working hours or location, and consider the necessity of adjustment. Some companies will focus on the need of staffs to adopt the "**flexible working time**" approach, in which employees can have a more convenient environment and comfortable emotions at work. However, before the implementation of this policy, we should consider whether it will affect the overall operation, and the problem of task convergence, and also try to avoid becoming the exception.

Another flexible adjustment method is the use of "**dispatched workers**" or part-time placement. This is for certain employees unable to work full-time, or the job position is a must, but it is routine, simple operation without affecting the company's core operations. In general, for dispatch workers or part-time positions, the company can significantly reduces on the burden of payroll and employee benefits, and is currently widely used model.

經驗與分享

員工的**遲到**與**早退**，對於管理者而言，通常是非常瑣碎而煩雜的事件，這種情況在剛開始也很容易被漠視或忽略，但若沒有一個良好的制度和管控，日積月累之後，辦公室的秩序和紀律受到影響，且導致一種普遍懶散的風氣，進而讓整體的士氣和工作效率低落。

員工若是經常性的遲到〔或早退〕，特別要去關心，以了解其原因和問題所在，並及時的解決和改善；有些時候，遲到是因為特殊性的原因所造成的，甚至是很普遍的現象，就需要去探討工作時段或地點的安排，是否需要調整；有些公司會針對員工需要，採用『**彈性工作時間**』的方式，讓員工能有個更方便的環境、與自在的工作情緒；但在實施這個政策前，應考慮是否會影響到整體業務的運作、及任務銜接的問題，並且盡量避免淪為特例。

另一種彈性的調整方式，就是採用『**派遣工**』或是兼職性質的職位安排；這是針對某些員工無法全時段的投入工作，或者該工作雖是必須的，但卻是例行、簡單操作而不影響到公司的核心營運；一般而言，對於派遣工或兼職的職務，公司在薪資和員工福利的負擔上較為減輕，目前也是普遍被採用的模式。

Tips in Management

Flextime System

Flextime (also spelled flexitime, flexi-time) is a variable work schedule, in contrast to traditional work arrangements requiring employees to work a standard 9 a.m. to 5 p.m. day. Under flextime, there is typically a core period (of approximately 50% of total working time / working day) of the day, when employees are expected to be at work (for example, between 11 a.m. and 3 p.m.), while the rest of the working day is "flexible time" in which employees can choose when they work, subject to achieving total daily, weekly or monthly hours in the region of what the employer expects, and subject to the necessary work being done.

A flextime policy allows staff to determine when they will work, while a flexplace policy allows staff to determine where they will work. Advantages include allowing employees to adopt their work hours to public transport schedules, to the schedules their children have, and that road traffic will be less congested, more spread out.

管理小偏方

彈性上班時間

彈性工作制（或稱為彈性工作時間）是一種可變通的工作時程，這不同於傳統的標準上，要求員工固定上午9點工作到下午5點天的工作安排。在彈性工作制當中，一天當中通常有一段核心工作週期（約佔美日總工作時數的50％），將所有員工都安排在工作當中（例如，上午11點和下午3點之間），而其餘的部分即是"彈性時間"，讓員工可以選擇其工作時段，以達到雇主所設定其每天、每週或每月總時數的預期範圍，並完成必要的工作。

彈性上班時間的政策，允許員工決定其工作的時間，而彈性工作地點的政策，則允許員工決定他們將在那裡工作。其優點在於讓員工調整自己的工作時間，以配合大眾運輸的時間表，及他們孩子的時間，且避開交通尖峰時段，分散交通擁擠的情況。

1-3 What a Messy Meeting
凌亂的會議流程

 ## Conversation 情境對話

It's 9:15 A.M. Time for a routinely construction progress meeting had already begun. A crowd of staff just rushed into the meeting room hastily. In the empty meeting room, it was only Robert there alone, who cleaned up the **clutter** on table and waited for others.

九點十五分，例行性工程進度會議的時間早已開始了，一行人才匆忙的趕到會議室內；這時空蕩蕩的會議室內，只有羅柏一人，一邊收拾著桌上的雜務，一邊靜靜的等待著大家。

Robert: "Since everyone is here finally. Let's take a look at what subjects we need to discuss with. Huh, Janet. Where's our **agenda**?"

經理：「大家總算都到了，就先看看我們今天會議要討論的議題吧！咦？珍娜！我們會議的議程表呢？」

When everyone **looks around**, Janet anxiously runs into the meeting room and sits down in panic. The colleague aside **drops** her **a hint**: "Agenda!"

正當大家東張西望的同時，這會兒珍娜才急呼呼的跑進了會議室，慌張的坐了下來；一旁的同事暗示著她：「議程表呢？」

Janet's brain suddenly went blank and was **unprepared**: "No, I didn't print it out!"

珍娜腦筋頓時一片空白，不知所措的說：「沒有，我沒有印出來耶！」

Robert felt frustrated and said: "Well, we might just adopt the file in my notebook, then figure out through the **projector**. Let's look at the screen to discuss."

經理有些無奈的說：「那就用我電腦裡的檔案，透過投影機放映出來，我們就看著螢幕來討論好了。」

Janet's ashamed: "I'm sorry. The projector had been **out of order**, and not yet repaired."

珍娜紅著臉說：「不好意思，投影機上週就已經壞了，目前還沒修好。」

Robert's speechless and put up with: "It's all right. Our meeting still needs to go on. What we can use is the **verbal** discussion. Now, John! We had mentioned in the last meeting for the problem of the serious construction delay in the pipeline area. How's the situation improvement going now?"

經理有些無言以對，只好將就的說：「好吧，會議還是要進行，只好用口頭討論的方式進行了。約翰，上次會議提及管線區工程進度嚴重落後的問題，現在改善的情況如何？」

John: "Well, I'm not sure! I didn't receive the agenda, and didn't recognize it's under our discussion today. That's why I didn't check it out yet."

約翰：「喔，我還不太確定！我還沒收到議程表，不知道今天要討論這件事，所以沒有去了解。」

Robert: "That's terrible. You're the supervisor of the pipeline area and should have some basic ideas for this topic, even without meeting agenda. As I know, the reason for such a situation has a partial relationship with the shortage of material supply from warehouse. Can anyone from the warehouse give us some explanations?"

經理：「真是糟糕！就算沒有議程表，你是管線區的組長，至少對這問題也該有些想法啊？我知道這情況的發生，部份跟倉庫的材料供應不足有關，是不是倉管組的人員可以說明一下？」

No one replied on this question, and the meeting suddenly became quiet for several minutes.

沒有人回應這個問題，會議室裡突然安靜了好幾分鐘。

Janet finally **breaks the silence**: "None of the warehouse team **participates** in the meeting. The supervisor there called me this morning and mentioned that he totally forgot about this meeting. Now he might be still in the supplier, and couldn't be back **in time**."

珍娜終於打破沉默的說：「倉管組好像沒有人來參加會議；早上他們組長才打電話給我，說他忘了有這個會議，目前人在供應商那邊，恐怕趕不及回來了。」

Robert has started to be impatient: "The meeting today is really a messy, because you all didn't care. But some serious problems still need to be solved immediately, like the improving **scheme** for the construction error of steel structure area, and the **overruns** of entitle construction cost. I wish that you could prepare well within the shortest time and summit the complete report before the meeting next week."

經理開始有些的不耐了：「今天會議進行的狀況實在很凌亂，似乎大家都沒真正的用心；但是有些問題還是要盡快處理，像是鋼構區發生建構錯誤部份的改善方案，以及整個工程費用超出預算的問題，希望用最短的時間準備，在下週的會議中提出完整的報告。」

After hearing this, a bunch of them yell **in unison**: "What? Meeting again!"

一群人聽到這些話，異口同聲的説：「什麼？還要再開一次會啊！」

Robert: "I hope that you'll be well-prepared and ready and then show up on time. Especially you, Janet! You shall tidy up the minutes of meeting, and summit together with the notice of next meeting to everyone."

經理：「我希望下次會議時，所有該準備的都已就緒，並且準時出席，尤其是珍娜！待會妳將會議紀錄整理好，連同下次的會議通知知會給大家。」

Janet: "But, Robert. I forgot to minute the meeting."

珍娜説：「可是，羅柏！我剛剛忘了做會議的紀錄耶！」

Vocabulary 字彙解析

- **clutter** *n.* 雜物、混亂

〔同義詞：chaos, confusion, mess〕

The attic is full of clutter.

There seems to be some clutter about which system does what.

- **agenda** *n.* 議程、議題

〔同義詞：topic, schedule〕

The question of nuclear weapons had been removed from the agenda.

Alter people's agendas so that no two contain any common item.

- **verbal** *n., adj.* 口頭上、言語

〔同義詞：oral, speech〕

The root of the problem is visual rather than verbal.

They had reached a verbal agreement.

- **participate** *vi., vt.* 參與、加入

〔同義詞：take part in, engage in, join in〕

Thousands participated in a nationwide strike.

The entire sales force participate the conference.

- **scheme** *n.* 方案、計劃

〔同義詞：program, plan, formula〕

The whole scheme is plunged into darkness, bar the light in Victor's house.

We need to give a full scheme of the job advertised.

- **overruns** *n., vt.* 超支、蔓延

〔同義詞：overspend, overflow, exceeding〕

The Mediterranean has been overrun by tourists.

He mustn't overrun his budget.

Phrase in sentence 片語和句型解析

■ **look around**　張望、環顧

〔同義詞：**peep, inspect, visit and observe**〕

The door was ajar and she couldn't resist looking around.

Young people look around decisions are made by others.

■ **drop a hint**　暗示、影射

〔同義詞：**imply, suggest, allude**〕

He has dropped a hint of his views.

She drops a hint to Jean, but never saying her name.

■ **out of order**　壞了、失靈、失序

〔同義詞：**shuffle, disorder, not work**〕

The machine in these days are mess and out of order.

The legal sanctions against oil spills are virtually out of order.

■ **break the silence**　打破沉默

〔或者說：breading the silence〕

The team's performance had broken the silence from outside critics.

The noise of car engine breaks the silence of mid-night.

■ **in time**　及時、準時

〔同義詞：**timely, promptly, on time**〕

He paid the fine in time.

Your help is just in time when we're in trouble.

■ **in unison**　異口同聲、齊聲

〔同義詞：**in one voice, in chorus, consistency**〕

The flutes play in unison with the violas.

"Yes, sir," said the girls in unison.

Practice in Management

Enterprise is a set of organized groups constituted by many people. Many communication and interaction among people are engaged through formal or informal meeting discussion. The meeting time had become a significant proportion to daily working hours. It's particularly true for the discussion of many formal meetings, which will determine and influence many important decisions of the company. Therefore, a comprehensive and adequate meeting preparation is an important issue. Such preparation includes something tangible like the arrangement of meeting time, place, participates, and related equipment and documents, and something intangible like the arrangement of agenda and procedures, advance notice of meeting, minutes of meeting, and the follow-up after meeting.

In the business organizations, conference is not only the essential activity, but also the important way for communication, problem solving and decision making. However, if there're too many meetings, especially those not necessary or not efficient, it's not only a waste of everyone's time, but will also reduce the efficiency of the work. Over the time, conference has become just a kind of formality, and peers just cope with the troubles and not really care about the conference discussion. So, a streamline and fully prepared meeting is much better than long and boring discussion. And on the other hand, effective implementation, and regular tracking to the resolution from meetings might be more important than the recurring meeting discussion.

經驗與分享

企業是一個集合多數人所構成的組織團體，許多人與人之間的溝通和互動，都是透過正式或非正式會議討論的模式進行著，在每日的工作時間中，會議就佔據了其中很大的比例，尤其許多正式會議的討論，更會決定和影響著公司的許多重要的決策；因此，周全而充分的會議準備，就更加的重要了，這包括了有形的事項如：會議時間、地點、與會人員、使用設備及相關文件的安排等，當然也包括了無形的要素如：議題與流程的安排、會前的通知、會議中的紀錄、及會後的追蹤等。

會議在企業組織中，是不可或缺的活動，也是溝通、解決問題和決策的重要方式；但是若會議太多了，尤其是過多沒有必要、或沒有效率的會議，這不僅是浪費了大家的時間，反而降低了工作的效率，長期下來，會議的進行已流於形式，反而讓同儕只是虛應其事，更不重視會議的討論內容。因此，精簡但充分準備的會議，勝過冗長而無趣的討論，另一方面，有效執行、與定期追蹤會議中所決議的內容，比起重複的會議討論，則更加的重要。

Tips in Management

Minutes of Meeting

Minutes, also known as **protocols** or, informally, **notes**, are the instant written record of a meeting or hearing. They typically describe the events of the meeting, starting with a list of attendees, a statement of the issues considered by the participants, and related responses or decisions for the issues.

Minutes may be created during the meeting by a typist or court reporter, who may use shorthand notation and then prepare the minutes and issue them to the participants afterwards. Alternatively, the meeting can be audio recorded, video recorded, or a group's appointed or informally assigned Secretary may take notes, with minutes prepared later. Many government agencies use minutes recording software to record and prepare all minutes in real-time. For private organizations, it is relatively important for the minutes to be terse and only include a summary of discussion and decisions. A verbatim report is typically not useful. For publicly held companies, the minutes of certain meetings such as a corporate board of directors, must be kept on file and are important legal documents.

管理小偏方

會議記錄

會議記錄，也被稱為**協議**、或簡稱為**會議筆記**，是有關會議或聽證會內容的即時書面記錄。會議記錄通常敘述著整個會議的內容，從參加者的名單，與會者所討論議題的說明，及與議題相關的回應或決定。

會議紀錄的產生，是在會議過程中透過紀錄員所記載，會議記錄的方式，可以先使用速記符號，然後再準備正式記錄，於會後分發給了與會者；此外，也可以運用錄音、錄影等方式錄製，或者是由一群人所指定、或非正式的委託給秘書抄錄筆記，隨後再來準備紀錄。許多政府機構都使用錄音軟體來記錄，並及時的準備會議紀錄。

在私人機構中，簡潔的會議紀錄是相對的重要，只是摘要各項議題的討論和決定的內容，因為逐字報告通常是沒有用的。但公開上市的公司，某些特定的會議記錄，如公司的董事會，會議紀錄則必須妥善保存，並視其為很重要的法律文件。

1-4 Office Murmur
辦公室的耳語

 ## Conversation 情境對話

In the corner of the office, several female colleagues get together whispering. They're rushing back to the seats when the manager **passed through** their side. But, shortly after that, they still secretly **convey** the message.

在辦公室的一角，幾個女同事圍在一起竊竊私語，看到了經理從走到經過，才匆匆的回到自己的座位上；但沒多久，幾個人又開始偷偷的傳遞著訊息。

These whispers had been **circulated** for days, gradually turn into vivid rumors, and then became rendered topics among colleagues privately. Therefore, Robert **congregated** all of them together.

這些耳語流傳了好幾天，慢慢像是繪聲繪影的謠言一般，成為同事間私下不斷渲染的話題。因此，經理將大家集合了起來。

Robert: "I know you're highly interested in certain topics recently, which made the office filled with whispers. But it's not really good. Why don't we just open the topic here sincerely, and clarify the truth to everybody. So now, Daphne, I heard you're always interested in this. You can first share what you know to us."

經理：「我知道最近大家似乎都很有興趣於某些話題，使得辦公室裡充滿了竊竊私語，但這種情況並不太好；不如就在這開誠佈公的講開來，讓大家清楚事情的真象。黛芬妮，我想妳對這是一直很感興趣，就先說說看妳所知道的事吧！」

Daphne **equivocated**: "I just **heard about** it. Well, it seems that Jenny was very busy these days and..."

黛芬妮有些支支吾吾的說：「我也是聽說的啦！嗯，好像珍妮這陣子很忙吧……！」

Daphne couldn't go on, and **drift** her sight **into** Grace at the side. Then Grace continued: "Yap! Everybody's curious to: Why Jenny always dressed up after work and then hurried to leave these days?"

黛芬妮有些說不下去了，眼角飄向了一旁的葛瑞絲；於是葛瑞絲接著說：「對啊，大家都很好奇：為何她這陣子下班時，總是特別盛裝打扮，然後匆匆忙忙地趕著離開？」

The topic seems to be opened up, and then Rose goes on with slight excitement: "For several times, she sat in the VP's car and leaved with him. We just don't understand the relationship between them is...?"

話題似乎被打開了，羅絲略帶興奮的接著說：「有好幾次，她就坐上副總的車子、跟著他一起離開；只是不知道她和副總之間，究竟是……？」

Queenie couldn't help to **interject**: "Well. Jenny is so pretty and considerate. So, of course, many men will like her. You know such kind of things. Just like sometimes in the past few days, she still stayed in the manager's room with Robert alone after work."

這時昆妮忍不住的插上了話：「唉，珍妮長得漂亮又善解人意，當然會有很多人喜歡她，這種事妳是知道的！就像這陣子在下班後，她不也經常和羅柏單獨待在經理室裡嗎？」

Queenie suddenly recognized herself **slip of the tongue**, and quickly stop the topic. Everyone just keeps the head down and silent, and the **ambience** is very embarrassed.

昆妮似乎發現自己說溜了嘴，趕緊停下了話題；大家突然鴉雀無聲的低著頭，現場氣氛似乎有些尷尬。

Robert says calmly: "As now we all **concern for** this issue, then why don't we just let Jenny stay here and clarify all the details."

經理心平氣和的說：「既然大家這麼關心這件事，我想就請珍妮進來，跟大家說清楚整個原由。」

Jenny comes in the meeting room and pleased: "I has been assigned to be the overseas business manager in Belgium next month. During this period of time, I'm very **grateful to** our VP for his **enthusiastic** arrangements for me in such a rare opportunity. In addition, I particularly want to thank Robert, who had spent several nights in giving me lots of **attentive** guidance and advice. All these do give me confidence and ready to compete for this position."

Robert followed: "Jenny's **energetic** and great effort help herself to win a better promotion. I'm very happy for her and give my most sincerely greeting."

Everyone's stunned and **dumb** after hearing such a big surprise.

珍妮進到會議室裡，愉悅的說著：「下個月我將被派到比利時，擔任駐外的業務經理；這段時間，我很感謝副總的熱心安排，讓我能爭取到這份難得的機會；此外，我也特別要感謝羅柏，花了好幾個晚上，給予我許多細心的指導和建議，讓我更充滿信心和準備，來爭取這份職位。」

經理接著說：「這是珍妮自己的積極和努力，讓自己得到更好的擢升；我很為她高興，也獻上最誠摯的祝福！」

這突如其來的轉變，讓所有人頓時目瞪口呆，驚訝得說不出話來。

Robert: "I believe, after this case, there're some issues for ourselves to reflect and review. In a group, false rumor and **arbitrary** transmission without proven sometimes can become the invisible killer to destroy our group."

經理說：「我相信經過了這件事後，是有一些我們自身要反省和檢討的課題。在團體生活當中，不實的流言，以及不經證實的肆意傳遞，往往就成了摧毀這團體的無形殺手。」

All these colleagues do feel ashamed. Yet Jenny's still pleased to give each of them a big hug.

在場的人全都羞愧的低下了頭。但珍妮還是開心的與每個同事一一擁抱。

Vocabulary 字彙解析

■ **convey** *vt.* 傳達、輸送、表達

〔同義詞：communicate, transport, express〕

Pipes were laid to convey water to the house.

He had conveyed his complete satisfaction.

■ **circulate** *vt., vi.* 流通、流傳、發行

〔同義詞：spread, release, despatch〕

The antibodies had circulated in the bloodstream.

Rumors of his arrest had been circulated.

■ **congregate** *vt., vi.* 集合、鼓起

〔同義詞：assemble, bring together, call up〕

More than 4,000 demonstrators had congregated at a border point.

The crowd had congregated outside the gates.

■ **equivocate** *vi.* 拐彎抹角、支應

〔同義詞：prevaricate, attend, cope,〕

She equivocated: "Not that we are aware of."

He seemed to equivocate when journalists asked pointed questions.

■ **interject** *vi.* 插嘴、突然插入

〔同義詞：infix, interfere, insert,〕

She interjects the odd question here and there.

These four layers are interjected by thick salty to sandy sequences.

■ **ambience** *n.* 環境、氣氛

〔同義詞：environment, mood, surrounding feeling,〕

The relaxed ambience of the cocktail lounge is popular with guests.

I lived in hostile ambience surrounded by religious bigotry.

- **enthusiastic** *adj.* 熱烈的、熱情的

〔同義詞：warm, zealous, animated〕

The promoter was enthusiastic about the concert venue.
The council was extremely enthusiastic in the application of the regulations.

- **attentive** *adj.* 細心的、殷勤的、注意

〔同義詞：careful, solicitous, warning〕

She never had such an attentive audience before.
I begged him to be more attentive.

- **energetic** *adj.* 積極的、有活力的

〔同義詞：vigorous, positive, active〕

He made an energetic identification of a glossy ibis.
I needed to change my lifestyle and become more energetic.

- **dumb** *adj.* 說不出話的、糊塗的

〔同義詞：mute, ludicrous, silent, speechless〕

He was born deaf, dumb, and blind.
He was dumb with rage.

- **arbitrary** *adj.* 獨斷的、隨便的

〔同義詞：wilful, casual, capricious〕

His mealtimes were entirely arbitrary.
It would be extremely arbitrary to make such an assumption.

Phrase in sentence 片語和句型解析

- **pass through**　通過、穿越

〔同義詞：**transit, pass, cut across**〕

A painting was damaged in passing through.

He has passed through the Atlantic twice.

- **hear about**　聽說、得悉

〔同義詞：**hear of, be told, learn about**〕

Most people heard about CFCs can damage the ozone layer.

Mary's heard about that she will bear a son.

- **drift into**　飄向、滑到

〔同義詞：**float, fleeting, wandering**〕

The cabin cruiser started drifting into downstream.

His sight drifted aimlessly into the narrow streets.

- **slip of the tongue**　口誤、說溜了嘴

〔同義詞：**gaffe, fault, error**〕

The judge made a slip of the tongue in his summing up.

I was slip of the tongue in the speech due to inexperienced and careless.

- **concern for**　關心、掛念

〔同義詞：**cares about, worry, be concerned about**〕

They don't concern for the human life.

I had always been concerned for the topics in history.

- **grateful to**　感激、感謝

〔同義詞：**appreciative, thankful, gratitude**〕

I'm very grateful to you for all your help.

　I don't need to be grateful to anybody.

Practice in Management

The environment of our workplace is just like a microcosm of society, and usually a relatively enclosed group. Within such a small environment, some like-minded peers, based on curiosity, boredom, together for warmth or other purpose, might pay close attention to the private actions of specific person (especially the managers or other particular person). Then, it became the private **whisper** or **gossip** among few friends.

Most of these issues are just harmless gossip or **complaint**, which will be vanished away soon, and thus might be difficult for managers to define and prevent. When such a situation continues over the time, however, these moves will lead those peers to become small intimate groups, or even derivative to be another faction within the whole group. That's one of the reasons for the phenomenon of infighting among peers or factions within some companies, and further more, becomes the fatal for companies' defeat eventually.

When these whispers go on persistently, or even exaggerated or rendered untruly to affect the interaction among peers, managers shall stop and clear up these situations timely to prevent the unfounded rumors. Therefore, the litigant and the harmony of entire organization can be protected from the crisis. Such critical situations cannot be resolved or defined by management theories and only rely on the wisdom and experience of managers to deal with.

經驗與分享

辦公室的環境像是一個小型社會的縮影,但這環境通常也是個相對較封閉的團體;同儕在這樣的小環境中,某些臭味相投的同儕,基於好奇、無聊、互相取暖或是某些目的,會對某些人的舉動或私事(通常是管理者本身或特定的人)特別的注目,甚至成為三五好友私下傳遞的**耳語**,或是茶餘飯後互相討論的**八卦**。

這類的問題,多數都只是無傷大雅的閒聊或**牢騷**,很快就煙消雲散,且管理者通常也較難界定與防範;然而長期下來,這群人自成為私密的小團體,甚至在整個團體中自成派系;這種現象也是許多公司會產生派系間明爭暗鬥的主因之一,甚至成為公司走向潰敗的致命傷。

但若這些耳語持續存在著,甚至有被誇大、或不實渲染的情況,開始影響同儕的互動時,管理者應該適時的澄清和制止,以避免成為無中生有的謠言,造成對當事人和整個組織和諧和運作;管理學理論無法解決、或定義這類的問題,惟有依靠管理者的智慧和經驗來處理了。

Tips in Management

The Office

"The Office" is originally an U.K. television comedy series that first aired on BBC2 in July 2001. The story takes place in a fictional city located in Slough paper company Wernham Hogg Paper Company, and the story described the daily life of the staff in the company. The content of the play is fictional, but the filming technologies of series take the form of a documentary.

U.S. version "The Office" series aired on NBC from March 24, 2005 to May 16, 2013. This series depicts the everyday lives of office employees in the Scranton, Pennsylvania branch of the fictional Dunder Mifflin Paper Company. To simulate the look of an actual documentary, it is filmed in a single-camera setup, without a studio audience or a laugh track. The show debuted on NBC as a mid-season replacement and ran for nine seasons, and 201 episodes.

管理小偏方

辦公室風雲

《辦公室風雲》是一部英國喜劇電視劇集，2001年7月在BBC2台首播。故事發生在一間位於斯勞市的虛構紙張公司Wernham Hogg Paper Company裡，劇情描述公司職員的日常生活。該劇內容雖然是虛構，拍攝手法卻採用了紀錄片的形式。

美國版《辦公室瘋雲》故事發生在位於美國賓夕法尼亞州斯克蘭頓一間虛構的紙業分公司（Dunder Mifflin），採取單機拍攝紀錄片的形式記述該公司職員的日常辦公室生活。本劇內容雖為虛構，但有別於其他情景喜劇並沒有搭配罐頭笑聲。《辦公室瘋雲》曾為NBC的收視率最好的節目之一，並在18-49歲收視人口群裡有高收視率。

1-5 Telephone Etiquette
電話禮儀

 Conversation 情境對話

The phone rings.

總機的電話響起來了。

Operator: "Fortune Investment. Who would you like to speak to?"	總機：「富國投資，你找哪位？」
The other side: "Hello, I'm William. May I speak to Ms. Lien. Thank you."	電話那頭：「妳好，我姓威廉，麻煩幫我轉連恩小姐，謝謝！」
Operator: "Lien who? We have several Ms. Liens here."	總機：「是哪個連恩啊？我們這邊有好幾個連恩小姐耶！」
The other side: "Oh, I'm sorry. But she didn't mention about her division and **extension**, so...!"	電話那頭：「喔，實在不好意思，但是她沒跟我說她是哪個部門，哪個分機，所以⋯⋯！」

The operator can't help muttering: "It's really **nasty**. How could I transfer the phone like this?"

總機開始嘀咕著：「真是討厭，這樣怎麼接啊！」

She dials an **intercom call** at the same time: "Mary, a phone call for you. It's from a **prolixity** poor old guy."

這同時她又撥了一個內線：「瑪莉，電話找妳的啦！一個囉嗦的糟老頭打來的啦」

Mary: "Is me you are **looking for**? What do you want from me?"

瑪莉：「你是找我嗎？有什麼事？」

The other side: "Ms. Lien? In regarding the case of **acquisition** you mentioned last time, I think we can make an **appointment** to talk about your idea."

電話那頭：「連恩小姐嗎？有關妳上次提的購併案，我想可以約個時間碰面談談，看看妳有些什麼樣的想法。」

Mary: "What acquisition? I'm totally confused. I wonder that you got the wrong one. You should back to the operator again."

瑪莉：「什麼購併案啊？我都搞糊塗了，我看你找錯人了，你再問問總機吧！」

Operator: "Fortune Investment. Who would you like to talk?"

總機：「富國投資，你找哪位？」

A little bit impatient tone comes from the other side: "Excuse me! Can you transfer for me to Ms. Lien. OK? Thank you!"

電話那頭開始有些不耐的口氣：「不好意思，可以幫我轉連恩小姐，好嗎？謝謝！」

The operator raises her voice and **clamors**: "Oh, it's you again! I had told you that we got many of Liens here. Why don't you **check** it **out** before the phone call? How can I transfer for you?"

總機提高了嗓門嚷嚷著：「喔，先生又是你喔！我不是說我們有好多個連恩嗎？也不查清楚就打過來，這樣我怎麼幫你轉接啊！」

Robert: just **passes by** the front desk and heard the yell of operator. He quickly **takes over** the phone.

這時羅柏正好經過櫃台，聽到了總機這般激昂的語調，趕緊將電話接了過來。

Robert: "Hello, this is Robert. What can I do for you?"

經理說：「您好，我是羅柏，有什麼我可以幫得上忙的嗎？」

The other side: "Oh, Robert? This is William from Gomatt Group."

電話那頭：「喔，是羅柏啊！我是高昇集團的威廉啦。」

Robert feels panic and hurries to say: "I'm really sorry for this plagued call, president William."

經理臉色一陣驚慌，連忙接著說：「是威廉總裁啊，真是不好意思讓這電話困擾著您。」

The other side: "I just try to make an appointment with Ms. Lien for the acquisition case. She got some great ideas and maybe she can give me another briefing. I thought your investment company shall be very professional. But in terms of the manner of forwarding phone from your staff, it seems that there are still many things that need to be reinforced."

Robert embarrassedly blushing: "We do need to improve our training. I'll visit you with Ms. Lien next time and present my **apology** personally."

The other side: "All right, ask her to book the appointment with my secretary. But, do you also agree that I'm a prolixity poor old guy? Hahaha!"

電話那頭：「本來我是想親自跟你們那位連恩小姐約的，上次她提出的購併案想法還不錯，或許找個時間再聽聽她的簡報。我本來還認為你們應該是個很專業的投資公司，但是你們員工轉接電話的態度，實在是有待加強！」

經理漲紅著臉、尷尬的說：「我們是該加強教育訓練的；下次我跟連恩小姐一起過去拜訪您，當面跟您致歉一下！」

電話那頭：「嗯，好啊，請她再跟我的秘書約時間。那你是否也認為，我是一個囉嗦的糟老頭呢？哈哈哈！」

 **Vocabulary 字彙解析**

■ **nasty** *adj.* 討厭、骯髒、污穢

〔同義詞：**dirty, filthy, disgusting**〕

The plastic bags were burn with a nasty, acrid smell.

Harry was a nasty, foul-mouthed old devil.

■ **prolixity** *n.* 囉嗦、冗長

〔同義詞：**windiness, lengthy, wordy**〕

Too much academic language is obscure and prolixity.

Before he finished his prolixity speech, everyone had left.

■ **acquisition** *n.* 獲得、收穫

〔同義詞：**gain, result**〕

Among the museum's acquisitions, he discovered a piece of furniture made 400 years Ago.

The mayor was accused of using municipal funds for personal acquisition.

■ **appointment** *n.* 約會、任命

〔同義詞：**date, engagement**〕

She made an appointment with my receptionist.

It won't be a formal appointment.

■ **clamor** *n., vt., vi.* 叫囂、鼓譟

〔同義詞：**rumpus, loud noise, uproar**〕

The questions rose to a clamor.

The surging crowds clamored for attention.

■ **apology** *n.* 抱歉、歉意

〔同義詞：**regret, sorry**〕

We owe you an apology.

She expressed her apology at Virginia's death.

Phrase in sentence 片語和句型解析

▪ intercom call　內線電話

〔同義詞：internal call〕

Some systems allow you to use another handset as for the intercom calls.

All the records of intercom calls are well finished and highly polished.

▪ looking for　尋求、找尋

〔同義詞：search, hunt for, seek〕

She looked for bus station on her return to the theater.

I'm looking for the answer among the textbooks, but there was nothing.

▪ check out　查證、退房、合格

〔同義詞：investigate, measure up, achieve〕

All the packages are scanned at the checkout counter.

We need to check out the room before 1 p.m.

▪ pass by　經過、路過、過去

〔同義詞：pass, travel by, go past〕

She passed by a rest area with a pay phone.

He had just passed by before you arrive.

▪ take over　接管、接替、兼併

〔同義詞：assume control, succeed, replace〕

As the company suffers from such a low valuation, it could also be a target of takeover.

He would take over Hawke as prime minister.

Practice in Management

Telephone communication is a very important interpersonal tool in the modern society. It's a important bridge of passing message or interactive with each other, when both parties in the distance, or can not talk face to face. That's especially important to the companies. For the visitors of incoming calls, the impression in their mind to this phone call might represent the image and spirit of the company. And, sometimes, it's the basis for them to decide whether a further interaction or doing business with the company. Therefore, good **telephone communication skill** is not only to transmit the message correctly and effectively, but sometimes even to create an unexpected niche.

In the areas of personnel training and management, many companies had paid attention to employee phone talking and answering skills, and continually provided on-job training in this area. In the fierce competition of modern commercial society, telephone communication skills are even treated as an important marketing and sales tool by many companies. **Telemarketing division** or even an independent telemarketing company has become an emerging professional marketing field.

經驗與分享

電話溝通是現代社會很重要的人際溝通工具,在遠距離或無法面對面談話的情況下,它就成為彼此互動和傳遞訊息的重要橋梁;這對於公司而言更為重要。對於來電的拜訪者而言,這通電話所帶給他的印象,就代表者公司的形象和精神,有時候更是他們是否進一步與公司互動的依據;良好的**電話溝通技巧**,不僅能正確有效的傳遞訊息,有時更能創造意想不到的利基。

在許多公司的人員訓練和管理領域當中,員工接聽或講電話的技巧日益受到重視,也不斷的提供員工在這方面的訓練課程。在近代競爭激烈的商業社會中,電話溝通技巧,甚至更被許多公司視為重要的行銷與銷售工具,**電話行銷**部門、甚至獨立的電話行銷公司儼然成為一個很新興的專業行銷領域。

Tips in Management

Telemarketing

Telemarketing is a method of direct marketing in which a salesperson solicits prospective customers to buy products or services, either over the phone or through a subsequent face to face or a Web conferencing appointment schedule during the call. Telemarketing can also include recorded sales pitches programmed to be played over the phone via automatic dialing.

The rise of telemarketing can be traced back to the 19th century telephones, or switchboard operators. Trans-cultural hiring of switchboard operators (mostly women) became especially popular in North America throughout the 20th century, partially due to popularity gained through advertising.

Cigna Life, for example, founded in 1989, reached customers through telemarketing, different from the practical way of face to face sales ways in general insurance company. In the early period, telemarketing could provide only limited services, because customers over the phone could not clearly know their rights and most of the online customer service specialist might require for immediate deals. After years of operation, regardless some arguments, the general public might not be glad but had gradually accepted this marketing approach. And then, some other life insurance companies decided to follow up and began to launch telemarketing business.

管理小偏方

電話行銷

電話行銷是一種直效行銷的方式,其銷售人員藉由電話,以爭取潛在的客戶購買產品或服務,並在電話中約定其後續交易經由面對面、或網路視訊會談的方法進行。電話行銷還可以藉由自動撥號方式,將預錄製好的銷售話術重複播放。

電話營銷的興起可以追溯到19世紀的電話或總機接線員,整個20世紀,跨文化招聘總機接線員(主要是婦女)在北美變得特別的流行,其部分原因是藉由廣告而取得了知名度。

例如成立於1989年的康健人壽,就以電話行銷的方式來接觸客戶,和一般的保險公司以業務員面對面的銷售手法不太相同;然而客戶透過電話無法明確知道自身權益,線上客服專員大多要求立刻成交,因此所提供之服務有限;初期雖然有所爭議,但經過多年經營,一般民眾雖不樂意但也逐漸接受此一行銷方式,且陸續也有其他壽險公司跟進,開始推出電話行銷業務。

1-6 Give a Hand
幫個忙

 ## Conversation 情境對話

Irene walks slowly into the office. Her face is pale and **gaunt**, and she seems very weak. A moment later, she **leans** weakly **against** the wall and almost passes out. Fortunately, she's found by Tina, who just passes **by chance**. Tina quickly helps her to the **infirmary** for rest and reports this to Robert.

艾琳緩緩的走進了辦公室，她的臉色蒼白而憔悴，身體非常的虛弱；不一會兒，她無力的倚靠在牆邊，幾乎就要昏厥了過去；所幸被正巧經過的提娜發現了，趕緊攙扶著她到醫務室休息，並且將這情況報告給羅柏知道。

Before long, Robert comes over to visit Irene.

沒多久，羅柏過來探望了艾琳。

Robert: "Feeling better now? Everyone is worried about you."

經理：「現在好一點了嗎？大家都為妳的健康感到很憂心！」

Irene: "Thanks for all your concern. I'm fine but just very tired. I do need a good sleep because I had been exhausted **for a while**."

艾琳：「謝謝大家的關心！我沒有大礙，只是身體很疲憊，這陣子可是累壞了，真的需要好好睡一覺。」

Robert: "What happened? I had found your **listlessness** in the office recently. Is there any trouble in the work?"

經理：「怎麼回事？最近我就發現妳在辦公室時，似乎有些無精打采的；是工作上遇到麻煩了嗎？」

Irene: "I'm sorry. My mother had a surgery not long ago. So, after work, I have to take care of her at the ward all night long."

艾琳：「實在很抱歉。前一陣子我母親住院手術，工作之餘，我必須徹夜守在病房照顧她。」

Robert: "It couldn't go on like this all the times for your health would be **tired out**. Is there anyone else who can **take turn** with you? Or you can find a caregiver."

經理：「這樣下去也不是辦法，妳的身體會累壞的！難道沒有其他人可以跟妳輪替，或者請個看護幫忙照顧嗎？」

Irene: "I'm her only relatives. I have been **overburdened** for the huge medical expense of her surgery. Then how can I find any **spare** capacity for a caregiver?"

艾琳：「我是母親唯一的親人，這次她手術要負擔的龐大醫藥費，已經讓我捉襟見拙了，怎麼還有餘力聘請看護呢？」

Robert: "Is there any insurance **coverage** available for your mother? "

Irene: "Her insurance policy is only partial coverage. I don't know the details, nor do I have the time to figure it out."

Robert ponders for a while and says: "So be it! I'll ask the staffs in personnel to help you check with Health Insurance Bureau or Bureau of Labor if there's any Medicaid. In addition, I'll tell all our colleagues regarding your situation, and try to support you more or less. Most importantly, I'll report to our Employee Benefits Committee. I do believe that you can get some help from our Employee Welfare Fund."

Irene: "Thanks so much, Robert! Your kindness made me feel very warm."

經理：「那妳母親沒有任何保險給付可以申請嗎？」

艾琳：「她的保險只能部份負擔醫藥費，至於其他的，我實在不清楚也沒時間去了解。」

經理思索了一下，接著說：「這樣吧！我會請人事部門的同仁幫妳去了解一下，如何向健保或勞保單位爭取一些醫療補助；另一方面，我也會將妳的情況告知所有同事，大家有能力救多少幫點忙；最主要的，我也會跟公司的福利委員會報告此事，相信我們的員工福利基金應該可以幫上忙。」

艾琳：「非常謝謝你，羅柏！你的好意讓我感到很溫馨。」

Robert: "But your routine needs to be changed. Otherwise, not only had your heath been collapsed, but also your work had been seriously affected. I suggest that you stop the work for a while and concentrate on taking care of your mother."

經理：「但是妳這樣的作息必須有所改變！否則不但身體會弄垮了，工作也會受到很大影響。我建議妳應該停止工作一段時間，專心照顧妳的母親。」

Irene: "But I do need this job."

艾琳：「可是我很需要這份工作的。」

Robert: "Don't worry! I'll report your situation to the executives. We might choose the way of retention without pay, and back till the recovery of your mother. Regarding your income during this period of time, I'll try my best to **strive for** you."

經理：「別擔心！我會跟上面報告妳的情況，或許用留職停薪的方式處理，等妳母親痊癒了再回來；至於妳這段時間的收入，我再盡力的爭取看看。」

Irene: "Really appreciated. Now can I ask your permission for a good sleep?"

艾琳：「真的很謝謝你，現在你可以批准，讓我好好的睡一覺嗎？」

Vocabulary 字彙解析

■ **gaunt** *adj.* 憔悴的、瘦弱的、疲累

〔同義詞：**haggard, drawn, thin, lean**〕

She was gaunt, painfully thin, and expressionless.

I trailed on behind, gaunt, and disheveled.

■ **infirmary** *n.* 醫務室、療養院

〔同義詞：**nursing house, convalesce, clinic**〕

Minimum health care or infirmary assistance is provided as needed.

She nursed the girl in the infirmary through a dangerous illness.

■ **listlessness** *n.* 萎靡、懶洋洋

〔同義詞：**dejected, listless, dispirited**〕

He was walking around in listlessness.

This afternoon was hot, quiet, and we all tired with listlessness.

■ **overburdened** *adj.* 不堪負荷、負擔過重

〔同義詞：**overwhelmed, overload**〕

They were overburdened with luggage.

An overloaded vehicle is very dangerous.

■ **spare** *adj.* 備用的、多餘的

〔同義詞：**backup, alternate, reserve**〕

Few people had spare cash for inessentials.

She was asked to attend on spare days.

■ **coverage** *n.* 涵蓋、範圍

〔同義詞：**cover, insurance coverage**〕

The grammar did not offer total coverage of the language.

It's a sequence of novels with the coverage from 1968 to the present.

Phrase in sentence 片語和句型解析

▪ lean against 倚靠、憑倚

〔同義詞：**rely, lean on, depend**〕
I know I can lean against your discretion.
He's the kind of person you could lean against.

▪ by chance 碰巧、萬一

〔同義詞：**by coincidence, fortunately, just in case,**〕
It's not by chance that this new burst of innovation has occurred in the free nations.
By the chance, no shots were fired and no one was hurt.

▪ for a while 一陣子、一段時間

〔同義詞：**for the moment, offhand, for a short time**〕
I had waited her for a while.
I still can't figure out a better answer for a while.

▪ tired out 疲憊、精疲力盡

〔同義詞：**exhausted, played-out, worn-out**〕
I was cold and tired out.
He had been tired out after a long trip.

▪ take turn 輪流

〔同義詞：**rotation, alternation**〕
All the children take turn caring of their illness mother.
He needs to take his turn in the ward.

▪ strive for 爭取、謀求

〔同義詞：**fight, compete for, endeavor**〕
The national movements were striving for independence.
He is striving for helping the Third World.

Practice in Management

Employee benefits are the rights of employee to enjoy because of his employment. Some benefits are offered directly by the employer, such benefits like special holiday bonus, employee travel, birthday celebration, performance bonuses, discount for employee, etc. Many companies will also set up the employee benefits committee, which might wide differently in organization and hierarchy for each company. Some workers' welfare may be provided by the government agents of health insurance, labor affairs, or related third party, such welfare like medical insurance, occupational injury, unemployment or disaster relief, etc.

In the employment environment nowadays, either employees or employers all pay serious attention in the issue of employee benefits and labor rights. This is not only a response to social trends and normative acts, but also a representation that the human resource will be regarded as a very important asset in the companies. Whenever subordinates face some difficulties in the family or health, the manager is willing to make all his best to assist and help subordinates, then, in return, he will obtain the subordinate identity and solidarity. On the other hand, when an employee needs temporary leave his work due to some personal factors, some companies might agree the "**retention without pay**" approach for employee. This approach should be adopted only for few unique exceptions, and must be discussed carefully within the company because this approach will create some practical harass for managers.

經驗與分享

員工福利，是僱員因為受雇工作而有權享用的福利；有些是由僱主直接給予的，例如三節獎金、員工旅遊、慶生會、尾牙、績效獎金、員工價等，許多公司也會成立員工福利委員會，但因為各公司的組織不同，而在層級上有著很大的差異。有些勞工的福利，也可能是由政府的全民健保、和勞工機構或第三者所提供的，例如醫療保險服務、職業傷害、失業或急難救助等。

在現今的就業環境中，無論是僱主或受雇者，對於員工福利與勞工權益，都非常的重視；這種情況不僅是因應時代的趨勢和法令的規範，也代表公司將人才視同很重要的資產。對於管理者而言，當部屬在家庭或健康上遇到了困難時，能盡全力的協助部屬取得協助，更能取得部屬的認同感和向心力。但在另一方面，當員工因個人因素而需暫時離開工作崗位，有些公司會讓員工採用『留職停薪』的制度；這個方式應是屬於很少數的特例、且必然是經過公司審慎的討論，因為這種方式的實施，對於管理者而言，將會造成一些實務上的困擾。

Tips in Management

Health Care System

According to the degree of involvement from government authority, there're three different kinds of system:

Public medical system: Use the United Kingdom as a representative. From 1948 to 1989 when the British health care reformed, physicians, employed in the civil service, public hospitals or medical expenses, were all budgeted by the government cope.

Social insurance system: Found in German. Medical expenses were paid by the sickness insurance funds, and the sources of sickness insurance are shared by the Government, employers, and people. The fund was financially independent, and not to be confused with other government expenditure. Thus the social insurance system could combine the functions of financial sustainability with medical efficacy and social equity.

Free insurance market: U.S. as the representative. The health care spending was afforded by private health insurer. The federal government provided only the health insurance of elderly and the low-income poor.

The National Health Insurance in R.O.C. was classified as **"single public social insurance"** health care system. The system integrated those old insurance systems, like public insurance, labor insurance, agricultural insurance, and the military security, into the new National Health Insurance system. Different identities had set different satisfied premiums rate by according to the industry they belong to, but nothing to do with their history of health problems. Each populace, with health insurance card, just paid the registration fee and partial burden of treatment cost while seeking treatment in the medical institutes. The medical institutions, based on the principal of capitation amount, reported the patient medical records to the National Health Insurance Bureau as to collar the medical benefits.

 管理小偏方

健康照護體系

根據政府公權力介入的程度，一般可以區分三種不同的體系：

公醫制：以英國為代表。自1948年起至1989英國醫療改革止，醫師為受雇於公立醫院的公務員，醫療開支由政府編列預算支應。

社會保險制：以德國首創，醫療開支由疾病保險基金所支付，而疾病保險基金的來源則由政府、僱主、民眾共同分擔。其特色為財務獨立，不與其他政府開支相混淆。由於社會保險製得以兼顧財務永續性、醫療效能以及社會公平性。

自由市場：以美國為代表。美國的醫療開支一般由民營的醫療保險公司負擔，聯邦政府僅提供老人與低收入窮人的醫療保險。

中華民國所實施的全民健康保險，在分類上屬於「公營單一社會保險制」的醫療照顧體系，將公保、勞保、農保、軍保的舊有保險體系整合納入全民健保中，不同身份的加保人不因健康病史問題而有不同保費，而是根據行業身份而有不同納保費率。民眾加保後，以健保卡到醫療院所就醫時即僅須負擔掛號費以及部份負擔費用。而醫療院所則是以量計酬，根據病患病歷就診紀錄向健保局請領醫療給付。

Section 2

Organizational Behavior

2-1 Fiery Quarrel
火爆的爭吵

 Conversation 情境對話

It's Time for the lunch break. On the walkway outside men's room, Elmer and Vincent suddenly loud up their dialogue. Then both men **groaned** to each other with heated arguments, as if they were about to start a fight at any moment. Many colleagues were scared of the **brawl** and stand aside helplessly.

午餐休息時間，在男用化妝室外的走道上，艾默和文森的對話突然大聲了起來，隨即兩人就面紅耳赤的叫罵著，互不相讓，眼看就要大打出手；許多同事被爭吵聲驚嚇著，卻不知所措的只能圍在一旁。

Robert, who is just back from meal outside, noted such a situation. He hurriedly requested the securities and several colleagues to pull them back, and then asked them to come to the manager's room and **dwell on** the conflict.

羅伯剛用完餐回來，見到此狀，趕緊要警衛和幾個同事將兩人架開，然後要兩人都到他的辦公室裡詳談。

Robert: "What's going on there? Why you both were such **pissed off**?"

經理：「剛剛到底怎麼回事？兩個好朋友為何要發這麼大的肝火？」

Vincent couldn't content himself: "I have always respected his leadership, because he is the project supervisor. But recently, I really cannot stand his **capricious** command. He sometimes asked us to do this way, and then, **all of a sudden**, got to change onto another approach. "

文森按捺不住的直說：「我一向是很尊重他的帶領，因為他是這個工程的主任；但最近實在受不了他反覆無常的命令，一下子要我們這麼做，一下子又得改變做法。」

Robert: "You just calm down first. Are there any difficulties or changes encountered for the project execution? But, after all, Elmer is the project supervisor, and should know the whole situation. So, what's wrong there, Elmer?"

經理：「你先耐住性子別生氣，是不是這個工程的進行遇到了什麼困難或是變化，但畢竟艾默是整個工程的主任，應該最清楚整個狀況的。艾默你說說看怎麼回事？」

Elmer replied with such a frustration: "We have no choice but this **workaround**. Because of the project schedule of another coordinated contractor had been seriously delayed, the owner temporarily requested us to modify our construction method in order to avoid the affection for the whole project."

艾默有些無奈的説：「這也是不得不的變通辦法，因為其他配合的承包商工程進度落後了，業主臨時要求我們修正一下施工方式，免得整個工程的進行受到了影響。」

Vincent shouted out **irascibly**: "Why don't you make it clear? We did perform very well originally; but now, all of a sudden, we have to change **drastically**. All the subordinates have been confused."

文森暴躁的説：「那你又沒講清楚！原本進行的都很順利，一下子又要大幅的改變，底下的夥伴們都有些無所適從了。」

After hearing this, Elmer **agitated**: "That's a temporary and urgent **contingency** approach, because I have to take into account the whole project. And you should support me, rather than **take the lead** to oppose and struggle in front of our partners!"

艾默聽了後也略帶激動的説：「這是臨時且緊急的應變做法，我必須顧及整個工程的進行，你應該支持我，而不是在夥伴面前，帶頭反對和抗爭啊！」

Robert: "I know you both work hard **for the sake of** the smooth project, but just neglect the key **minutiae** at the critical moment."

經理說：「我知道大家都是為了工程的順利進行著想，但卻都在節骨眼中疏忽了一些細節。」

Elmer and Vincent then were silent with a gentler mood.

艾默和文森兩人默默不語的，情緒似乎稍微平緩了下來。

Robert: "Elmer! The way owner suddenly changes the construction procedure might cause serious effect to us. You should clearly negotiate with them again, or we go together, if necessary. But the most important thing is you should describe clearly the situation to partners, or at least give some hints to your **cadres** in advance even if the time's running out."

經理：「艾默，業主突然修改施工的程序，這對我們可能會造成很大的影響，建議你再跟業主溝通清楚，必要的話，我們一起去了解一下；最重要的，是你要跟你的幹部說明清楚原由和你的想法，就算時間緊迫，至少也要讓他們心裡有些準備。」

Vincent muttered: "That's it! Why not just speak out."

文森嘀咕的說：「對啊，也不講清楚。」

Robert: "But, Vincent. You also need to think about what you have done. Any decision from Elmer should have its reason because he takes on the responsibility of this project. You should report first to Elmer in private if any question had been **popping up**. Just image! How would you feel if your subordinates had also struggled with you in public? You might be promoted to be a leader of a higher level in the future, so you should think over the issues of **ethics**, respect, and leadership in the workplace."

經理：「但是，文森，你也要想一下！艾默既然擔負工程的責任，他這樣的決定必定有其理由的，有什麼疑問，應該是先在私下跟艾默反映的。假如有一天你的夥伴也像今天這樣當面對你抗爭，那你又做何感想？有一天你會成為更高階的領導者，你要好好思考一些職場上應有的倫理與尊重，和一些領導統御的方法。」

Vincent feels embarrassed: "Maybe I'm too impatient, sorry."

文森不好意思的説：「或許是我太急了，實在很抱歉。」

Robert: "The case itself is no big deal, but there is no good communication between you both, especially behaving toward such an irritable emotion and manner. It's detrimental to be good friends, and competent cadres."

經理：「這件事情本身並沒有很大障礙，但你們兩人之間缺乏良好溝通，尤其是用這暴躁的情緒和方式處理，那就有愧於兩人是好友，也都是公司得力的幹部了！」

🗒 **Vocabulary 字彙解析**

- **groan** *vt., vi., n.* 呻吟、哼

〔同義詞：**moan, hum, croon**〕

Marty groaned and pulled the blanket over his head.

James slumped back into his chair, making it groan and bulge.

- **brawl** *vt., vi., n.* 爭吵、打鬧

〔同義詞：**quarrel, bicker, dispute**〕

How can it get better if we are always engaged in fighting and brawling with each other?

She had seen victims of bar fights and street brawls.

- **capricious** *adj.* 任性、善變

〔同義詞：**changeable, unpredictable**〕

This party is capricious and often brutal administration.

The weather here will be capricious, with rain at times.

- **workaround** *n.* 解決辦法、變通方法

〔同義詞：**solution, settlement**〕

There are no easy workaround to financial and marital problems.

The unions succeeded in reaching a paying workaround.

- **irascible** *adj.* 暴躁的、易怒的

〔同義詞：**irritable, impatient, choleric**〕

She was tired and irascible.

In a heat wave, many people become increasingly irascible.

- **drastic** *adj.* 果斷的、大刀闊斧的

〔同義詞：**intensive, crucial, decisive**〕

The Supreme Court voided the statute by a drastic 7–2 vote.

He was drastic of many U.S. welfare programs.

- **agitated**   *adj., v.*   激動的；使焦慮不安

〔同義詞：exciting, anxious, disturbed〕
There's no point getting agitated.
The theory of death agitated him extremely.

- **contingency**   *n.*   偶發性、不可測的意外

〔同義詞：chance, fortuity, accident〕
This is a detailed contract that attempts to provide for all possible contingencies.
To be pregnancy was a contingency.

- **minutiae**   *n.*   細節、瑣事

〔同義詞：detail, niceties, trivia〕
She was never interested in the minutiae of Greek and Latin.
We shall consider every minutiae of the bill.

- **cadres**   *n.*   幹部、核心

〔同義詞：team, group, core〕
This team is the cadres of our film-producing industry.
What we need is just a small cadre of scientists.

 Phrase in sentence 片語和句型解析

- **dwell on**   詳談、流連

〔同義詞：recount, dilatation, linger over〕
I dwelled on the tale to Steve.
She dwelled on the yard, enjoying the warm sunshine.

- **piss off**   激怒、惹惱、滾開！

〔同義詞：infuriate, rage, get out of here!〕
Her speech pissed him off.
Piss off and leave me alone!

■ all of a sudden 突然、一下子、倉促

〔同義詞：suddenly, all at once, hastily〕

The ambassador died all of a sudden.

All of a sudden, he changed the subject.

■ take into account 顧及、考慮、兼顧

〔同義詞：take into consideration, think〕

They agreed a ceasefire to take into account the government.

Each application needs to take into account on its merits.

■ take the lead 帶頭、率先

〔同義詞：lead, be the first, set an example〕

The US is now taking the environmental lead.

This lady is going to take the lead for the rest of the tour.

■ for the sake of 為了……緣故、為求……

〔同義詞：due to, in order, because of〕

For the sake of survival, we need to flight back.

He donated the huge money for the sake of saving the tax payment.

■ pop up 跳出來、突然出現

〔同義詞：crop up, jump up, pop〕

The corks popped up, glasses tinkled, and delicate canapés were served.

Juliet popped up and ran away.

Practice in Management

The operating promotions in most companies are the result of a group action. Just like baseball or basketball athletic activities, each position plays a different role and function by different individuals. As for the actions of the team, each member has his or her individual cognitive and idea, which might be different to others; therefore, sometimes this results in friction or conflicts. But there's one team goal, and team actions also need to be consistent. It's an important task for managers to know how to get the same in differences, and to resolve the confliscts among them.

Interpersonal management issues, in practice, involve many complex factors. These are issues that managers deal with every day, and discuss repeatedly among studies of management science. For example: organizational behavior and mass psychology among peer interaction, leadership skills to the subordinate, set up for organizational and individual work goal, implementation steps and process specifications, and resolving of conflict and deviant behavior, etc.

No matter under any practical or **managerial issue**, good interpersonal communication is the best way to promote inter-friendly peer interaction and cooperation, and also the foundation of success for all management and organizational objectives. Without good communication, any excellent management system or method will become less effective or even futile.

經驗與分享

絕大多數公司的**營運推動**，都是一種團體行動的結果，就像是棒球或籃球等競技活動一樣，每個位置由不同的個人扮演其不同的角色和功能；對於團隊的行動，每個人都有其個別的認知和想法，彼此間必定有其差異性，有時會因此而產生了摩擦或衝突；但團隊的目標只有一個，團隊行動也必須一致，如何在異中求同、化解分歧，這是管理者很重要的課題。

人際上的管理問題，在實務上涉及到很多複雜的因素，是管理人每天都會面對的問題，更有許多管理學上被一再討論的議題。例如同儕間互動的組織行為、群眾心理，主管對部屬的領導統御，組織目標與個別工作方針的設定，執行步驟與流程的規範，以及衝突與偏差行為的處理……等等。

但無論是在任何實務情況下、或是**管理議題**中，有良好的人際溝通，才是促進同儕間友善的互動與合作最好的方法，也是所有管理與組織目標成功的基礎；沒有好的溝通，任何優異的管理制度或方法，也都將會事倍功半，甚至徒勞無功。

Tips in Management

Interpersonal communication

Interpersonal communication refers to the mode of transmission of two-way communication between people. It shares and sends messages between two, or among more people or groups. Studies found that expression through words passes only 7 percent of the meaning. Through tone conveyance can reach 38%, while nonverbal communication can convey 55%. One word expressed by two people might result in different recipients' perception. It's mainly caused by the differences between various cultures, selective acceptance, and awareness of people to the messages, factors of ambivalent, psychological defense and environmental interference.

Organizational communication

Organizational communication refers to communication among several individuals or groups, and acts the behavior to convey information between the upper and lower levels of organization. In the business management, organizational communication is one of the necessities to maintain relationships within the organization. The purpose is, through the mutual contacts among internal members of the organization, to enhance mutual trust and understanding, to judge efficiently the status of their own actions and activities, to serve as the coordination and consistency of actions, and to achieve the condensate goals within the organization.

管理小偏方

人際溝通

人際溝通指的是人與人之間的雙向溝通的傳播方式,通過2人以上或團體之間分享而傳送訊息。經研究發現,詞語表達僅能傳遞7%的意思,聲調可以傳達38%的意思,而非語言溝通則能傳達55%的意思。兩個人所表達同樣一個詞語,但傳遞出來給接受者的認知可能不同,主因是在於各種文化彼此間差異、人們對訊息選擇性的接受與認知、模凌兩可、防衛心理及環境干擾等因素所造成。

組織溝通

組織溝通指的是好幾個人或團體之間的溝通,是組織上下之間傳達資訊的行動或行為。組織溝通在企業組織管理是維繫組織內部人員關係的必要條件之一,其目的在於透過組織內部成員的互相聯繫,增進彼此信任與了解,有效判斷本身行為與活動狀態,以作為協調與一致性行動,來達到組織內部擬定的目標。

2-2 Request for Salary Adjustment
要求調薪

 ## Conversation 情境對話

The Christmas and New Year holidays are **approaching,** and the office has been filled with joyfulness and **relaxation**. Everyone's discussing the plan of holidays, while some of them are enthusiastic about the year-end bonuses and salary adjustment for the coming year.

聖誕節和新年的假期即將到來，辦公室裡充滿了愉快和輕鬆的氣氛；大家討論著假期的計劃，也有些人熱烈的討論著年終獎金和來年調薪的問題。

Queenie and Mary seem more concerned about the issue of salary adjustment. They're whispering together all day long, and Queenie even constantly tries to **inquire about** others' salary. Finally, they decide to talk to Robert.

昆妮和瑪莉似乎一直對調薪的事很在意，兩人整天竊竊私語的，昆妮還一直向別人打聽薪水的情況。最後，她們決定一起去找羅柏談談。

Robert: "I believe the reason you both come to me today is about the salary. I heard from some colleagues. All right, what is the problem now?"

羅柏：「今天兩位來找我，相信必然是有關薪水的事，我聽幾個同事提起過了。來，說說看有什麼問題？」

Queenie: "The situation is that I have worked in the company for almost two years, but my salary has never been adjusted. I'd like to know whether it's going to get a raise next year."

昆妮：「是這樣的：我來到公司都快兩年了，但薪水一直都沒有調整，不知道明年是否會增加？」

Robert: "I can't give you an explicit answer. For issues of promotion and salary, the company has the **appraisal** system, which mainly depends on the employee's attendance, performance, **seniority** and also the operational status and future plans of the whole company."

羅柏：「這我無法給妳明確的答案。關於升遷和調薪的問題，公司有一定的考核制度，主要是要看員工的考勤、績效、年資和公司的營運狀況與未來計劃，最後才能決定。」

Queenie: "But I heard that someone has been promoted within one year. Are you willing to **strive for** me, too?"

昆妮：「可是我聽說公司有人才來一年，就被調高了薪水，是不是你也願意幫我爭取看看呢？」

Robert: "I think making comparison of the salary with others is not right. I am willing to strive for you, of course. But the most important thing is your work performance. There's always a good chance if you have outstanding performance. But, **frankly speaking**, there's still a large space for your **advancement**. Now, Mary! You have the similar problem like Queenie?"

羅柏：「我認為薪水的事，實在不適合一直拿來和別人做比較。至於妳的薪水，當然我也希望能幫妳爭取，但最主要的還是看你工作上的表現，有好的表現，自然就有機會。但是坦白說，我認為妳還有很大等待進步的空間。那麼，瑪莉！妳也像昆妮一樣，有相同的問題嗎？」

Mary: "It's not necessarily the same. What I like to know is not just about my own salary, but also about the entire team. Our team had developed a series of application software, and I do believe that it had helped the company to achieve a great performance goal this year."

瑪莉：「倒也不盡然相同。我想了解的不單只是我個人調薪的問題，也包括我們整個團隊的人。今年，我們團隊幫公司開發出的那一系列的應用軟體，相信已經幫公司創造出不少的業績。」

Robert: "This achievement, without any doubt, was the effort of the whole team. That's why the president has **praised** the team publicly in the annual meeting of the company."

羅柏：「這件事情，無庸置疑的，是整個團隊努力的成果，所以總裁也在公司的年度會議中，公開的表揚。」

Mary: "What I like to know is whether the executives will have any incentive reward or **exalt** plan for such achievement of the team. And by the way, whether there's any specific consideration in grading and welfare for who's been assigned to the upcoming Chicago division."

瑪莉：「我想知道的是，公司是否會針對團隊的表現，給予些激勵性的獎賞、或是擢升的計劃？另外，對於即將被外派到芝加哥新公司的人，是否在職級和福利等方面，也會有些特別的考量呢？」

Robert: "That's a good question. For the outstanding performance of our team this year, I'm **convinced** that the executives will certainly have an incentive program, and you don't need to worry about this. However, because the new division in Chicago is **on the verge of** establishment, and some colleagues from the team is likely to be part of the expatiators. However. the executives might need a little more time to facilitate a more comprehensive plan."

羅柏：「這是個很好的問題。關於團隊在今年這樣優異的表現，我相信公司肯定會有個不錯的獎勵方案，這點妳不用擔心；只是因為芝加哥的新公司即將設立，團隊裡有些同仁極可能會被外派，所以需要再多一點的時間，以便於更完整的規劃。」

Mary: "I do think so, too. But I just wish that would not be **dragged on** for too long. All the colleagues are highly expecting, and might become more sensitive and anxious."

瑪莉：「我也是這樣想，只希望不要拖太久，同仁們期待很高、相對的也比較敏感和不安。」

Section 2
Organizational Behavior

Robert: "I like to emphasize again: The issue of salary is something **take to heart** for everyone, and could be very private and sensitive. Therefore, it's not suitable for inquiring the salary of others, and especially **forbidden** to discuss and compare all around. Otherwise, it might be **derived** lots of unnecessary misunderstanding or distress, and then hurt the harmony of team-work."

羅柏：「最後我還是再強調：薪水的事，每個人都會在意，也是很隱私和敏感的，因此不太適宜一直去詢問別人的薪水，尤其是很忌諱將此一話題到處的討論和比較，否則會衍生出許多不必要的誤解或困擾，反而傷害了團隊的和諧。」

Vocabulary 字彙解析

- **approaching** *adj., n.* 接近、逼近、將至

〔同義詞：**propinquity, next, upcoming**〕

All politicians are nervous on the approaching election.

He's afraid that his approaching might lead him into temptation.

- **relaxation** *n.* 放鬆、休閒、鬆弛

〔同義詞：**slack, laxity, letdown**〕

There has been a relaxation of the restrictions.

She found relaxation in gardening.

- **appraisal** *n.* 考核、評估、鑑定

〔同義詞：**assessment, evaluation, estimation**〕

The report has been subject to appraisal.

She carried out a thorough appraisal

- **seniority** *n.* 資歷、年資、排行

〔同義詞：**qualification, ranking, superiority**〕

There ought to be a proper sequence according to seniority.

Pay and benefits rise with seniority.

- **advancement** *n.* 進步、發展、演化

〔同義詞：**progress, headway, evolution**〕

Their lives were devoted to the advancement of science.

The future advancement of socialism needs input from young activists.

- **praise** *v., n.* 稱讚、表揚、誇獎

〔同義詞：**approval, acclaim, admiration**〕

We praise God for past blessings

The novel received extremely high praise from critics.

■ **exalt** *n.* 尊崇、表彰、擢升

〔同義詞：extol, acclaim, esteem〕

We are talking about people who exalt the effort to preserve slavery.

The party will continue to exalt its hero.

■ **convince** *v.* 說服、信服、誘使

〔同義詞：persuade, satisfy, assure〕

He failed to convince her that he was being honest

The director had a hard time convincing him to take the part.

■ **forbidden** *adj.* 被禁止、嚴禁

〔同義詞：prohibited, un-allowed, banned〕

You can find out some magic and monsters in this forbidden book.

In the Islands, forests are always forbidden places.

■ **derive** *v.* 衍生、導出、獲得

〔同義詞：extract, attain, glean〕

The source of confusion usually derives from oneself.

This calculation derives from another formula to solve a differential equation.

Phrase in sentence 片語和句型解析

■ **inquire about** 打聽、探詢

〔同義詞：**ask about, query, find out**〕

We inquired about food preparation at the table.

The students inquired about the details of scholarship.

■ **strive for** 爭取、追求

〔同義詞：**struggle, fight**〕

He always strives for perfection.

We must strive for steady growth

■ **frankly speaking** 老實說、坦白說

〔同義詞：**straightforwardly, forthrightly, openly**〕

Frankly speaking, all these plans are wrong.

To most of the people I was, frankly speaking, too scary and horrid.

■ **on the verge of** 即將、瀕臨、行將

〔同義詞：**on the eve of**〕

He was on the verge of turning professional at one time.

My voice has got so loud that it is on the verge of breaking.

■ **dragged on** 拖延、一拖再拖、偷生

〔同義詞：**delay, hang up, hold off**〕

Larry was turning out to be a drag on her career.

He took a long drag on his cigarette.

■ **take to heart** 認真、在乎

〔同義詞：**care, mind, notice**〕

You take to heart very deeply for him.

When you say you take me to heart, I feel loved.

Practice in Management

For all corporate employees, undeniably, the payroll package is definitely one of the issues that everyone cares the most. Everyone is working hard for better remuneration. Therefore, the issue of salary will not only be deeply interested by us, but also provokes our sensitivity. If not handled appropriately, the issue of private payroll will become a topic of argument. This situation is likely to be a great distress on management, or even mischief to the team.

One of the main factors to bring about salary argument is lack of enough institutionalized, or no consistent standard in the salary structure and adjustment method of the enterprise. Some companies even don't have any rules to formulate or adjust the salary levels, and only in accordance with the benchmark what the boss set says. Or there're always exceptions outside the rules. Employees might have an unfair feeling under these situations, holding the grudge to their companies or having an unpleasant feeling among peers.

Another factor for salary argument is failed to protect the confidentiality of payroll. Whenever there are too many discussion sand comparison among colleagues, then whispers, rumors, and emotions will be overspread, or even result in some events out of control, such as sabotage without warning, emotional reaction intensively, or group resignation. That's really a very tricky surprise to managers.

經驗與分享

對於所有企業的員工而言，無可諱言的是，薪資和福利絕對是大家所最關心的事情之一，大家辛勤地工作，無非就是希望能得到更好的報酬；因此，薪資的議題不僅讓大家深感興趣，也會挑起大家敏感的神經，如果沒有妥善處理，讓薪資的私事成為議論紛紛的話題，這種情況很可能成為管理上很大的困擾，甚至產生團隊上的傷害。

薪資問題會造成員工間的議論，其主要的原因之一，是在於公司薪資結構和調整方法，其本身的不夠制度化、或沒有一致的標準；有些企業對於員工的敘薪和調整，並沒有真正的規則可依循，完全依照老闆本身的設定為基準，或者在規則之外有太多的特例；在這種情況會造成員工感覺到不公平，使得對公司心生不滿、或者同儕間有所芥蒂。

另一個造成薪資議論的原因，就是薪資機密性的保護不夠，同事間不斷的討論和比較著薪資，許多的耳語、謠傳和情緒就會不停的滋生著，甚至會造成失控情況，例如：無預警的怠工、強烈的情緒化反應或是集體離職等，讓管理者感到很棘手、或是措手不及。

Tips in Management

Human resources management

Human resources management is the managerial tasks to complete the personnel related matters. It's increasingly important in the modern enterprise management. In a mature developed economic system, human resources management must meet for the best resource efficiency, buildup human resource platform, role as a communication and gathering information channels, integrate the views of all other parties to deal with compensation and benefit matters. The most important objectives are training and human resource development.

The main functions of human resource management include: recruitment, training and development, compensation and benefits administration, performance appraisal, employee relations, and corporate culture.

1. Manpower planning: Base on the expected future manpower needs, then establishes the recruitment employee, training, re-deployment and severance or dismissal procedures to ensure that companies within the specified time have adequate and appropriate personnel.

2. Recruitment and selection: recruit and attract talented people for the position posted, and then pick up the most suitable candidates.

3. Training and Development: to enhance the capacity of work for employees in all aspects, such as professional skills, interpersonal skills and problem-solving ability, and then improve their performance.

4. Performance Appraisal: Assessing staff performance.

5. Compensation and Benefits Management: developing effective compensation and benefits system to attract and retain talent, and motivate employees to work hard.

In the general category of human resource management, payroll and benefits administration are most sensitive and concerned by employees. However, to protect the privacy of individual employees, and also to avoid unnecessary distress management, the salary will be paid in a confidential manner and not publicly released.

 管理小偏方

人力資源管理

人力資源管理是指為了完成管理工作中涉及人或人事方面的任務所進行的管理工作，其在近代企業管理中愈來愈被重視。在經濟發展成熟的體系下，人力資源管理必須配合以爭取最佳的資源效益，建立人力資源平台，作為溝通及搜集資訊渠道，將各方意見綜合，捨短取長，以處理薪酬、福利等事宜。人力資源最重要的工作是培訓及發展。

人力資源管理主要職能包括：人員招募、培訓及開發、薪酬及福利管理、績效考核、員工關係、與企業文化。

1. 人力規劃：根據企業所設定的未來人力需求，建立員工招募、訓練、重新部署與遣散或解僱等程序，確保企業在指定時間內能有足夠和合適的人員。

2. 招聘和挑選：招攬和吸引具備才能的人應徵有關職位，並從中挑選最合適的申請人。

3. 培養和發展：從各方面提升員工的工作能力，例如專業技能、人際關係技巧和解難能力等，從而改善他們的工作表現。

4. 工作表現評核：評估員工的工作表現

5. 薪酬和福利管理：制定有效薪酬和福利制度，以吸引和保留人才，並激勵員工努力工作。

在一般的人力資源管理範疇中，通常薪資與福利管理，是員工最為關注和敏感的部分；但為保障員工個人隱私，也避免管理上不必要的困擾，對於個人薪資和福利內容，都將之列為保密，採取薪資保密發放的方式，不會公開公布。

2-3 Attributing Appreciation to the Subordinates
讓部屬表現出來

 ## Conversation 情境對話

In the annual business conference, all the executives of the company had **prepared well** in advance, and cautiously participate in the meeting. The president of the company **presides** the conference by himself.

公司年度的經營會議上，集團內所有的高階主管都預先做足了準備，戰戰兢兢的列席參加會議，而會議由總裁親自主持。

President: "This year is very difficult and toilsome for all of us. We did encounter a lot of operational challenges from economic **depression** and also the changeable consumption behavior in technology. Fortunately, we launched a series of new application softwares in the middle of this year. It's not only been critically acclaimed, but, **leaped up** our operating performance just like a **booster**."

總裁：「今年是一個非常艱辛的一年，大家辛苦了；整個經濟環境的蕭條，加上科技消費行為的多變，我們今年的營運的確遇到了很大的挑戰。所幸，我們在年中推出了一系列嶄新的APP應用軟體，不僅深獲好評，也讓我們的業績突飛猛進，有如營運上的強心針一般。」

At the same time, a wealth of application from this new software was just presenting in the big screen.

同一時間，大螢幕上正呈現著這新軟體豐富的應用。

The president then continued: "This series of software was fully developed by our business promotion division, which gives me a special surprise and **admiration**. I like to invite the division manager, Robert, to share with us."

總裁接著說：「這一系列的軟體，全是由我們的業務推廣部門所開發出來的，這讓我特別感到驚喜和敬佩。是否就請部門的經理羅柏來跟我們分享一下。」

Robert: "Thanks to our president. I do really enjoy working in the team, and I'm also honored to be one of them. However, this achievement was entirely **carried through** the ongoing efforts of these hard working partners. If you don't mind, I would like to invite them in and introduce them to you."

經理：「非常謝謝總裁的厚愛；能在這樣一個團隊裡工作很享受，也很榮幸能成為他們的一份子，但這項成果，完全是由我們一群不斷的努力而得來的，如果各位容許，我想邀請他們進來，讓大家認識一下。」

Then Peter, Mary and several young men, walked into the huge conference hall nervously. Then the audience burst into applause.

這時彼得、瑪莉和幾個年輕人，略帶緊張得走進碩大的會議廳內，現場響起了熱烈的掌聲。

President: "What a **vibrant** group of young people. Now, Robert. Can you share with us what's special about this software?"

總裁：「真是充滿朝氣的一群年輕人；羅柏，現在是否跟我們分享一下，這個軟體有什麼不一樣的地方。」

Robert: "This research was the effort from these partners. I'll recommend that they explain by themselves on the stage and answer all the related questions for you. Peter and Mary can be the **representatives**."

經理：「這項研發是這群夥伴辛苦得到的成果，我想就由他們上台來為各位解說，並且回答使用上的問題。我們就請彼得和瑪莉代表吧！」

Peter: "For the development of this series of software, it's originally came from the experienced demand when we **contact with** some customers. So we always reflect and search from the users' **point of view**. We're glad, after months of team brain storming, to get this effort eventually, just like the **nurturing** of our own child."

彼得：「當初會開發這系列，是我們在接觸客戶時所體驗出來的一些需求，所以我們一直都站在使用者的角度來思考和研發，很高興經過數個月的團隊腦力激盪，像孕育自己的孩子一樣，終於得到這項成果。」

Mary: "Now please allow me to explain for you the application and **distinguish** of the software. With just some simple operation, it's very easy for everyone to get started."

瑪莉：「接下來我就透過螢幕，為各位說明這項軟體的應用與特色；只要藉由簡單的操作，每個人都可以輕鬆上手。」

President: "This achievement is really cool, and I can't wait to learn, too. Are you willing to spend some time in my office to teach me alone as practical operation?"

總裁：「這真的是很酷的研發，我也迫不及待的想要學會；你們願意花點時間，到我的辦公室裡來，單獨的教教我如何操作嗎？」

Peter's excited and **aroused**: "You're so **polite**, Sir. It's our pleasure!"

彼得興奮又激昂的說：「總裁您太客氣了，這是我們的榮幸。」

President: "These young guys are so **terrific**, and share us with vitality and hope. Thanks Robert for guiding these young partners, too. I wonder if I had chance to join this team and work with them?"

總裁：「這群年輕人太棒了，讓我們感受到活力和希望，也謝謝羅柏為我們帶領這群夥伴；不知道，我是否也可以加入這個團隊，跟他們一起工作呢？」

Everyone there is laughing.

現場的每個人，都哄堂大笑了起來。

Vocabulary 字彙解析

■ **preside** *vt.* 主持、擔任主席

〔同義詞：**take charge of, direct, chairman**〕

Bishop William presided at the meeting.

No longer was there a need for the composer to preside at the keyboard.

■ **depression** *n.* 蕭條、沮喪、不景氣

〔同義詞：**dismay, recession, slump**〕

Antipyschotics may also be used to treat severe cases of depression.

Economic depressions are predominantly the result of insufficient demand.

■ **admiration** *n.* 敬佩、讚賞

〔同義詞：**gloat, respect, appreciation**〕

Their admiration for each other was genuine.

The director had a lot of admiration for Douglas as an actor.

■ **vibrant** *adj.* 充滿活力的、朝氣的、熱鬧的

〔同義詞：**spirited, lively, energetic**〕

She joined a vibrant team of reporters.

He has a vibrant personality.

■ **nurture** *vt., n.* 敬佩、讚賞

〔同義詞：**gloat, respect, appreciation**〕

John was nurtured by his parents in a close-knit family.

I'm interesting in study the nurture of fishes.

■ **arouse** *vt.* 激發、喚起、啟發

〔同義詞：**stimulate, excite, inspire**〕

Something about the man aroused the guard's suspicions.

She had been aroused by the telephone.

Phrase in sentence 片語和句型解析

- **prepare well** 做好準備、充分準備

〔同義詞：**ready, adequate preparation, fully prepared**〕
We had prepared well a brief summary of the article.
The spare transformer was prepared well for shipment.

- **leap up** 跳起來、躍起、飛竄

〔同義詞：**jump up, squander, skip**〕
The cat leaps up to the table.
She began to leap up the path.

- **carry through** 完成、貫徹

〔同義詞：**complete, accomplish, fulfill**〕
The planes carried through their mission.
He carried through his ambition to become a journalist.

- **burst into** 衝進、闖入、爆開

〔同義詞：**stormed, break, arouse**〕
The ice had burst into the lake.
The computer game was burst into poor programming.

- **contact with** 連繫、接觸

〔同義詞：**connect, communicate with, approach**〕
The electrodes were contacted with a recording device.
Transportation planning should be contacted with energy policy.

- **point of view** 觀點、看法、角度

〔同義詞：**perspective, view, angle**〕
I'm trying to get Matthew to change his point of view.
Most guidebook history is written from the editor's point of view.

Practice in Management

In the field of **business management**, **leadership** is not only a very complex, but also very important knowledge. For managers, as the leader of intermediate level, especially those who need to study through the techniques of leadership. Manager's act as leader and guider to the grassroots subordinates, the manager of managers and their mentors, but the company owner or executives, the managers and, on the other side, managers then became the subordinates and executors to the top. Managers play a very important bridging role between the top and the grassroots levels. On the one hand, managers need to carry out the direction of high-level instructions and convey to the subordinates. Then, on the other hand, managers help the subordinates to solve the problems and reflect to the top.

Because of the different perceptions in managerial role and leadership styles, each manager acts totally different to others in the role of bridging function between levels, especially to reflect the aspirations and needs of the grassroots. Some managers might rather try his best to cover up the good performance of his subordinates and then attributed the outstanding performance as to their own. Some managers always report to the top nothing but good news. Still some managers will shirk out the responsibility when the problems or troubles happened. All these cases, after a period of time, might lead the subordinate to forfeit the willingness of cohesion and then increase the barriers to management. It's the issue that needs to be reconsidered by managers.

經驗與分享

在**企業管理**的領域中，**領導統御**不只是一門很複雜、也是很重要的學問，這對身為中階管理的經理人而言，更是需要深刻去體會其中的技巧，因為對基層部屬而言，經理人是他們的管理者與指導者，但對於公司老闆或高階主管而言，經理人又成了別人的部屬和執行者；尤其經理人身處在高階與基層之間，居間扮演著極為重要的橋樑角色，一方面要貫徹高層指示的方向，並向下傳達，另一方面又要幫助基層部屬解決問題，並向上回報與反應。

基於對管理者角色認知不同、和領導統御模式的差異，經理人對於這種橋樑的功能，特別是反映基層的心聲與需求，實際的運作卻是大異其趣。有些經理人在面對部屬有所好表現時，或者是盡力的將之掩飾而不讓高層知道、或甚至是直接歸功於己，有些經理人對上層的回報永遠是報喜不報憂，也有些經理人在遇到問題或錯誤時，會將責任推脫於外；這些情況在久而久之後，部屬會對經理人失去了向心力，也增加了管理上的障礙，值得經理人的三思。

Tips in Management

Leadership

Leadership has been described as a process of social influence in which a person can enlist the aid and support of others in the accomplishment of a common task. For example, some understand a leader simply as somebody whom people follow or as somebody who guides or directs others, while others define leadership as "organizing a group of people to achieve a common goal".

The study of leadership can be dated back to Plato, Sun Tzu, and Machiavelli; however, leadership has only become the focus of contemporary academic studies in the last 60 years, and particularly more so in the last two decades. Leadership study is a multidisciplinary academic field of study that focuses on leadership in organizational contexts and in human life. Leadership studies has origins in the social sciences (e.g., sociology, anthropology, psychology), in humanities (e.g., history and philosophy), as well as in professional and applied fields of study (e.g., management and education). The field of leadership studies is closely linked to the field of organizational studies.

As an academic area of inquiry, the study of leadership has been of interest to scholars from a wide variety of disciplinary backgrounds. Today, there are numerous academic programs (spanning several academic colleges and departments) related to the study of leadership.

管理小偏方

領導統御

領導統御,乃定義為透過社會影響力,讓其中一人可以得到另一群人的協助與支持,以共同完成任務的一種過程。有些人將領導者定義為:眾人所追隨的人、或是指揮與指引他人的人;也有人將領導統御定義為:「將一群人組織起來,以實現一個共同的目標」。

領導統御的研究,可以遠溯至柏拉圖、孫子和馬基維利等時代;然而在過去60年間,特別是過去的20年,領導統御才慢慢成為現代學術研究的焦點。領導統御的研究,是一種橫跨多種學術領域,且側重於針對於在組織背景、和人類生活中的領導統御。而領導統御的淵源,來自於社會科學(如社會學,人類學,心理學),人類學科(例如,歷史和哲學),以及在專業和應用領域的研究(例如,管理和教育)。因此,領導統御的研究,與組織研究的領域息息相關。

當做為學術調查的領域之一,領導統御的研究,一直吸引著來自不同學術背景學者的興趣。在今日,許多學院的課程(跨越幾個學科院系)都有領導統御相關的研究。

Section 2 Organizational Behavior

2-4 Strive for Your Team
為部屬據理力爭

 Conversation 情境對話

Thanks to the successful development of new APP software, the company's performance had finally **turned up**. Therefore, the executives had decided to set up a dedicated software design and development division. Then, they plan to recruit some professional **talents**, and select some candidates for the training course in Japan. This important business direction will be formally announced in the coming yearly business meeting.

由於新款APP軟體的成功開發，讓公司的業績終於止跌回升，高層也決定成立一個專責的軟體設計開發部門，除了招聘一些專業人才進來，並遴選部份的人選到日本受訓；在新年度的經營會議當中，也正式宣布了這項重要的經營方向。

President: "In the past years, the development of application software worldwide was extremely fast, and the competition is more and more intensive. You can have a **profound** experience from our operating situation last year. Therefore, we hope to set up an independent professional software design and development division, which acts as a strong operating generator for the whole group. Now please welcome our senior vice president Rudolph, who's **in charge of** this project. He'll give us a further illustration."

總裁：「近幾年來，全世界應用軟體的發展極端的快速，競爭也更加的激烈，若我們從去年公司的營運情況來看，相信會有很深的體會；因此，我們希望能成立一個專業獨立的軟體設計開發部門，讓整個集團能增加新的動力。現在就請負責這個專案的資深副總魯道夫為我們進一步說明。」

Rudolph: "The purpose to setup this new division is not only for the developing of new software products, but also hoping to **spur** the sales of all accessories consumables. It's very important to the future of company. And now, we're recruiting some professional talents."

魯道夫：「這個部門成立的目的，不僅是要開發新軟體商品，更希望藉此能帶動所有週邊耗材的銷售，對公司未來的發展很重要，因此我們正在招募一些專業而傑出的菁英。」

President: "**In addition to** the recruiting, there should be some further plans."

總裁：「除了人才招募外，應該還有進一步的計劃吧！」

Rudolph: "Yes. After the work of recruiting and **team up** had reached a certain extent, we hope to select some core candidates to have trainings in Japan. We wish that the strength and developing direction of the whole team will be more superior and clear then."

魯道夫：「是的！等人員募集整隊到一個程度後，我們希望能遴選一些核心人員到日本受訓，好讓整個團隊的實力和發展方向，更加的精實和明確。」

While all the members are exciting in discussion, Robert suddenly raised his hand to speak.

正當大家很興奮的討論著時，羅柏突然舉起手來準備發言。

Robert: "In regarding the **configuration** of this new division, I don't know if I could make some suggestions. I think it might be better if we can **transpose** some good talents from inside the company to enhance the new team."

羅柏：「關於這個新部門的配置，不知道我可否提出一些建議。我認為是否應該從公司內部調一些不錯的人才過來，以增加這個團隊的實力。」

President: "You got someone in your mind?"

總裁：「喔！那你可有些想推薦的人選嗎？」

Robert: "Yes. I believe that Peter and Mary from our sales team will be qualified candidates."

羅柏：「是的！我相信我們營業部門的彼得和瑪莉，都是很不錯的人選。」

Rudolph: "I know they are excellent in selling. But what this division needs is some talents with professional software development technique and creativity, and I'm afraid that their basic training might be not good enough."

Robert: "Do you still remember the software series which had created a **brilliant** achievement for the company last year? That's the effort from this team. Although their backgrounds were not major in software design, I have confidence that they're absolutely **competent** because of their creativity and hard working, especially **base on** their **familiarity** with our business model and clearly **mastery** to the needs of consumers. I believe that all these are necessary and very important to the new division."

President: "I know these young guys. They're good. But, **after all**, they are from your division. We need a further consideration whether a recommendation from you is appropriated. And, furthermore, it might be a loss of your division if they're transposed to the new team."

魯道夫：「我知道他們的業務能力很不錯；但是這部門需要的，是具有專業的軟體開發技術和創意的人才，我擔心他們的基礎訓練，恐怕還不太夠。」

羅柏：「大家還記得去年為公司營造出亮麗成績的那一系列軟體嗎？那就是他們這個團隊努力的成果。雖然他們並非軟體設計科班的背景，但我相信以他們的創意和努力，絕對可以勝任的；尤其他們不僅了解公司的營運模式，更能清楚掌握消費者的需求，我相信這些對於新團隊而言，都是必備、且非常重要的。」

總裁：「我知道這群年輕人，他們很不錯。但是他們畢竟是你部門的人，你的推薦是否合宜仍有待進一步思考，但若將他們調到新部門，是否反而會造成你部門裡的損失？」

Robert: "I'm glad that we have such outstanding talents in our team. But they are not just talents of mine or our division, they're the human resources belonging to the whole company. And we should not **obliterate** their growing space."

President: "I see. This issue will be assigned to Rudolph for further discretion and planning. You can fully discuss the **feasibility** of implementation. And please let me know if there's any conclusion."

Robert: "Thanks for your consideration. **Even though** they're not easy to be transposed to the new team in eventually, I also believe, if we assign them to join the training program in Japan and then participates the initial planning processes of new division, it will be definitely a great help to the company as a whole."

羅柏：「我很高興在我的團隊裡，有這麼優秀的人才，但是他們並非只是我的、或我們部門的人才，他們應該屬於整個公司的資源，我們也不應該抹煞了他們的發揮空間。」

總裁：「我了解了。這事就請魯道夫好好的去斟酌和規劃，你們仔細的去討論執行的可行性，有任何的結論，務必讓我知道。」

羅柏：「謝謝您的體諒！我想即使他們不便於轉調到新團隊去，如果能讓他們一起到日本受訓，並且參與團隊初期的規劃過程，相信對公司整體而言，絕對會有很大的幫助。」

Vocabulary 字彙解析

▪ talent　*n.*　天賦、才能、人才

〔同義詞：talented person, endowment, ability〕

He possesses more talent than any other player.

She tried to promote the talent of a Chair of Psychiatry.

▪ profound　*adj.*　深刻的、深切的、奧妙的

〔同義詞：intense, keen, wise〕

We present our profound thanks to whoever save us.

She's a profound and studious young woman.

▪ spur　*vi., vt., n.*　鞭策、帶動、骨刺、馬刺

〔同義詞：drive, stimulus, incentive〕

She spurred her horse toward the hedge.

The profit was both the spur and the reward of enterprise.

▪ configuration　*n.*　構造、格局、組態

〔同義詞：arrangement, layout, geography〕

The broad configuration of the economy remains capitalist.

Flint is extremely hard, like diamond, which has a similar configuration.

▪ transpose　*vi., vt.*　轉調、移位、顛倒

〔同義詞：reverse, interchange, transfer〕

The captions describing the two state flowers were accidentally transposed.

The problems of civilization are transposed into a rustic setting.

▪ brilliant　*adj.*　輝煌、精彩、燦爛

〔同義詞：glorious, splendid, shining〕

Robert is a brilliant young mathematician.

The sun shone brightly, illuminating the garden with a brilliant ray of light.

■ **competent** *adj.* 勝任、能幹、稱職

〔同義詞：qualified, capable, professional〕

I could only judge this young man a competent candidate.

I'm quite competent of taking care of myself.

■ **familiarity** *n.* 熟悉度、簡略的行為

〔同義詞：acquaintance, extravagance, informality〕

Advertising can increase customer familiarity with a product.

He enjoyed the familiarity of the occasion.

■ **mastery** *n.* 掌握、征服、精通

〔同義詞：conquest, proficiency, comprehension〕

She played with some mastery.

He demonstrated his mastery in Chinese.

■ **obliterate** *vt.* 抹殺、否定、忽略

〔同義詞：blot, cross out, write off〕

The memory was so painful that he obliterated it from his mind.

The writing was messy and obliterated.

■ **feasibility** *n.* 可行性、可能性

〔同義詞：possibility, odds, eventuality〕

The scientist had tried the feasibility of a manned flight to Mars.

It's the theoretical feasibility of a chain reaction.

 # Phrase in sentence 片語和句型解析

■ **turned up** 調高、交替上升、抖擻

〔同義詞：increase, dig up, stir up〕

They try to turn a slightly up for his voice.

Car use is turning up at an alarming rate.

■ **in charge of**　負責、掌管

〔同義詞：**responsible for, accountable for, in control of**〕

The department is in charge of the education affairs.

The supplier of goods or services can become in charge of contract in a variety of ways.

■ **in addition to**　除了、此外

〔同義詞：**except, besides, furthermore**〕

In addition to a quiet charm, this species is an easy garden plant.

She began with simple arithmetic, in addition to the subtraction.

■ **team up**　組隊、聯手

〔同義詞：**ally, together, associate with**〕

He teamed up with the band to produce the album.

The band teams up with a variety of musical influences.

■ **base on**　基於、立足於、憑著

〔同義詞：**depend, go by, lean against**〕

Differences in earnings are based on a wide variety of factors.

I know I can base on your discretion.

■ **after all**　畢竟、到底、終究

〔同義詞：**eventually, in the end, at last**〕

After all, I arrived at the hotel before midnight.

The largest firms, after all, may become unstoppable.

■ **even though**　即使、儘管、雖然

〔同義詞：**even if, although, notwithstanding**〕

It wasn't that warm even though the sun was shining.

Nothing much changed even though he was away.

Practice in Management

For managers, leadership is the art and skill with people, just like the leading in the army. No matter how rich the experience and knowledge in the professional areas, how familiar with a variety of management techniques, the most effective managing way to managers is still the sincerely mutual interaction with the subordinates and unites the team cohesion. Especially when the subordinates got the potential or better opportunities of promotion in the company, do the managers have such magnanimity willing to help subordinates go upward and strive for subordinates? Thus mind is a rare magnanimity in leadership.

In a reality environment, what the most managers are concerned about is the performance of their own team. When subordinates have a very good ability and potential, the managers naturally wish that he could summit a greater contribution to the team in order to enhance the team's performance. Even when the sight extended to the whole enterprise, many managers still choose to keep the subordinates as the assets of team's, or use as the chips to show their management performance. When the manager's view focuses on the development of enterprise as a whole, it's still not known if there's any help to the manager himself, but a great thing for subordinates with potential to play out on a higher stage.

This is a question worth pondering, maybe everyone has a different answer.

經驗與分享

對於企業的經理人而言，領導統御是種帶人的藝術，就像帶領一支部隊一樣，無論經理人在其專業領域的經驗和知識是如何的豐富，或者他是多麼熟悉各種的管理技巧，但最有效的管理方式，仍是與部屬間真心的**互動**，以凝聚**團隊的向心力**；尤其當部屬有些值得開發的潛質、或是在企業裡有更好的發展機會，經理人是否有這種氣度，願意協助部屬向上提升，並盡力的為部屬設想和爭取，這種胸襟，是一種很難得的領導者氣度。

在實際的環境中，對多數經理人而言，最關心的還是自己所帶領團隊的表現，當部屬有很不錯的能力和潛力時，自然希望他能在團隊中有更大的貢獻，以提升團隊的績效；即使將目光擴展到整體企業時，許多經理人仍會選擇將好部屬視為這個團隊的資產、或是用來展現自己管理績效的籌碼。能夠將眼光放在整體企業的發展上，對於經理人本身的升遷是否有所幫助，並不得而知，但讓有潛力的部屬在更大的舞台發揮出來，卻是很棒的一件事。

這是一個值得玩味的問題，或許每個人都有不同的答案。

Tips in Management

Positive reinforcement

Behavior modification and the concept of positive reinforcement was created by B. F. Skinner. Positive reinforcement occurs when a positive stimulus is presented in response to a behavior, increasing the likelihood of that behavior in the future.

The following is an example of how positive reinforcement can be used in a business setting.

Assume praise is a positive reinforcement for a particular employee. This employee does not show up to work on time every day. The manager of this employee decides to praise the employee for showing up on time every day the employee actually shows up to work on time. As a result, the employee comes to work on time more often because the employee likes to be praised. In this example, praise (the stimulus) is a positive reinforcement for this employee because the employee arrives at work on time (the behavior) more frequently after being praised for showing up to work on time.

The use of a positive reinforcement is a successful and growing technique used by leaders to motivate and attain desired behaviors from subordinates. Organizations, such as Frito-Lay, 3M, Goodrich, Michigan Bell, and Emery Air Freight have all used reinforcement to increase productivity. Empirical research covering the last 20 years suggests that reinforcement theory has a 17 percent increase in performance. Additionally, many reinforcement techniques, such as the use of praise are inexpensive, providing higher performance for lower costs.

管理小偏方

正向鼓勵

有關行為矯正和正向鼓勵的概念，是由B. F. Skinner所創建的。正向鼓勵的發生，乃源自於當對於某個行為所產生出的正面刺激時，未來類似的行為將越來越可能不斷出現。

下列的例子即在説明正向鼓勵如何應用於實務的企業環境之中。假設獎賞對特定員工而言是一種正向鼓勵；該員工原本並非每天準時上班，經理人於是決定：當這員工每天都準時上班時，將給予員工獎賞的經理決定讚美員工每天員工實際顯示了上班時間顯示出來的時間。如此一來，員工將會有更多的時候能準時的來工作，因為員工喜歡這獎賞。在這個例子中，獎賞（刺激）對員工是一種正向鼓勵，因為該員工在得到獎賞後，就更經常的準時上班（行為）。

正向鼓勵的使用，對於領導人用於激勵、及誘導部屬以達到特定的方面，是一種成功且日益增加的管理技巧。許多公司組織，例如Frito-Lay、3M、固特異、Michigan電話公司、及Emery航空等，都使用這種激勵方式以提高生產率。在含蓋著過去20年的研究中顯示，這項激力理論可提高17%的績效。另外，許多項獎賞這類得激勵方法算是很廉價的，用很低的成本就能提昇許多的績效。

2-5 Request from the Boss
老闆的要求

 ## Conversation 情境對話

Robert is the new manager of Engineering Department, and still trying to get familiar with the new work. But the partners he needs to lead are a bunch of **veterans** who always **ignore** his requirement or **prevarication** to **stall**. Robert feels very frustrated, and, without any choice, comes to his superior Simon, the VP, for help. Simon promises to attend the department meeting, and will help him timely.

羅柏是工程部新任的經理，對於剛接觸的業務還在熟悉當中，但他所帶領的夥伴，卻是一群資深的同仁，對於他的一些要求並不太理會，總會找些理由搪塞，這讓羅柏感到非常挫折；羅柏只好向他的上司賽門協理求救，賽門答應他列席參加部門會議，並適時的幫他一把。

Robert: "Our project progress was delayed 20% this month, and also that's lagged behind for three or four months consequently. Although I just **took office** not long ago, I knew it's **a** serious **matter of concern** to the Company. It needs our greater efforts to catch up the schedule. Elmer, you're the supervisor of the entire project, and understood the whole situation. What's your opinion?"

Elmer: "Well, it's really helpless. That's so while Manager Howard was here."

Robert: "Isn't there any other more efficient way to improve such a **plight**?"

Elmer: "Robert. Maybe you're new here, and don't quite understand the situation. There're so many difficulties and **variables** therein. All we veteran partners for years are aware of that it's not an easy job."

羅柏：「這個月的工程進度又落後了20％，我們已經連續落後三、四個月了，雖然我剛到任不久，但我知道這是公司很重視的問題，希望我們能加把勁，將進度趕上來；艾默，你是整個工地的主任，最了解整個狀況，你有什麼看法？」

艾默：「唉，這也是沒有辦法的事，以前豪爾經理在的時候就是如此了。」

羅柏：「難道沒有其他更有效率的方式，來改善這種困境嗎？」

艾默：「羅柏，或許你剛來不久，並不清楚很多情況；這中間有太多的困難和變數，我們這些待了好多年的夥伴，都知道這沒那麼簡單啦！」

Robert: "Additionally, the inventory of warehouse material after counted seems to have a big **discrepancy** too, compared with the computer data. The executives worry about the loss or theft, too. Vincent, you've been in charge of warehouse for some time. Isn't there any better way?"

羅柏：「另外，倉庫那邊的物料，盤點出來的數據，似乎一直都跟電腦資料上有很大的落差，公司也很擔心是否有漏失或是失竊的情形；文森，你管理倉庫一段時間了，有沒有什麼更好的辦法呢？」

Vincent: "The inventory data of warehouse has been a mess for long time and I could never check it out. Why don't you figure out that by yourself, if you don't believe it."

文森：「倉庫那個資料的數據，早就是一團混亂了，再怎麼對也對不上來，不信的話，不然你就自己來對看看就知道了。」

Robert says helplessly: "But, at least, you should have some preventive measures for the problem of loss and theft."

羅柏無奈的說：「但是那漏失和失竊的問題，你總該有些預防的管理方法吧！」

Vincent: "What can I do? I just **shove** the material to the position of what it should be. And I totally can't control how they apply those materials."

文森：「能有什麼辦法？我就把物料擺在該擺的位置上，至於他們怎樣領用物料，我也實在很難完全的控制。」

Finally, Simon could not help but stand up and walk into the front of meeting room.

這時賽門終於忍不住，起了身走到會議室的前面。

Simon: "The topics you guys just discussed have been noticed by the executives for a long time. What Robert had said is not only his personal opinion, but also the requirement by executives. Robert's just taken office shortly. I don't want to see any **indolent** or prevaricate **mentality** as of veteran. You can come to me directly for any question. But, in the same time, I'll request you execute what's the expectation of Company, especially Elmer and Vincent. How do you both feel?"

賽門：「剛剛各位討論的議題，都是公司已經注意很久的事了，而羅柏所說的話，並不只是他的意思，這是公司的要求！現在羅柏剛上任不久，我不希望再看到這種倚老賣老、搪塞怠惰的心態了；如果大家有問題也可以直接來找我，但我也會要求各位好好執行公司的期待，尤其是艾默和文森，兩位覺得如何？」

Elmer and Vincent look at each other, and then sit upright by silence.

艾默和文森互相望了一眼，正襟危坐地不敢說話。

Simon: "For the previous issues, I want you both summit the improving plan to Robert's office and also send a copy to me. Then you propose the executive report of these projects in the meeting next week."

賽門：「針對剛剛的問題，我要兩位在三天內提出改善計畫，送到羅柏的辦公室，也給我一份副本，下週的會議中，你們再提出這些專案的執行報告。」

Vocabulary 字彙解析

- **veteran** *n.* 老兵、老手、老資格

〔同義詞：old hand, past master, vet, 〕

The new players have provided tough competition to the veterans in the field.

He's a veteran at keeping his whereabouts secret.

- **prevarication** *n.* 推諉、支吾

〔同義詞：Evasiveness, equivocation, lies〕

I say this without any prevarication.

There're truth and also prevarication of her legend in our society.

- **stall** *vt., vi., n.* 使進退兩難、失速

〔同義詞：suffer, endure, stand〕

Her car stalled at the crossroads.

These cities have stalled through the war.

- **plight** *vt., n.* 困境、地步、發誓

〔同義詞：dilemma, predicament, ensure〕

We must direct our efforts toward relieving the plight of children living in poverty.

People often face the plight of feeding themselves or their cattle.

- **discrepancy** *n.* 差異、出入

〔同義詞：difference, divergence, diversity〕

There's a discrepancy between your account and his.

Here was considerable discrepancy in the style of the reports.

- **shove** *vi., n.* 推擠、猛撞

〔同義詞：push, thrust, squeeze〕

Police started pushing and shoving people down the street.

She gave him a hefty shove and he nearly fell.

- **indolent** *adj.* 懶惰的、怠惰的

〔同義詞：**lazy, idle, slothful**〕

They didn't want any competition in the lazy and indolent stakes.

Prostate cancer is an indolent disease in most men.

- **mentality** *n.* 心理、心態、思維

〔同義詞：**psychology, mood, viewpoint**〕

It's hard to express your highly developed and sensitive mentality.

He appeared to be in a very good mentality about something.

 ## Phrase in sentence 片語和句型解析

- **take office** 就職、上任

〔同義詞：**assume a post, assume office**〕

Obama took an office as the president of U.S.A.

It's a bright opportunity of growth when our new chairman takes office.

- **a matter of concern** （令人）關注的問題（事情）

〔同義詞：**concerns, care**〕

Oil reserve is a matter of concern for the Energy Department.

It's a matter of concern for him to pay attention in the spelling mistakes.

Section 2
Organizational Behavior

🔖 Practice in Management

The managers are positioned in the **intermediate level** among the organization of whole enterprise, and play the role of nexus in facing different levels. There exist significant differences among different levels for many affairs cognition and expectations. While caught in between, managers often face a great challenge in management and task. But from another perspective, at some points when faced with the obstacle from upper or lower level, they might base on the advantages of the bridging role, use with the power or influence of upper or lower level to negotiate or pressure onto another level, so that the goal intended to reach and go on smoothly.

In the practice of organizational behavior, this approach is uncommon, forced method of organizational management. Most of the time, when the managers (especially new managers) encounter some malicious subordinates challenging the authority of new leaders, managers might be forced to use the coercive power of the higher level to push or improve the mission. Occasionally, the managers may use the collective voice of the grassroots to reflect views of certain issues toward the top.

Of course, these approaches are not long-term viable models, and managers will eventually need to establish good communication and understandings through interaction and mutual trust to jointly promote the goals set by the organization, so that the management process can be returned into the normal track.

經驗與分享

經理人在整個企業組織當中屬於**中階**的主管，扮演著承上啟下的角色，也同時面對著其上與其下不同層級的族群，而不同的層級，對於許多事務的認知與期許，通常都存在著極大的差異，夾在兩者之間，經常讓經理人在管理和任務的推動上，形成很大的挑戰；但換個角度來看，在某些時候，當經理人面臨著某個層級的阻礙，卻也可以運用其橋樑的優勢，藉由其上層、或下屬某個層級的力量或影響力，來向另一個層級的人進行溝通或施壓，讓所想要進行的任務能順利的推動。

在實務上，這種方式的運用，在組織行為學當中，是一種較為不常見、不得不的組織管理方法；多數的時候，是當經理人（尤其是新就任的經理人），面對有些部屬惡意的不配合、或對管理者的挑戰時，經理人不得已，只得藉由高層的強制力，讓任務能順利的推動或改善；有少數時候，經理人也可能藉由基層集體的聲音，向高層反映對某些議題的看法。

當然，這些方式並非長遠可行的模式，經理人終究要透過互動和互信，建立良好的溝通與默契，共同推動組織所設定的目標，讓管理回歸正常的軌道。

Section 2
Organizational Behavior

Tips in Management

Middle management

Middle management is the intermediate management of a hierarchical organization that is subordinate to the executive management and responsible for at least two lower levels of junior staff. Middle managers' main duty is to implement company strategy in the most efficient way. Their duties include creating effective working environment, administrating the work process, making sure it is compliant with organization's requirements, leading people and reporting to the highest level of management.

Middle manager is a link between the senior management and the lower levels of the organization. Due to the involvement into day-to-day running of a business, middle manager has an opportunity of reporting valuable information and suggestions from the inside of an organization. Moreover, middle manager is a channel of communication within the organization, as he passes on major decisions of executives and main goals of an organization to lower levels of employees. This contributes to better coordination between workers and makes a company more united.

Primary responsibility of a middle manager is to implement a strategy, created by the executive level, in the most efficient way possible. In order to reach the target goals, manager may effectively adjust and clearly interpret the initial plan to the subordinates.

管理小偏方

中階管理者

中階管理者在組織階級中，一方面是高階主管的部屬，另方面又需管理和負責至少兩個下級的基層員工。中層管理者的主要職責，是以最有效的方式，落實公司的策略。他們的職責包括建立有效的工作環境，管理工作流程，確保工作流程符合組織的要求，領導部屬並向高層回報等。

中層經理是高層管理人員和組織的低階員工之間的連結。由於其實際參與到企業日常的運行，中層管理人員有機會從組織的內部，提供有價值的訊息和建議。此外，中層管理者是組織中的一個溝通橋樑，因為他將高層重大的決策、和組織的主要目標，傳達給較低階層的員工。這個功能，將有利於員工之間更好的協調，也使公司更加團結。

一個中層經理的主要職責，是以其所可行最有效的方法，來實踐由高階主管所建構出來的策略。為了有效達此目標，中階管理者需要清楚的將高階的想法，有效的調整、及清楚的説明給下層的部屬。

2-6 Job Rotation
職務輪調

 Conversation 情境對話

During the mid-night, the power control **panel** located in the **guard post** of office building has appeared **intermittently** unusual flash for three consecutive nights. When the security chief arrives, the security of night shift constantly complained to him that the day shift security doesn't seem to know the situation in night, including the control panel case.

午夜時分，辦公大樓警衛哨的電力控制面板上，已經連續三個晚上出現了間歇性、異常的閃燈。

保全組長來到警衛哨站，夜班的執勤人員就不斷的跟組長抱怨著，似乎日班的警衛都無法了解夜間的狀況，所以包括這控制面板在內的許多問題，都遲遲沒有處理。

After being noticed, Robert invited the security chief Russell to the guard post on the next morning. They **came along** to conversation with the day shift security and inspected the power panel.

羅柏得知此事，便在隔天的上午，約好保全組長羅素，一同來到哨站和日班警衛聊聊，順便了解一下電力面板的情況。

Russell: "I have checked the panel, Robert. It seems that the lines inside might be way too old and results in poor contact. Finding someone to fix them would surely solve the problem. It should be enough to find someone for repair."

羅素：「羅柏，我已經檢查過這個控制面板了，可能是裡頭的線路太過老舊，因此產生接觸不良的情況，只要找人來維修一下就能解決了。」

Robert: "This problem has been there for three days, and why didn't anyone take care of it? Aren't you the day shift security, Simpson? What's going on here?"

羅柏：「這種情況不是已持續三天了，怎麼都沒想辦法找人來處理？辛普森，你不是這日班的警衛嗎？這到底是怎樣的情況？」

Simpson: "The night shift guy didn't clearly mention about the control panel problem. I had no idea what happened at night, so it's hard to explain to the maintenance **vendors**. **On the contrary**, some vendors complained to me that no one answering the door sometimes, when they delivered the cargoes to the outpost at night."

辛普森：「夜班的警衛也沒說得很清楚那控制面板的問題，我也不知道當晚是怎樣的情況，所以很難跟維修的廠商說明。倒是有些廠商跟我抱怨那晚班的警衛，他們有幾次晚上送貨到哨站時，結果都等不到有人來應門。」

Russell: "Really? It might **happen to** the timing when the guards are under **patrolling**. Someone should be back very soon, if the vendors could just wait for a while."

羅素：「是嗎？會不會是正巧碰到警衛四處巡邏的時段，只要稍微再等一下，應該就會有人回來處理了。」

Robert: "It appears that there's a gap between these two shifts, and lack of mutual understanding. We need to improve this right away."

羅柏：「這樣看來，這兩輪班的警衛之間，彼此似乎都缺乏了解，中間也橫著些鴻溝，以至於溝通上產生了些斷層。我們可能要立即改善這樣的情況。」

Russell: "That's also what I'm thinking now. But, what can we do to make the communication and interaction between two parties more efficiently?"

羅素：「我也正在思考這個問題。該怎麼做才能讓兩班的人員之間，溝通和互動更有效率些。」

Robert: "First of all, we need to completely estimate the '**duty journal**' **together with** the list of equipment and operating manual, and make some adjustment to make it **integrated**. And then we execute some re-training programs, if necessary."

羅柏：「我想首先要進行的，是仔細地再去檢視他們『勤務日誌』的內容，並且連同設備清單和相關的操作手冊，再調整得更完整一些。必要的時候，就這些勤務的內容，規劃一些再訓練的課程。」

Russell: "But they did write the 'duty journal' every day."

羅素：「但是他們每天都有填寫『勤務日誌』啊！」

Robert: "It has gradually become a **superficial** daily work. That's another reason for the poor communication. I think the key point is how to use these documents and records to enhance the quality of communication on both sides, especially in the item of '**duty transition**'. As a supervisor, we need to review and **follow closely** to the situation among colleagues at any time."

Russell: "Thanks, Robert! That's **indeed** a need for improvement, and I will follow-up right away."

Robert: "Secondly, You may consider the feasibility of 'shift rotation' approach for security duties."

When he heard of this, Simpson speaks out loudly: "Wow! That will make a big difference to our lifestyle."

羅柏：「但好像慢慢變成了一種形式上的工作吧！這就是彼此溝通不良的原因之一了。我想最重要的是如何運用這些文件和紀錄，增進兩邊溝通的品質，尤其是在『勤務交接』的項目內；而我們身為主管，就是要隨時檢視和關心同仁之間的狀況。」

羅素：「謝謝你，羅柏！這的確是個需要加強的方向，我會立刻著手進行。」

羅柏：「其次，你可以考慮將警衛的勤務採取『輪調班』方式的可行性。」

辛普森聽到這個想法，大聲的說著：「哇！那我們的生活作息不就大大受到影響了嗎？」

Robert: "Just calm down! The benefit of 'rotation' is to help both the day shift and night guards to be familiar with the situation and problems for **respective** periods. In this way, the communication for both sides will be much easier, and all securities will not **confine** to their vision. In fact, job rotation can be done in various ways. It could be regular or occasional rotation, normality or flexibility rotation, which all depends on the necessity of actual situation. You may discuss about that in further."

羅柏：「你先別急！『輪調班』的好處，是讓日班和夜班的警衛，都能熟悉各別時段上，可能會遇到的狀況和問題；如此一來，兩邊在勤務的溝通上將更加容易，也不會侷限自己的想法。其實『輪調』可以有很多種方式進行：可以採取定期輪調、或不定期的，可以是常態式的、或機動式的，這就看實際的狀況需要而定，大家可以進一步討論看看。」

Vocabulary 字彙解析

■ **panel**　*n.*　面板、鑲板、翼片

〔同義字：**faceplate, pane, sheet**〕

A layer of insulating material should be placed between the panels and the wall.

The loose panels creaked as I walked on them.

■ **guard post**　*n.*　崗亭、哨站、崗哨

〔同義字：**sentinel, sentry box, hillock**〕

The security was peering through the window of the guard post.

Following the guard post until the track, you can meet a forestry road.

- **intermittent**　*adj.*　斷斷續續、間歇、間斷

〔同義字：**desultory, fitful, snarchy**〕

They were questioned about their intermittent dealings.

The police interpretation of the law was often intermittent.

- **integrated**　*adj.*　整體、綜合、完整

〔同義字：**overall, whole, complex**〕

The recession effect of global economy is integrated.

This college offered an integrated list of courses.

 Phrase in sentence 片語和句型解析

- **on the contrary**　反之、相反的、反而

〔同義字：**otherwise, contrast, instead**〕

On the contrary, we would be unable to acquire knowledge.

Do not use lotions, but put on a clean dressing on the contrary.

- **happen to**　恰巧、碰巧、剛好

〔同義字：**by chance, occurred in, exactly**〕

They 're happen to meet each other in the market.

The accident was happened to occur at about 3:00 p.m.

- **together with**　再加上、連同、一起

〔同義字：**jointly, conjointly, collectively**〕

It's a famous report prepared together with Harvard and Yale universities.

The darkness always came together with the affright and trepidation.

- **follow closely**　關注、緊盯、密切注視

〔同義字：**close attention, keep in step, press**〕

He was requested to follow closely the serious mistakes happen in the division.

The policeman stood to follow closely when the suspects arrived.

Practice in Management

In the practical operation management, **job rotation** will be applied to different organization with different purposes. Many institutes or agencies, especially in the public sectors, might request the rotation of certain positions, especially some important positions, from time to time. The main purpose is to prevent malpractices or ills of certain positions if it's under the same person for long time. But for most businesses, job rotations typically focus on staff training, especially new staffs. Through the experiences of working in different positions, the employee will not only be more familiar with the overall operation, but also enhance the cooperation and understanding among different positions.

But the implementation rotation, sometimes, will face with the problem of poor convergence. Each new job is taken under the strange circumstances, and then accumulated the experience gradually. And the long established work comprehension should be started over again. On the other hand, some rotation might involve the change of working hours and circumstance. We need to consider and check regularly the adjustment problem of employees in daily life and psychological adjustment problems of employees to avoid any distress.

經驗與分享

在經營管理的實務上，**職務輪調**多少都會應用在許多不同的企業組織當中，但其中也有著不同的目的。有許多的機構（特別是公家機構），會在每相隔一段時間之後，就要求某些職務（通常是重要的職位）的輪調，其主要的目的，在於防止某些職務，若由相同的人在位太久，容易產生一些弊端或沉疴。但對於多數企業而言，職務的輪調通常著重於員工的培訓（尤其是新進人員），藉由不同職務的歷練，讓員工更熟悉整體的運作，也增進不同職務間的謀合和默契。

但是實施職務的輪調，有時會面臨銜接不良的問題，每個新接手的工作，都是陌生的情況下，再慢慢累積經驗，而原有已經長期建立的工作默契也要從新開始；另一方面，有些輪調涉及到工作時間與環境的改變，員工的生活與心理調適問題，也是需要先行考量、並定期檢視的管理工作，避免產生困擾。

Tips in Management

Job Rotation

Job rotation is a management technique that assigns trainees to various structures and departments over a period of a few years. Surveys show that an increasing number of companies are using job rotation to train employees. There are both positive and negative effects involved with job rotation that need to be taken into consideration when a company makes the decision to use this technique. Organizations that use job rotation tend to be successful innovative companies and organizations with a growth and development agenda.

Job rotation is also a control to detect errors and frauds. It reduces the risk of collusion between individuals. Organizations dealing with sensitive information or system (e.g. bank) where there is an opportunity for personal gain can benefit by job rotation. Job rotation also helps in business continuity as multiple people are equally equipped to perform a job function. If an employee is not available other can handle his/her position with similar efficiency

There are different reasons a company may choose to use job rotation. Research suggests that there are significant benefits that may outweigh the costs involved with training employees for diversified positions. As a learning mechanism, employees are given the opportunity to learn necessary skills which can help them to advance within a company. This employment opportunity also has the effect of boosting morale and self efficacy. The company may benefit from using job rotation by having the ability to staff key positions within a company. This practice may allow a company to run more efficiently, and as a result, become more productive and profitable.

管理小偏方

工作輪調

工作輪調是在一種針對新進人員，在前數年間到各個部門工作的管理技術。調查顯示，越來越多的公司都運用工作輪調方式來培訓員工。當公司考慮採用這種管理技術時，應先考量其正面和負面的效應。通常採用工作輪調的組織，往往是一些成功的創新型企業，或者組織已有了成長和擴展的計畫。

工作輪調也是一個用以檢測錯誤和欺詐行為的控制機制。它可減少個人之間串通的風險。當某些敏感的資訊或系統（如銀行）可能成為個人利得時，組織可藉由工作輪調方式得到幫助。當有幾個人都具備執行同樣任務的功能時，輪調也將有助於業務的持續進行。

公司可能基於不同的理由而採用工作輪調。研究顯示，訓練員工從事不同的職位，其中有許多顯著的好處是遠超出所投入的成本。就學習機制而言，員工有機會學習到必要的技能，這可以幫助他們在公司內的進步。這樣的職場機會，可以鼓舞士氣，讓員工有自我成就感。而公司可能藉由輪調，讓公司內的員工獲得關鍵性的工作的能力。這種做法，可以使公司的運行更有效率，且以結果論，公司將變得更有生產和獲利能力。

Section 3

Processing Management

3-1 Warehouse Processing
倉儲流程

 Conversation 情境對話

7:30 A.M. Many workers **congested** in front of the site warehouse. Some of them clamored to exchange the tools, while others were anxious to get the material. It's really rushed and uproar. After around 10 minutes, workers quitting en masse, left only Vincent who **bewildered** alone to look at a pile of damaged equipment and messy materials. At the same time, Robert and Elmer just walked forward to the warehouse. They were surprised at such a mess and then approaching to Vincent.

清晨7:30。工地倉庫前擠滿了一堆的工人，有人嚷嚷著要換工具，有人急著要領材料，大家七嘴八舌亂哄哄的；約莫十分鐘後，工人一哄而散，只剩下倉管員文森，一臉茫然的望著一堆損壞的機具和凌亂的材料。此時羅柏和艾默也正走向倉庫，看到這一片的狼籍，不禁大吃一驚，趕緊過去向文森了解這個狀況。

Robert: "What happen here, Vincent? The equipment and materials are scattered everywhere, as if it's after a battle."

羅柏：「文森，這裡到底發生了什麼事？機具和材料到處散落著，就好像經過了一場戰役似的。」

Vincent: "Oh, don't mention it! You didn't see the bunch of workers who just surrounded here like hungry wolves. They were neither line up nor to fill out the forms, but just go anxiously for materials or put aside the broken equipment. It's really a headache to put these back in order."

Robert: "Aren't there any required procedure or documents needed for **collaring** material or **refunding** for repair in warehouse? No wonder the record of inside warehouse has been chaotic and never checked up. Then, what's going on for the large number of damaged equipment?"

Elmer: "Most of them are new types of **drilling** machines and **welding** machines, and it seems the damages are from poor **artificial** operations."

文森:「唉,別提了!剛剛你沒看到一群工人像餓虎撲羊般的圍在這裡,每個人要不急著領材料,要不就把壞掉的機具丟在一旁,大夥既不排隊也沒填單子,光是要收拾這些東西就夠傷腦筋的了。」

羅柏:「這些領用材料或是退倉送修的動作,難道都沒有一些規定的流程和單據嗎?難怪你那倉庫裡頭的帳目,一直都是雜亂無章的,根本就對不起來。那麼,這麼多損壞的機具又是怎麼一回事?」

艾默:「這些多數是些新型的鑽孔機和焊接機,看來都是因為操作不良所造成的。」

Section 3 Processing Management

Robert: "It's really bad, and might take lots of money to repair. Isn't there anyone to teach them how to use them, or support some operating manuals?"

羅柏：「這樣看來很糟糕，光是要修復這些機具，可是要花上不少錢；難道沒有人教他們如何使用，或是提供些操作手冊之類的東西嗎？」

Elmer: "There's an operating manual when the equipment is initially imported, but it's written in a foreign language. So, no one can ever understand."

艾默：「當初原廠進來時，是有附一些標準的操作流程說明，但那些都是用外國文寫的，所以沒人看得懂。」

Robert: "Why don't we find someone to **translate** it as soon as possible. Then set up a detailed welding demonstration for all the operating workers."

羅柏：「那就盡快找人翻譯，然後將操作工人都集合起來，一塊做個詳細的使用說明焊示範。」

Vincent: "That's really necessary! Otherwise, these machines might become **scrapped** in no time. It's tiring to deal with."

文森：「那實在太需要了！否則這麼新型的機具，沒兩下就故障或報廢了，處理起來可就累人了。」

Robert: "Not only the operating **guidelines** for machines, but the warehouse needs a complete 'Standard Operation Procedure', which covers the all procedures of picking, refunding, and approval, and also some reports for material storage, turnover, inventory, and checking."

Vincent: "Gosh! It's really troublesome."

Robert: "These are all basic but important managerial tools. Otherwise, the warehouse operation will always be a mess, and never really be on track."

Elmer: "Don't worry, Vincent! I'll find someone fully support you."

羅柏：「不單是這些機具的使用，倉庫更是需要有個完整的『標準作業流程』出來，包括進退貨及簽核程序等。另外像是物料儲存、進出、盤點及報表核對等也應該都包含在內。」

文森：「哇，要這麼麻煩啊！」

羅柏：「這些都是很基本、但很重要的管理工具，否則你那倉庫的進出和盤點作業，永遠都是一團亂、無法真正上軌道的。」

艾默：「別擔心，文森！我會找人來全力協助你的。」

Section 3 Processing Management

Vocabulary 字彙解析

■ **congested** *V.* 擁擠、聚集、積蓄

〔同義字：**overcrowd, cluster, accumulate**〕

They congested the holes with sticky tape.

We have to congest the information for our study.

■ **bewildered** *adj.* 茫然、惶恐、不知所措

〔同義字：**apprehensive, overwhelmed, confused**〕

She was utterly bewildered about what had just happened.

He felt bewildered about going home.

■ **collar** *v.* 領取、侵佔、攝取

〔同義字：**receive, grab, conquer**〕

She jumped up and collared his arm.

I need all the money I can collar.

■ **refund** *v.* 退回、償還、退款

〔同義字：**retreat, return, compensate**〕

We guarantee to refund your money in full.

The investors should be refunded for their losses.

■ **drilling** *n., v.* 鑽孔；鑽探、演進

〔同義字：**auger, corkscrew, gimlet**〕

His cutting device was a drilling without spurs.

The plane was drilling toward the earth.

■ **welding** *n.* 焊接、焊機、焊合

〔同義字：**soldering, jointing, welding machine**〕

His efforts in welding together the religious parties ran into trouble.

These joining methods may include welding, brazing, soldering, riveting, or bolting.

- **artificial** *adj.* 人工的、偽造的、虛假的

〔同義字：**false, fake, phoney**〕

The test can produce artificial results.

They have illegally entered the UK using artificial travel documents.

- **translate** *adj.* 翻譯、轉換、移轉

〔同義字：**interpret, conversion, change**〕

The German original has been translated into English.

She had been translated from familiar surroundings to a foreign country.

- **scrapped** *adj.* 報廢、取消、廢除

〔同義字：**repeal, cancel, discard**〕

They decided to make the fleet entirely scrapped.

The clothes she like most has become scrapped.

- **guideline** *n.* 指南、導引、方針

〔同義字：**principle, direction, advice**〕

The Health and Safety Executive also issued guidelines for working safety.

Under his guideline, the college has developed an international reputation.

 # Phrase in sentence 片語和句型解析

- **quitting en masse** 一哄而散

〔同義字：**spread out, scattered, disperse**〕

The students had been quitting en masse from the yard before teacher arrived.

The audience had rush to quitting en masse when the heavy rain falls.

Practice in Management

In the past, the management of warehouse related works has been seriously neglected by executives or management team and was thought of as only rough jobs of tally and heavy loading. So, the works of warehousing was relatively arduous under poor environment. In this case, the quality of the warehouse staff couldn't be enhanced and the turnover rate of staffs was very high. Therefore, the work efficiency and accuracy couldn't be significantly improved.

But in these years, the importance of warehousing has been duly noted gradually. Thanks to the intensive market competition, the changes in consumer habits, and the booming **logistics industry**, which's became a very important business services. It's especially true for those new emerging businesses, who had tried to apply with integrated workflow planning tools and complete scientific information in warehousing operations, combine their business with the factors of logistics, transportation, customer service, marketing and others, and then create a whole new business opportunities under the slowdown economic environment.

These new business models are all base on the build-up of a complete and accurate "standard operating procedures". Based on this foundation, they developed the whole management system and specification of business prototype, and then realized the business achievement eventually.

經驗與分享

過去在**倉庫管理**的工作領域中，一直被經營者或管理階層忽視，認為其只是理貨和搬重的苦差事，工作吃重、環境也較為差；在這種情況下，倉管人員的素質無法提升，流動率非常高，相對的作業效率和精確度都無法提高。

但在這近年來，由於市場競爭激烈、和消費習慣的改變，**物流業**逐漸成為很重要的商業服務領域，倉儲作業的重要性才逐漸受到了重視；尤其許多新興的業者，運用了整合的資訊工具和完整科學化的作業流程規劃，將倉儲作業，結合了物流、運輸、客服、行銷等因素，創造出了全新的商機出來，在一片低迷的環境中，像雨後春筍般冒了出來。

而這些新的商業模式的基礎，則建構在一套完整而精確的「標準作業流程」之中，並在這基礎下，發展出龐大的管理系統與事業規範的雛形，最後再逐漸實現事業經營的成果。

Section 3
Processing Management

Tips in Management

Standard Operating Procedure

The term standard operating procedure, or SOP, is used in a variety of different contexts, including healthcare, aviation, engineering, education, industry, and military. The U.S. military sometimes uses the term Standing — rather than Standard — Operating Procedure, because a military SOP refers to a unit's unique procedures, which are not necessarily a standard for another unit. "Standard" could imply that there is one (standard) procedure to be used across all units.

Procedures are ongoing processes with unlimited ending time frames, while projects have definite starting and ending points. Installing a unit, or establishing a business, is a project with tasks that ends at point the unit or business is "standing". The term SOP means the procedures that are executed after the unit or business "stands". SOPs get usually applied in the pharmaceutical processing and for related clinical studies. There the focus is always set on repeated application of unchanged processes and procedures and its documentation, hence supporting the segregation of origins, causes and effects. SOP's can also provide employees with a reference to common business practices, activities, or tasks. New employees use an SOP to answer questions, such as how an operation is performed, without interrupting supervisors.

The international quality standard ISO 9001 essentially requires the determination of processes (documented as standard operating procedures) used in any manufacturing process that could affect the quality of the product.

管理小偏方

標準作業流程

標準作業流程（或稱為SOP），被廣泛應用在各種不同的領域中，包括醫療，航空，工程，教育，工業，軍事等。在美軍的慣用術語裡較常用「常態」（而非「標準」）作業流程；因為軍事上的SOP，是指一個單位的獨特程序，對另一單位而言就不一定是標準了。而「標準」，則意含著對所有單位都適用唯一（標準）的流程。

流程是無止盡持續進行的一種過程，而任務則是有明確的起點和終點。設立一個單位、或建立一個企業即是一項任務，其工作在單位或企業設立之時，即告完成了。在此處，SOP這名詞代表著單位或企業在設立之後，所開始要執行的程序。

SOP通常應用在一些醫藥程序、和相關的臨床研究方面。其注視的焦點幾乎都在於，就不會變的流程和程序，做不斷重複的應用，以及所相關的文獻紀錄，藉此來支持其所離析出來的病源、病因和其影響。SOP的也可以做為員工一種日常商業行為、活動或任務的參考。新進員工對於某項工作該如何運作等類似問題，則可運用SOP來自我解答、而無需去打擾上司。

近數十年，SOP的重要性更形明顯，國際社會已發展成國際品質認證的標準。例如：國際品質標準ISO9001，其基本上在於規範著：針對在任何製造過程中，所有可能影響產品品質之流程的應用程序（即所謂的標準操作程序）。

3-2 Inventory Management
庫存管理

 Conversation 情境對話

Susan brings the merchandise inventory list for the past two months to Robert's office, and then both of them discuss against some specific items for a long time. Then, Robert looked over Peter and his assistant, as well as the warehouse keeper Sean for further discussion.

蘇珊拿著前兩個月的商品庫存明細表，來到了羅柏的辦公室內，兩人針對一些品項的數量和金額討論了很久；於是羅柏就將彼得和他的助理，以及倉管員史恩找了過來一起討論。

Robert: "Susan and I had discussed some inventory problem today. I'm not sure if there's any mistake there, but we do need your help to clarify for the Accountancy division."

羅柏：「今天蘇珊和我討論了一些庫存方面的問題，我不確定這其中是否有什麼錯誤，但需要大家協助會計部門釐清一下。」

Susan: "The first issue is about some items of computer accessories. We had found out that the purchase cost of some items seem different in **before and after**."

蘇珊：「首先的問題，是關於一些電腦耗材方面的品項；我們發現這其中，有些相同品項的進貨成本，前後似乎不太一樣。」

Peter: "Ya! The rate of replacement for these accessories is very fast, so the price changed a lot."

彼得：「對啊！這些耗材的汰換速率很快，價格的變動也非常大。」

Susan: "But, **according to** the shipping records, your shipment doesn't seem to follow the order of purchasing, for the unit number and cost had become very confusing. It's very difficult for bookkeeping and estimating the operating profit."

蘇珊：「但就出貨的紀錄來看，你們似乎沒按照進貨先後的順序來出貨，所以貨號及成本價格就顯得很混亂，實在難以記帳、和估算營運利潤的情況。」

Queenie: "Well, I just followed the packing notes from warehouse to record, and didn't pay particularly attention on this."

昆妮：「我就根據倉庫出貨的單據輸入紀錄，倒沒有特別留意到這些。」

Section 3
Processing Management

Susan: "It's not only a problem of cost confusion. The point is that the replacement rate of these accessories is too fast to become **unsalable** goods, if not been shipped out ASAP. That's why we always use the 'FIFO, first in first out' format to compute the inventory for such merchandise."

蘇珊：「這問題不單只是成本不清楚而已，最主要的是這類的耗材更新太快了，不盡快出貨就很容易成為滯銷品；這也是為甚麼我們對這類商品的庫存品，都會採用『先進先出』的方式來計價。」

Sean: "But it's too **bothersome**. I have to adjust the storage position of products consequently."

史恩：「但是這樣太麻煩了，我勢必要不斷調整商品倉儲的位置。」

Susan: "There's still another question. In the last season, we had purchased some high priced LED computer equipment. But in this season, with only two pieces of product selling out, we purchased near 10 pieces of same item again. In the long run, it may cause a huge **hoarding** pressure in both of the capital and inventory."

蘇珊：「另外還有一個問題；上一季我們進了一批單價很高的LED電腦設備，這一季才賣不到兩件，最近卻又進了將近十件同樣的商品。這樣下來，可能會造成我們在資金和庫存上很大的囤積壓力。」

Peter: "It's might because of being overly optimistic from the initial expectation of salesmen."

彼得：「或許是銷售人員當初的預估太過樂觀了。」

Robert: "For such high-priced products, we probably need to setup some specific procurement standards and restrictions. Or, it would be a **thorny** problem to deal with those expensive unsalable goods."

Susan: "I would suggest applying the 'zero inventory' mode of operation, if the supply of goods is abundant and convenient to delivery. We can, for example, order the merchandise from supplier only after the customer's **reservation**. It's also called 'Just in Time' inventory management mode."

Sean: "There might be only few products to apply in such a reservation order mode. But for the majority products, we still need to prepare some quantity of stock. Once the products are **out of stock**, we might not only lose some business opportunity, but also are prone to be **stricken** from customers' complaint."

羅柏：「針對這類高單價的商品，或許應該特別設定一些採購的標準和限制，否則光要處理這些昂貴的滯銷品，那可是非常麻煩的事。」

蘇珊：「假如這類商品的貨源供應很充沛，配送也很便利的話，我會建議盡可能採用『零庫存』的運作模式，例如可以先接受顧客的預訂，然後再跟供應商採購，這就是所謂『最及時』的庫存管理方式。」

史恩：「或許有極少數的商品，可以採用這種預約訂貨的方式，但絕大多數的商品，可能還是要有一定量的庫存，否則一旦斷了貨，不旦失去了銷售的商機，而且更容易遭致顧客的抱怨。」

Section 3
Processing Management

Robert: "We do need an overall review and adjustment for the **commodity** inventory. We need Sean to **sort out** a merchandise inventory list first. With the list, we filter and classify them **itemized according to** criteria as the functional, price level and **turnover** rate of goods, and then clearly mark out in related storage position. For each classification of merchandise, it refers to the relationship between the period of delivery and selling, we setup the minimum quantity of stock, **procurement** cycle and mode of shipping. That will be much easier for the inventory management."

羅柏：「我們是需要針對商品的庫存，做一番通盤的檢視和調整。史恩先整理出一份商品庫存清單，然後我們再逐項的過濾，將商品依照其功能的屬性、價位、和迴轉速度等條件，歸屬於不同的類別，並且在倉儲的位置上清楚標示出來；每個類別的商品，再參考其供貨期和銷售之間的關係，設定出最低基本庫存量、採購的周期、和出貨的方式。這樣就比較容易做商品庫存的管理了。」

Vocabulary 字彙解析

- **unsalable** *adj.* 滯銷的、賣不出去的

〔同義字：**unsold, unmarketable**〕

Many services provided within private households are considered to be unsalable.

Even after discounted, many copies of the book still remained unsalable goods.

- **bothersome** *adj.* 麻煩的、傷腦筋的、令人焦急的

〔同義字：**knotty, troublesome, anxious**〕

Jason is a bothersome student for all teachers in school.

She was extremely bothersome about her exams.

- **hoard** *v.* 囤積、滯銷、窖藏

〔同義字：**store, overstock, accumulate**〕

There were thousands of antiques hoarded by the compulsive collector.

Don't hoard the kitchen with too much food.

- **optimistic** *adj.* 樂觀的、開朗的、看好

〔同義字：**roseate, sanguine, hopeful**〕

He is optimistic about prospects for the global economy.

She was an optimistic, outgoing girl.

- **thorny** *adj.* 棘手的、多刺的、荊棘

〔同義字：**prickly, spiky, knotty**〕

The white rose stands out against the green thorny branches.

The garden was paneled in thorny pine.

- **reservation** *n.* 預約、定位、保留

〔同義字：**retention, maintenance, preservation**〕

We have to call for reservation of theatre seats before Friday.

Australia has a huge wildlife reservation.

■ **stricken** *adj.* 被侵害、失措、災害

〔同義字：**affected, struck, afflicted**〕

The pilot landed the stricken aircraft.

Scientist had applied moist heat to the stricken area.

■ **commodity** *n.* 〔大宗〕商品、貨物、物品

〔同義字：**merchandise, goods, article**〕

This store offered wild range of commodity.

Export of primary commodities is very important to Brail economy.

■ **itemized** *adj.* 詳細的、列舉的、明細的

〔同義字：**breakdown, details**〕

I need the itemized tasks for this morning.

We shall consider the itemized paragraph of the bill.

■ **turnover** *n.* 迴轉、營業額、成交率

〔同義字：**revenue, movement, rate of replacement**〕

It's very important to raise substantial turnover of the company.

The turnover rate of inventory depends on the consumers' demand.

■ **Procurement** *n.* 採購、搜羅、購買

〔同義字：**purchase, buy, acquirement**〕

There're still thousands of videos available for procurement.

We had to find more money before the procurement of house.

Phrase in sentence 片語和句型解析

■ **before and after** 前後、之前和之後

〔同義字：**front and rear, around**〕

There's a big different meaning for this item before and after.

The character of oxygen is consistent before and after the experiment.

■ **according to** 根據、依照、比照

〔同義字：**on the basis of, in the light of, in accordance with**〕

The outlook for investors is not bright, according to financial experts.

The product is disposed of in according to federal regulations.

■ **out of stock** 斷貨、缺貨

The inventory of store is almost out of stock.

It's easily to be out of stock without check up the inventory periodically.

■ **sort out** 整理、清查、搜索以排序

〔同義字：**check up, clear up, put in order**〕

She sorted out the clothes, some to be kept, some to be thrown away.

The cargoes are sorted out according to the classification.

■ **mark out** 標示、註明、標註出

〔同義字：**indicate, label, tag**〕

The dotted lines mark out the margins clearly.

She marks out the parcels neatly in capital letters.

Practice in Management

The problem of **inventory** in business, just like the liver in human body, will not send any message (because it's always silent with the pain) if you don't pay attention to it. But, on the other hand, whenever it does send a message to you, it's definitely a very serious danger, or, in many cases, it's already too late. The quality of inventory management becomes significantly important, especially for the pricing characteristics of products are seasonal, timely, or fiercely changeable under competition.

This problem is quite common in many electronic or semiconductor companies. Due to the severe competition in global market and expeditious replacement in product, the value of goods in stock might be sharply impaired within a very short period of time. For those businesses, the real challenges are: first, how to sell off the inventory to the customers in the most effective time? Second, how to truly reflect the value of existing inventory and then present the real status of operational profitability? This is also a key question for the majority of investors in public.

Inventory management is extremely important for many businesses with diverse merchandise or groceries, for example: fresh foods, supermarkets, bookstores, and drug store, etc. When dealing with so many merchandises with different classification, duration, module of storage, and transportation, we eagerly look for more rigorous scientific management approaches. In the western countries and Japan, the experiences of inventory management had been developed and proofed for long time. These experiences can be used as our excellence reference. For example, Japanese companies have developed the "**color management module**" for inventory.

經驗與分享

企業的**庫存**問題，有時候像人體的肝臟一樣，當你不注意它的時候，它也不會發出任何訊息（因為它不會痛），但一但它發出了訊息，就都是嚴重的危險訊息，許多時候已經為時已晚了。如果商品的價格特性，是屬於季節性、時效性、或隨著競爭有激烈變動的時候，庫存管理的良莠，就更顯得重要了。

這種情況，在許多電子、或是半導體產業，都是很普遍存在的問題；由於國際市場競爭太激烈，產品汰舊換新速度太快，以致於商品庫存的價值，很快的就被折耗掉了。對於業者的挑戰在於，其一，如何在最有效的時間內，將庫存商品出脫至客戶手中；其二，如何能真實反映其庫存商品的現有價值，讓營運和獲利情況真實呈現？這也是許多廣大投資者當注意的課題。

庫存的管理，對許多商品多樣、雜貨類的業者，例如生鮮、超市、書局、藥妝等等，更形的重要，因為面對那麼多不同屬性、期效、儲運方式的商品，是需要一套更縝密的科學管理方法；這在西方和日本商業社會中，已有長久的發展和實證，可作為參考與效仿，例如：日本企業曾發展出「顏色管理法」。

Tips in Management

Inventory Management

Inventory management is a science primarily about specifying the shape and percentage of stocked goods. The scope of inventory management concerns the fine lines between replenishment lead time, carrying costs of inventory, asset management, inventory forecasting, inventory valuation, inventory visibility, future inventory price forecasting, physical inventory, available physical space for inventory, quality management, replenishment, returns and defective goods, and demand forecasting. Balancing these competing requirements leads to optimal inventory levels, which is an on-going process as the business needs shift and react to the wider environment.

Inventory management involves a retailer seeking to acquire and maintain a proper merchandise assortment while ordering, shipping, handling, and related costs are kept in check. It also involves systems and processes that identify inventory requirements, set targets, provide replenishment techniques, report actual and projected inventory status and handle all functions related to the tracking and management of material. This would include the monitoring of material moved into and out of stockroom locations and the reconciling of the inventory balances.

Management of the inventories, with the primary objective of determining/controlling stock levels within the physical distribution system, functions to balance the need for product availability against the need for minimizing stock holding and handling costs.

管理小偏方

庫存管理

庫存管理,是一個主要是確定應庫藏商品的型態和比例的科學。它的應用範圍包括了補貨的前置時間、積壓成本、資產管理、庫存預測、存貨估價、庫存監控、庫存未來價格預測、實際庫存、可用於庫存的空間、品質管理、補貨、退貨和瑕疵品、及需求預測等。就在這許多相互影響的條件中尋求到均衡點,以引導出最佳的庫存水平;這是一個持續進行的過程,因為經營的需要不斷改變、並要因應整個大環境。

在零售業理,庫存管理包括了業者在取得、並保持商品相當的豐富性,同時也要檢視訂貨、運輸、處理,以及相關的成本。它也是一種系統和流程,用之於判定庫存需求、目標設定、補貨技術、實際和設定庫存狀況之報告、並處理有關於材料的跟踪與管理之所有相關因素。這些也包括了材料進出庫房地點倉儲地的監控、及庫存餘額的核對。

存貨的管理,基於其在實體物流系統內確定、與控制庫存水平為首要目標之下,必須產品供貨需求、及降低存貨之持有與處理成本之間,尋求到均衡點。

Section 3
Processing Management

3-3 Store Display Management
店舖陳列管理

 Conversation 情境對話

Robert is the manager of a chain book store. Almost 10 a.m., the branch store was about to open. Robert went close to the shop door and **gazed** at the window posters, then looks **dejectedly** into the store. On the way through rows of bookcases, he watched at a clerk who is sorting books in the floor of corner. He **went around** the dressing room behind counter, then moved into a small office and, alone, pondered speechlessly for a moment. Eventually, he asked the supervisor and several clerks to the office.

羅柏是一家連鎖書店的經理。接近上午十點，這家分店已經準備開始營業了，羅伯走到店門口、望了望櫥窗的海報，然後神情黯然的走進店裡頭；沿途他經過一排排的書櫃，看了一下在一角整理書本的店員，然後繞到櫃台後頭的化妝室，最後走進狹小的辦公室內，獨自不發一語的沉思了好一會兒。終於，他將店長和幾個店員叫到了辦公室內。

Robert: "Today, I do find out lots of things happening here, even just a brief inspection. Firstly, I'd like to figure out what's the poster inside showcase all about?"

羅柏：「今天我僅稍微的檢視，似乎就發現了這邊許多的狀況。首先，我想先了解一下櫥窗上海報的內容是什麼？」

Molly: "Oh! It might be the new released book poster of 'Harry Porter III', and the other one was for the event of discounted promotion."

茉莉：「喔，好像是哈利波特第三集的新書海報，還有一張是促銷折扣的活動。」

Robert: "The 'Harry Potter' series had released out the fifth **episode**, but the poster for the third episode was still on the window. And the promotional activities on the showcase poster already ended in the last month. I really don't know for how long you haven't renewed the showcase display. Besides, I'd like to know who is sorting books in front of the closet."

羅柏：「哈利波特都已經出到第五集了，第三集的海報卻仍貼在櫥窗上，而櫥窗海報上的那個促銷活動，在上個月就已經結束，我實在不知道，你們有多久沒去更新櫥窗的佈置了；另外，我很想想知道，剛剛在壁櫃前整理書本的是誰？」

Jessica: "It's me. I'm Jessica, just served here since last month. So, I'm still not really clear about the classification of books."

潔西卡：「是我，我叫潔西卡，上個月才來報到的，所以對於書籍的分類還不是很清楚。」

Section 3
Processing Management

Robert: "It doesn't matter for the **green hands** if they're still not familiar with the work. You will **get started** after a period of time. But I must tell all of you, not just Jessica, never put the books upon the ground directly whenever you are in a bookstore. It's a big taboo for all bookstore employees."

羅柏：「剛來到書店工作還不熟悉，這倒是沒關係，一段時間後自然就上手了；但我要告訴大家，不只是潔西卡，在書店裡，無論何時絕對不可以將書本放在地面上，身為書店的從業人員，這是很大的忌諱。」

Daphne: "I'm sorry about that. Jessica hasn't worked in the bookstore before. And which is what I should teach her."

黛芬妮：「實在很抱歉，潔西卡才剛到書店工作沒多久，這是我應該教導她的事。」

Robert: "You're right, that's your responsibility as a supervisor. But I do see something that needs to be improved. For example, some books on the bookshelves, are not only **crooked**, but also misplaced. And, it's dusty in the corner."

羅柏：「妳說得沒錯，這是妳身為店長的責任。但今天我的確看到了許多有待改進的地方，譬如說我看到了書櫃上的書本，不但是東倒西歪，還有放置錯誤的；另外在書櫃的角落積了不少的灰塵。」

Molly: "But we only have 30 minutes to prepare before opening every day. It's really not enough."

茉莉：「但是我們每天營業之前，只有三十分鐘的準備時間，根本就不太夠。」

Robert: "It's a managerial issue to organize and arrange the time schedule of clearance, and to allocate the work efficiently in limited time. We still have many other branch stores, and maybe you can **look around** there in your free time. Yet, the most unacceptable place of all is the dirty and smelly dressing room. It's really terrible!"

Michael murmurs: "It should be no big deal for dressing room. After all, there might be only few people using the toilet and not for a long time. Customers wouldn't be really care about it.

Robert: "Your **notion** is a very serious mistake! In all kinds of stores, the clearance of dressing room is most easily overlooked, but, on the customer's **point of view**, it is the most important concern. Try to imagine: When you go shopping in a store with fantastic decoration, but find out that the dressing room is full of dirt stains and **debris**. Then, how will you evaluate this store?"

羅柏：「如何安排整理和清潔的時間，以及如何在有限時間內將工作有效的分配，這是分店裡管理上的問題；我們有很多其他的分店，或許可以利用閒暇時間，過去參觀學習一下。但今天最讓我難以接受的，就是那間既髒又臭的化妝室，這是很糟糕的事！」

麥可喃喃自語的說：「化妝室應該沒啥關係吧！畢竟上廁所的人很少、時間也不長，客人應該沒太在意吧！」

羅柏：「你的觀念是個很嚴重的錯誤！在所有賣場和商店的經營裡，化妝室的清潔往往是最容易被忽略的，但是就顧客的觀感而言，卻是最重要的一件事；試想一下，如果你到了一家裝潢美侖美奐的商店裡頭消費，卻發現那邊的化妝室滿是垢漬和雜物，你對這家商店的評價又會如何？」

Section 3 Processing Management

Daphne: "I'm really sorry, Robert. I have to agree with you, and it's all my responsibility."

黛芬妮：「實在很抱歉，羅柏！我想你說得沒錯，而這些都是我應盡的責任。」

Robert: "It's not only your personal responsibility, but also the common goal for all of us. When we're going out, for example, we always keep neat, clean and **decent**. It's similar to the store operation. We might not use the most luxurious decoration, but need to operate **diligently** for each detail. That's the most important factor for succeed."

羅柏：「這不單是你個人的責任，而是我們要共同努力的目標；就如同我們出門時一定會將自己整理得非常整齊、乾淨和得體，而在經營商店時也是如此，賣場不一定要用最豪華的裝潢，但要能用心去經營每個細節，這才是成功最重要的要素。」

Vocabulary 字彙解析

- **gazed** *v.* 凝視、注視、盯住

〔同義字：**stare, watch, ogle**〕

He could only gaze at her in astonishment.

He sat on the carpet gazing his image in the mirrors.

- **dejected** *adj.* 黯然、苦悶、沮喪

〔同義字：**dispirited, listless, downcast**〕

He stood in the street looking dejected.

Their happiness wedding made Anne feel even more dejected.

- **episode** *n.* 情節、集、插曲

〔同義字：**plot, collection, interlude**〕

The animated series carried on the complex episodes of the graphic novel.

It's one of the best episodes of European poetry.

- **green hand** *n.* 新手、生手、初學者

〔同義字：**new hand, tiro, novice**〕

He was a complete green hand in foreign affairs.

We should be cautious with investigative reports by a green hand.

- **crooked** *adj.* 彎曲的、歪斜的、屈曲

〔同義字：**askew, curved, bent**〕

His teeth were yellow and crooked.

The door was hanging crooked on one twisted hinge.

- **notion** *n.* 概念、主張、觀點

〔同義字：**concept, claim, proposition**〕

Children have different notions about the roles of their parents.

She had a notion to call her friend at work.

■ **debris**　*n.*　廢墟、瓦礫、碎片

〔同義字：**ruins, rubble, fragments**〕

The bomb hits it, showering debris from all sides.

Two buildings collapsed, trapping scores of people in the debris.

■ **decent**　*adj.*　體面的、正經的、合適

〔同義字：**dignity, serious, appropriate**〕

She's never had a decent job.

They thought the stage no life for a decent lady.

■ **diligently**　*adv.*　用心、勤奮、努力

〔同義字：**intention, strive, industriously**〕

She works diligently in pointing out every feature.

He diligently provides every amenity for his guests.

Phrase in sentence 片語和句型解析

■ go around　巡迴、到處、環行

〔同義字：tour, circuit, roam〕

He went around through the narrow streets.

The vessel went around from Libya to Ireland.

■ get started　上手、開始、入門

〔同義字：overhand, begin, start〕

He takes over as chief executive now even he just got started last year.

Theorists just get started to address these complex questions.

■ look around　張望、環顧、參觀

〔同義字：peep, visit, inspect〕

The door was ajar and she couldn't resist look around.

They look around my outside paintwork for cracks and flaws.

■ point of view　觀點、看法、角度

〔同義字：perspective, argument, angle〕

I'm trying to get Michael to change his point of view.

Most guidebook history is written from the editor's point of view.

Practice in Management

In the industry of store selling, all the **presentation** in the shop displaying, like our dress up to go out, will be the most direct impact to customers, and is also on behalf of the respect for the customers. Therefore, many chain stores, such as some convenience stores, telecommunications outlets, etc., have a strict and consistent requirement for the displaying and labeling of goods in shops. These requirements, including staff uniforms or even relevant jargons, are used to present the unique entrepreneurial spirit of the enterprise.

In addition to the store display and layout, the most straightforward impact to customers is the **attitude of the sales staff** and the **ambience in the store**. For a long time, some Japanese department stores have paid close attention in the training and requirements of service for their sales person. These requirements indeed enhance the store's style and quality. That's one of the main reasons why their businesses has pressed ahead of the Western and other Asian countries successfully and become the goal to emulate.

In the stores, regardless of what the commodities are or how the display is designed, neat and clean ones are always the fundamental factors. What customers experienced was always from the subtle and remote corner, which is the most easily overlooked. The customers might forget the stores with pretty decoration, but always remember the store with stinking dirty toilets.

經驗與分享

在店面銷售的服務業當中，店舖**陳列**所的一切，就像我們出門的妝扮一樣，是讓顧客的感受最直接的媒介，也是代表著店家對商品、與對顧客的尊重；因此，許多連鎖經營的店舖，例如便利商店、電信門市等，對於店舖內商品陳列和標示等，都有其一致性的嚴格要求，甚至也包括員工制服或相關話術等，這些都在於展現該公司獨特的企業精神。

但對顧客而言，除了商品陳列、或賣場布置外，讓他們感受最直接的，卻是**銷售人員的服務態度**，以及**賣場環境所呈現的氣氛**；日本一些百貨業者，長久以來，對於賣場人員的服務訓練和要求，都是相當嚴格和重視，這些要求確實提升了商店的格調，也是他們能打進西方、和其他亞洲國家消費市場的原因之一，並成為他國業者學習和效仿的對象。

對於賣場環境的氣氛而言，無論經營的商品、店舖陳列的設計為何，整齊和清潔卻是永遠不變的要件；顧客的感受，永遠是來自最細微、偏僻的角落，因為那是最容易被忽略的地方；在那麼多商店當中，顧客或許記不得那家店很漂亮，卻永遠記得那家店的廁所又臭又髒。

Tips in Management

Retailing

Retailing is the sale of goods and services from individuals or businesses to the end-user. A retailer purchases large quantities of goods or products directly from manufacturers or through a wholesale. And then sells smaller quantities to the consumer for a profit. Retailers are a part of an integrated system called the supply chain.

Retailing can be done in either fixed locations like stores or markets, door-to-door or by delivery. Retailing includes subordinated services, such as delivery. The term "retailer" is also applied where a service provider serves as the needs of a large number of individuals, such as for the public. In the 2000s, an increasing amount of retailing is done online using electronic payment and delivery via a courier or postal mail.

Shops may be on residential streets, streets with few or no houses, or in a shopping mall. Shopping streets may be for pedestrians only. Sometimes a shopping street has a partial or full roof to protect customers from precipitation. Online retailing, a type of electronic commerce used for business-to-consumer (B2C) transactions and mail order, are forms of non-shop retailing.

管理小偏方

零售業

零售業是個人或企業向最終用戶銷售商品和服務的一種行業。零售商從廠家經由直接、或透過批發方式購買大批的商品或產品,然後以小量方式向消費者銷售,以賺取利潤;因此,零售商是屬於在一個商品供應整合系統中的一部分。

零售業的型態可以是固定的位置,像商店或市場,或者是以到府送貨的方式。因此,零售的範圍也包括了其附屬的服務,例如送貨在內;而“零售商”這個名詞,也包含了一個提供給大多數個體之需求的服務提供者,諸如用於公共服務。在2000年代,藉由線上付費及快捷郵寄,使得零售業有了很大的增加量。

而商店可能是座落在住宅區的街道,極少或根本沒有房子的街道,或者在購物商場內。而購物街則可能是只限行人通行;有時候,在購物街的一部分或全部,設置了屋頂以確保客人不被淋濕。網上零售業,是一種用於企業對消費者(B2C)的交易和郵購的電子商務型態,是一種無店舖的零售形式。

3-4 Brain Storming
腦力激盪

 Conversation 情境對話

The 2nd quarter earnings report has just released, but the result is really unsatisfyiing, with a decline of 30% compared with the same period last year. Robert feels worry and confused after reviewing the data. He's puzzled by the tactics of discounted pricing, which was often used in the past, and didn't have the expected marketing results. So he tried to find out the fundamental **crux** of the problem, and also wished to hear more **diversified** ideas in the meeting.

第二季的業績報告剛出爐了，但結果非常的不理想，整整比去年同期衰退了30%。羅柏看到了這樣的數據，心中有些擔憂和困惑，他不解過去所運用的價格折扣策略，為何沒有預期的行銷效果？於是決定要在會議中試圖找出根本的問題癥結，也想聽聽更多不同想法。

Robert: "Guys! Our performance in the past six months had a significant recession, which is a very serious warning to us. Therefore, I hope that we can **brainstorm** together and everyone offers some ideas and advices for us."

羅柏：「各位夥伴，我們這半年來的業績有著明顯的衰退，這是個嚴重的警訊；所以，希望大家能夠集思廣益，提供每個人的想法和意見。」

Jonathan: "We have been using the discount and promotional pricing strategies very successfully in the past, right?"

強納生：「過去我們一直運用的價格和促銷折扣策略，不是一直都很成功嗎？」

Robert: "That's the key problem we need to discuss. Why these strategies are no longer successful, or even **evolved into** an **obstacle** that leads to recession? So I wish that we all **laid aside** completely the thinking patterns in the past, and do our best for some innovative ideas. Hopefully, we can find out some feasible directions."

羅柏：「這就是我們要探討的問題所在：為何這些策略不再成功了，甚至是造成衰退的障礙？因此我希望，大家都完全拋開過去的思考模式，竭盡所能的提出一些創新的想法，希望能找到一些可行的新方向出來。」

The meeting suddenly became silent for some time, and everyone had stocked to cudgel his brains."

會議頓時安靜了一段時間，所有人都陷入了苦思。

Annie finally broke the silence: "I think the result of long-term price war in the past had not only lead to the constantly follow-up by competitors, but also the sense of weariness by consumers."

安妮終於打破了沉默：「我認為過去長期打價格戰的結果，不但讓競爭對手也不斷的跟進，消費者也早已經厭倦了。」

Jonathan: "But price competition on the market is already a **widespread** phenomenon. If there're no **concessions** on the price, we might even become less competitive."

強納生：「但價格競爭早已經是市場上普遍的現象了；如果沒有價格上的優惠，那我們不就更沒有競爭力了嗎？」

Mary follows: "In addition to pricing strategies, our brand image should **bring about** something different and closer to the consumers. For the ongoing discounts, it's better to develop some innovative gifts to stimulate the purchase of consumers."

瑪莉跟著說：「除了優惠價格的策略外，我們的品牌似乎應該帶給消費者一些更不一樣、更貼近他們的形象；與其不斷的打折，不如多開發一些創新的贈品來刺激消費者的購買。」

Peter: "I agree with Mary. Maybe we need to find a suitable brand **advertising person**. Through the fresh and friendly image of an advertising person, we can reshape the awareness of our brand and reversing the **cognitive** impression in consumers' minds."

彼得：「我認同瑪莉的想法。或許我們該找一個適當的品牌代言人，透過他清新和親切的形象，來重新塑造我們品牌的知名度，扭轉消費者心中的認知印象。」

Alex: "Maybe we need to re-design a brand new product packaging, too. And then, we can take a series of image advertising and **propagate** extensively through television or internet media."

亞歷:「或許我們也需要設計一套嶄新的產品包裝;還有呢!再拍攝一系列的形象廣告,透過電視或網路媒體,廣泛的宣傳。」

Annie: "Both changing the package and mass media advertising are very expensive, and we won't get results immediately. Why don't we just **pay the attention on** the cultivation of membership, such as conducting more site activities for members, or developing some exclusive **propaganda** gifts for members."

安妮:「改換包裝和大量的媒體廣告都很花錢的,而且效果也不一定馬上看得到;不如我們就多花些心思在會員的經營上面,例如多舉辦一些會員的現場活動,或是多設計一些會員專屬的文宣贈品。」

Lisa: "The consumers nowadays **are inseparable from** mobile phones and computers in their daily life. We can enhance the **functionality** of our website, and develop some software applications easy to download and use in connection with the characteristics of our product. All these will be more convenient for consumers to find and buy our merchandise."

麗莎:「現代的消費者,生活裡都離不開手機和電腦,我們可以加強網站的功能,並且針對我們商品的特性,開發一些容易下載與使用的應用軟體,讓消費者更方便搜尋和購買我們的商品。」

Section 3 Processing Management

Everyone discusses ardently at the meeting, and many innovative ideas constantly have been **stimulated out**. The meeting seems non-stop.

大家在會議中熱烈的討論著，許多創新的想法不斷被刺激了出來，似乎也讓會議停不了。

Robert: "Guys! Thanks for all your warmly discussion, and it seems like we can't get enough at the meeting. However, the time is limited and the meeting needs to be suspended. After our brainstorming this time, I believe that some great and workable ideas had aroused. I suggest that you each rearrange the ways in your own mind, or hear from others and consider possiblility, into a marketing plan proposal. Then in our meeting next week, organize them further into viable marketing plans. Okay?"

羅柏：「各位！謝謝大家熱烈的討論，這場會議實在是有些意猶未盡，但時間實在是有限，也必需要暫告一個段落；經過我們這次的腦力激盪，相信這其中會有許多不錯而可行的創意出現。我建議大家各自將自己想到的、或聽到而認為可行的方法，在我們下週的會議中，重新整理成一份可行的行銷方案；好嗎？」

🗂 Vocabulary 字彙解析

■ **crux**　*n.*　關鍵、癥結

〔同義詞：**nub, key, essence**〕

The **crux** of the matter is that attitudes have changed.

We had only the bare **crux** in the way of gear.

■ **diversify**　*vt.*　多元化、多樣化、分散

〔同義詞：**diversification, dispersion**〕

The trilobites **diversified** into a great number of species.

Some seeds rely on birds to **diversify**.

■ **brainstorm**　*n.*　腦力激盪、集思廣益

〔同義詞：**brainwave, search**〕

The survey revealed that few rated **brainstorms** or discussions at work with colleagues.

Jane had a **brainstorm** and started flirting at question time.

■ **obstacle**　*n.*　障礙、阻力、絆腳石

〔同義詞：**barrier, hurdle, stumbling block**〕

The major **obstacle** to achieve that goal is money.

There are many **obstacles** to overcome.

■ **widespread**　*adj.*　廣泛的、普及的、廣博的

〔同義詞：**general, extensive, common**〕

There was **widespread** support for the war.

Salt and pepper are the two most **widespread** seasonings.

■ **concession**　*n.*　讓步、優惠、特許

〔同義詞：**reduction, allowance, discount**〕

The strikers returned to work after having won some **concessions**.

Many stores will offer a **concession** on bulk purchases.

- **cognitive** *adj.* 認知的、認識

〔同義詞：**understanding, perceptive, knowledge**〕

The noise might keep you **cognitive** at night.
People expect their doctor to be **cognitive**.

- **propagate** *vt., vi.* 繁殖、傳播、宣揚

〔同義詞：**broadcast, cultivate, spread**〕

He's trying **propagating** his own houseplants from cuttings.
The policemen **propagated** the idea that the group was violent.

- **propaganda** *n.* 促銷、宣揚、宣傳活動

〔同義詞：**promotion, advertising, publicity**〕

He was charged with distributing enemy **propaganda**.
Most movie audiences are receptive to **propaganda**.

- **functionality** *n.* 功能、實用性

〔同義詞：**practice, functionary, pragmatic**〕

I like the feel and **functionality** of this bake ware.
It's a new software with additional **functionality**.

 # Phrase in sentence 片語和句型解析

- **evolved into** 演化成、發展成了

〔同義詞：**become, evolution**〕

The company has evolved into a major chemical manufacturer.
The motion pictures evolved into mass entertainment.

- **lay aside** 擱置、拋開、丟下

〔同義詞：**fling off, set aside, throw down**〕

The plans to reopen the school have been laid aside.
He picked up the debris and laid it aside.

■ **cudgel one's brains**　苦思、絞盡腦汁

〔 同義詞：rack one's brains, tax one's ingenuity 〕

I cudgel my brain to the question of what clothes to wear for the occasion.

He sat on the carpet and cudgeled his brain in front of the mirrors.

■ **bring about**　實現、導致、造成

〔 同義詞：cause, lead to, result 〕

This disease can bring about blindness.

He brought about his ambition to become a journalist.

■ **pay attention on**　注意、重視、理會

〔 同義詞：note, advert, emphasize 〕

He had failed to pay attention on the consequences.

She couldn't pay attention on his reasons for marriage.

■ **be inseparable from**　形影不離、緊密、不可分

〔 同義詞：close, indivisible, indissoluble 〕

Research and higher education are inseparable from each other.

Privilege was inseparable from responsibility.

■ **stimulated out**　激發、刺激出來

〔 同義詞：excite, arouse, motivate 〕

The women are given fertility drugs to stimulate out their ovaries.

The energy of an electron is sufficient to stimulate out the atom.

Section 3　Processing Management

∞ Practice in Management

Nowadays, the consumer behaviors and habits are constantly changing, and the technology and creativity are innovated increasingly. When many companies are still stick to the existing business model and methods, or rely on single or few people's judgments in the decision-making process, they might face some enormous frustration and obstacles and easily lose a competitive advantage. Such a challenge will be more obvious in the high-tech and creative design industry, or in the highly competitive field of media marketing. There's a vivid example that traditional grocery stores had entirely been replaced by the convenience stores.

As the saying goes: "two heads are better than one". Sometimes companies may try the "brainstorming" model to break through the bottleneck. Through the brainstorming among peers everyone tried to think entirely different from the old framework, without any restrain to imagination or limitation to ideas been put forward during the discussion, might inspire incredibly spark and find a way out to overcome the barriers.

Not all new ideas are implementable, of course. We need to review these concepts carefully after brainstorming. In addition to vetting the pros and cons of each new idea, the most important thing is their feasibility, as well as procedures and methods to achieve them. Sometimes we can try a small-scale experimental activities, and finally become an effective new method after repeated verification.

經驗與分享

在現今的時代中，**消費行為**和習慣不斷的在改變，科技及創意也跟著日益求新求變，許多的企業仍固守著既有的經營模式和方法，或是在決策過程中，僅靠著單一或極少數人的想法和判斷，許多時候都會面臨極大的挫敗和阻礙，也很容易就失去了競爭的優勢；這種情況，在高度競爭的高科技、創意設計產業，或是在媒體行銷的領域中，就更加的明顯了。過去傳統的雜貨店，如今已被處處可見的便利商店所取代，這就是個活生生的例子。

俗話說：三個臭皮匠，勝過一個諸葛亮。為突破決策的瓶頸，有些時候企業可運用『腦力激盪法』的模式，透過同儕間的集思廣益，試著完全跳脫舊有的思考框架，大家天馬行空的想像，不設限的提出各種可能的想法，有時在這個過程中，會激發出異想不到的火花，尋找到了可以突破障礙的方法出來。

當然，並非所有新的想法都是可行的，在大家的集思廣益之後，應該再將這些概念仔細的檢視一番，除了檢核每個新想法的優劣之外，最重要的就是這些想法的可行性，以及實現它們的步驟與方法，有時可以嘗試著小規模的實驗活動，經過反覆驗證後，最後才能成為有效的新方法。

Tips in Management

Brainstorming

Brainstorming is a method designed to stimulate creativity and strengthen thinking. This method is pioneered by the United States BBDO (Batten, Bcroton, Durstine and Osborn) advertising company founder Alex Osborne (English: Alex Faickney Osborn) in 1938. This experiment can be performed by one person or a group of people. Participants get together and is free to proposed ideas pop up related to the topics, and then re-sorting the insights. Throughout the process, no one can interrupt or criticize regardless how ridiculous or absurd those views might be, and then it might result in a lot of new ideas and problem-solving methods. Its purpose is to encourage all participants to have an equal say in the process, thereby generating a series of ideas.

The participants were asked to write down their ideas anonymously. The moderator collected these ideas and group voting. Then members of the group or groups may be at the forefront of his mind again for further brainstorming. Each sub-group discussed on the list of topics after the final summary of the whole group again. The idea became implementable only if it had finally been recognized by absolute majority of the participants.

管理小偏方

腦力激盪法

腦力激盪法（Brainstorming），又稱為頭腦風暴法，是一種為激發創造力、強化思考力而設計出來的一種方法。此法是美國BBDO（Batten, Bcroton, Durstine及Osborn）廣告公司創始人亞歷克斯・奧斯本（Alex Faickney Osborn）於1938年首創的。

這個實驗，可以由一個人或一組人進行；參與者圍在一起，隨意將腦中和研討主題有關的見解提出來，然後再將大家的見解重新分類整理。在整個過程中，無論提出的意見和見解多麼可笑、荒謬，其他人都不得打斷和批評，從而產生很多的新觀點和問題解決方法，它的目的在於鼓勵所有參與者在整個過程中擁有均等的話語權，藉此用來鼓勵生成一系列的主意。

參與者被要求匿名寫下他們的主意，主持人收集這些主意並進行小組表決，接著小組或分組成員可能會重新對位於前列的主意進行進一步的腦力激盪。

每個分小組對列表上的主題討論後最後整個小組再匯總，直到最後得到絕多數參與者的認同，這個主意才是可進一步實施的方案。

3-5 Follow up
後續追蹤

 Conversation 情境對話

Jenna sent the meeting notice to Robert's office. Robert reminded her of adding the last **minutes of meeting**, and notify all members who will participate in the meeting to be **well-prepared** in advance.

珍娜送來了會議通知單到羅柏的辦公室，羅柏提醒了她要補充上次的會議記錄，並知會所有參加會議的人做好事先的準備。

Before the meeting, Robert had **read through** the contents of minutes of meeting and prepared well the topics to be discussed in the meeting.

在會議之前，羅柏已詳細研讀了會議紀錄的內容，充分準備著會議中即將討論的議題。

Robert: "I am sure that you guys had read through the related articles of last minutes of meeting. Today, we need a **thorough** discussion **in connection with** these problems. First, with respect to the **backlogged** problem of power distribution project, Elmer please explains the update situation of improvement."

羅柏：「相信各位已經看過了上次的會議紀錄了，今天將針對這些問題，好好的討論。首先，關於配電工程進度落後的事情，請艾默說明一下目前的改善狀況。」

Elmer: "Yes. I had coordinated with the supervisor from project owner, and he agreed to offer us some time to improve the progressing. The **partial** material has been delivered into the site last week. The progress of works should have been slowly caught up some more."

艾默：「嗯，我已經有跟業主派來的監工協調，對方同意給我們一段時間來改善及追上進度，上周也有部份的材料送到工地了，工程的進度應該是慢慢趕上了一些。」

Robert: "It seems like the case had been improved. But it's not enough. Did you **grasp** how long the tolerate period given by the supervisor? How much progresses we had caught up? When will those lacking main material be **supplemented**?"

羅柏：「聽起來這問題似乎在改善當中，但這還不夠！你可有掌握到監工給予的容許期間有多久？我們目前追趕的進度有多少？那些欠缺的主要材料又何時能補充進來呢？」

Elmer: "I'm sorry, Robert. I need a further understanding for these issues."

艾默：「不好意思，羅柏！這些問題我還要進一步的了解。」

Robert: "I will suggest you to build up the project table of schedule as soon as possible, and **identified** particularly some unusual problems and addressed the improving status. This can help you to **keep track on** some specific important issues. Next, I will also like to know about the status of warehouse material shortages and differences. Vincent, can you briefly explain about this?"

羅柏：「我會建議你盡快的建立起工程進度表，並且特別標明一些異常的問題與解決情況，這樣可以幫助你持續的追蹤特定的重要事項。另外，我也想了解一下倉庫物料短缺和差異的情況如何；文森，你可以說明一下嗎？」

Vincent: The situation of theft had somehow improved after last two outland workers had left. But I'm not quite sure the actual number of materials. Those engineering guys had been asking some of the materials, but I really don't know when will those material be **put in storage**."

文森：「之前那兩個外來的工人離開後，失竊的情況是有些改善；但目前物料實際的數量，我並不清楚；工程部的人一直在詢問著某些材料，但我也不知道東西何時會入倉。」

Robert: "I think this is the similar problem. First of all, you shall re-establish a complete table of material put in and out and their inventory, and then check clearly the filed data of each item with the number of actual inventory.

Elmer: "That's it! Many important materials had been **out of stock** for a long time, and the workers are very anxious."

Robert: "That's the key point I want to mention! This issue has been raised in several meetings, but they seem to have no follow-up progress. You should regularly update the inventory checklist, fully **mark out** the unusual materials and their problems, and continuously track the status of improvement. By the way, regarding the batch of equipment you are waiting for, shouldn't that be approached two months ago? Why there's no follow-up since then?"

羅柏：「我想這也是相同的問題。首先，你應該重新建立一套完整的物料進出與盤存表，好好的將每個品項在檔案資料上的數據，以及實際盤點的數字核對清楚。」

艾默：「對啊！有好多項重要的材料都缺好久，工人急得都快跳腳了。」

羅柏：「這就是我要說的重點！這個問題，已經在好幾次會議中提出了，但似乎都沒有後續的進展。你應該定期的更新盤存檢核表，將異常的物料和其問題，詳細的標示出來，並且持續性的追蹤改善狀況。對了，有關你們等待的那批機具，不是應該在兩個月前就開始接洽了嗎？為何至今完全沒有後續的動作？」

Queenie heard the question Robert mentioned, and reply in panic: "I had contacted with the exporter since that time, and they mentioned to arrange the shipment first."

昆妮聽到羅柏的問題，驚慌的回答著：「我那時候有跟出口廠商連繫，廠商説會先安排船期。」

Robert: "And then?"

羅柏：「然後呢？」

Queenie replies timidly: "Then, no one from engineering or warehouse mentioned to me again. I thought it's not so urgent.... So..., and then...! I had forgotten about this matter."

昆妮膽怯的回答著：「後來，工程部和倉庫都沒有人再跟我提起，我想應該沒那麼急…；所以…，然後…，這事我就忘了。」

Robert's enraged: "That's **ridiculous**! For such an important issue after two months, the handling person did not follow up any further arrangements, the engineering staffs did not react positively, and the warehouse staffs just waited there quietly. And then, the issue had been **stagnated** at the origin, or even long been forgotten."

羅柏生氣的説：「真是太扯了！這麼重要的事，經過了兩個月的時間，承辦的人完全沒有進一步的安排，工程部的人完全不會積極的反應，倉庫的人只會靜靜的等待，然後事情就停滯在原點，甚至早就被遺忘了！」

It's **rare** to see Robert's so angry, and everyone is afraid and silent.

難得看到羅柏如此的動怒，大家都緊張的不敢出聲。

Robert: "That's our key issue. Sometimes when the meeting is over, we're so easy to forget the issues we just discussed when the meeting is over for days. All the memories seem to just stay in the minutes of meeting and no one would go on tracking. That's why I repeatedly reminded you to 'build up the procedures, respond to **anomalies**, and keep on tracking' in this meeting."

羅柏：「這就是我們的關鍵問題！許多時候，會議中所討論過的問題，當會議結束了，我們也就跟著忘了，所有的記憶似乎只是留在會議紀錄上，沒有人會再去追蹤。這也就是在今天的會議當中，我一再要求各位『建立流程，反應異常和持續追蹤』的用意了。」

 # Vocabulary 字彙解析

■ **minutes of meeting** *n.* 會議紀錄、紀要

〔同義詞：**conference record, record of processing**〕

All the discussion and resolution shall be written in the minutes of meeting.

The policy of employment will be discussed first according to our last minutes of meeting.

■ **backlog** *n.* 積壓、待辦事項

〔同義詞：**overstock, pileup, accumulation**〕

There is a traffic backlog and vehicles move at a snail's pace.

The gradual backlog of soot can seriously affect the chimney performs.

■ **partial** *adj.* 部份的、局部的、偏倚的

〔同義詞：**fractional, sectional, biased**〕

It's only the partial answer for questions we need to answer.

We will not tolerate this partial media coverage.

■ **grasp** *vt.* 掌握、了解、領會

〔同義詞：**predominate, understand, clasp**〕

She was grasped by a feeling of excitement.

He didn't grasp a word I said.

■ **supplement** *vt. n.* 補充、輔助、副刊

〔同義詞：**replenish, assist, addendum**〕

She took the job to supplement her husband's income.

The handout is a supplement to the official manual.

■ **identify** *vt.* 鑑定、辨認、認出

〔同義詞：**recognize, evaluate, associate**〕

The judge ordered that the girl not be identified.

He was equivocal about being identified too closely with the peace movement.

■ **ridiculous** *adj.* 荒謬、可笑、滑稽

〔同義詞：**preposterous, comic, laughable**〕

If it didn't make me so angry, it would be ridiculous.

It's ridiculous that I have been fined.

■ **stagnate** *vt.* 停滯不前、滯留

〔同義詞：**become stale, fester, putrefy**〕

Teaching can easily stagnate into a set of routines.

Relationships have to keep moving forward or they stagnate and die.

■ **anomalies** *n.* 不規則、異常〔的人〕

〔同義詞：**abnormal, oddity, peculiarity**〕

There are a number of anomalies in the present system.

There is evidence that fraud and anomaly continue on a large scale.

Phrase in sentence 片語和句型解析

■ **read through**　通讀、仔細閱讀、讀完

〔同義詞：**read over**〕

I've read through the gas meter.

He has spent countless hours in libraries to read through art history books.

■ **in connection with**　針對、連接、聯繫

〔同義詞：**against, contra, contrary to**〕

The electrodes were in connection with a recording device.

Oscar had been in connection with other construction firms.

■ **keep track on**　跟蹤上、追蹤、明了

〔同義詞：**follow, trail, trace**〕

Secondary radars had kept track on the aircraft.

She went back into the house, and Ben kept track on her.

■ **put in storage**　入庫、入倉

〔同義詞：**warehousing**〕

The executive had approved to put in storage of the new product.

It is almost as expensive to hold, and put in storage as to produce.

■ **out of stock**　缺貨、斷貨

〔同義詞：**out-of-stock, run out of**〕

The store has a very low turnover and almost out of stock.

It is recommended to use a steady rest from out of stock.

■ **mark out**　註明、標示、標記

〔同義詞：**mark off, indicate**〕

Use the dotted lines to mark out the text's margins.

The treatment is likely to be marked out severely depressed patients.

Section 3
Processing Management

經驗與分享

In addition to the correct direction, strong resources and outstanding experience and profession, the key factor of success for a business or team is the **continuous execution**. It's also an indispensable driving force. Ironically, even with some good ideas, a lack of execution is "thinking like a giant, but acting like a dwarf." Therefore, the manager needs to strengthen the ongoing execution of team. For every issue handled by himself or his subordinates, the manager shall be consequently tracking, reviewing, evaluating, and correcting to ensure the quality and progress of implementation.

It's especially true for some important matters, or the issue covered by a longer period of time. After a period of time, sometimes these issues can easily be overlooked or forgotten, or getting lost the sharp reaction, and then resulting in a management oversight. While in such a situation, the most effective reinforcement is to keep a complete record of the conference resolution, and, in accordance with the resolutions and the significance of issues, regularly tracking and vetting the implementation of the follow-up implementation. And alternatively, you can design some suitable spreadsheets for recording and vetting, or setup the automatic check point, to prevent the oversight from the human being and then reinforce the efficiency of management work.

經驗與分享

一個企業或是團隊成功的要素，除了來自於其有正確的經營方向、堅強的專業實力和資源外，最重要的，有著**持續不斷的執行力**，方是真正不可或缺的原動力；令人感到諷刺的是，有再好的想法，若缺乏執行力，就好像是『思考的巨人、行動的侏儒』。因此對經理人而言，如何能加強團隊的持續執行力，對於自己和部屬所處理的每件事情，能不斷的追蹤、檢視、評估和修正，以確保執行的品質和進度。

尤其對於一些重要的事務、或是所涵蓋的期間較長遠的，有時因為時間的關係而容易被忽略或遺忘，或者漸漸的失去了敏銳的反應，造成管理上的疏漏；面對這樣的情況，較為有效的補強方法，首先就是要有完整的會議決議紀錄，並且依決議內容和重要性，定期的追蹤和檢核後續執行的成果；另外也可以設計出適用的紀錄與檢核的表格文件，或是設定自動檢核點，以防止人為的疏漏，補強管理上的工作。

Tips in Management

Management science

Management science is concerned with developing and applying models and concepts that may prove useful in helping to illuminate management issues and solve managerial problems, as well as designing and developing new and better models of organizational excellence.

Application of management science is abundant in industry as airlines, manufacturing companies, service organizations, military branches, and governments. The range of problems and issues to which management science has contributed insights and solutions is vast.

It includes: scheduling airlines, including both planes and crew, deciding the appropriate place to site new facilities, such as a warehouse, factory or fire station, managing the flow of water from reservoirs, identifying possible future development paths for parts of the telecommunications industry, establishing the information needs and appropriate systems to supply them within the health service, and identifying and understanding the strategies adopted by companies for their information systems

Management science is also concerned with methods called soft-operational analysis for strategic planning, strategic decision support, and Problem Structuring Methods (PSM). In dealing with these sorts of challenges, mathematical modeling and simulation are not appropriate or will not suffice.

管理小偏方

管理科學

管理科學一種是關於制定與應用許多模型和概念的學科，而這些概念對於點亮並解決管理上的問題，以及規劃並啟發出應用在組織上更優質與卓越的模型，可以被證明出有著明顯的幫助。

管理科學已應用在很廣泛的產業之中，譬如航空業、製造業、服務業、軍事部門和政府機關等。而運用管理科學所能發掘出的方案、和解決的問題，其涵蓋的領域是非常廣泛的。這些領域可能包含了：航空公司的調度，包括飛機和機組人員；設置新裝備設立位置的確認，如倉庫、工廠或消防局；水庫的水流量管理；識別出電信行業所用的裝置，其在未來所可能發展的途徑；在健康服務的內部供應上，建立出所需求的資訊和有效的系統；針對公司的資訊系統，闡釋出適用於公司的策略。

管理科學同時也注重被稱為軟運營分析的方法，應用於策略規劃、決策支援和問題構建方法（**PSM**）等等面向。在處理這些各種各樣的挑戰，只運用數學模型或模擬，其實是不恰當、或是不夠的。

Section 3
Processing Management

3-6 Job Overlap
工作重疊

 ## Conversation 情境對話

Robert received again a customer complaint report from the Customer Service Department. It's the third one this week, and this really bothers him. Some customers complained about too many salesmen had contact with them consequently, sometimes even push for the **duplicated** items. There also some complaint to salesmen for the **dodger** of after-sale service.

羅柏又接到了一份來自客服部門的客訴報告，這已是此週的第三份了，讓他非常傷腦筋；有些客戶抱怨著公司裡太多的業務人員陸續來跟他們接洽，甚至是推銷重複的東西，也有客戶抱怨業務人員對一些商品的售後服務，卻是推託給別人。

Robert determines to convene a meeting to clarify the problem and solve them completely.

羅柏決定召集大家來開會，將問題釐清，徹底的解決。

Robert: "Recently, we had received some customers' complaints. You can read the related information in your **hand out**. I like to hear your commend if there's any better solution. Tony, you tell us first."

經理：「最近我們接到了一些客戶的抱怨，各位手上都有相關的資料，我想聽聽各位的看法，看能否找出較好的解決方案。東尼，你先說說看。」

Tony: "Some of them are our customers who distribute our IT **accessories.**"

東尼：「這有幾個的確是我們的客戶，都是跟我們經銷資訊周邊耗材。」

Noah refutes: "It's not right! You are responsible for the accessory distribution in Eastern area. But some of these customers are located in Western area, and should be the customers of our Application Software division."

諾亞反駁：「這就不對了！你們是負責東區的耗材經銷，但這其中有些客戶是位在西區，應該是我們應用軟體部門的客戶啊！」

Tony then loudly replies: "These agents are introduced by our original customers, and, of course, they now have become our customers, too. On the contrary, your salesmen push not only software, but also the accessories to customers. That's truly **out of bound**!"

東尼也大聲回應：「但這些都是我們原有的客戶轉介紹的，當然也是我們的客戶了；倒是你們部門的人，除了推銷軟體，又跟客戶推銷耗材，這才是撈過界了。」

Section 3
Processing Management

Noah's unpleased: "Some customers need the software, but still lack of **opportune** accessories. It couldn't be work without **collocation**. That's call matching service, got it?"

諾亞不悅的説：「有些客戶想買軟體，卻沒有適當的周邊耗材，如果不搭配起來，根本就無法操作；這是配套服務，懂嗎？」

Tony replies angrily: "Isn't that rushing to sell our product? If so, how do we promote our work?"

東尼氣急敗壞的説：「那不就是搶賣我們的商品，這樣我們的業務如何推動啊？」

Noah is also **outdone**: "Don't you grab our Eastern customers, too? And then, what's that all about?"

諾亞不甘示弱的説：「你們不也搶了我們西區的客戶嗎？這又該怎麼説！」

While both guys arguing, Enya, the customer service division staff, who sits aside, couldn't stand anymore."

兩人面紅耳赤的爭論著，這時在一旁客服部門的恩雅終於忍不住了。

Enya: "You guys just calm down, and don't rush for the domain. Some customers had complaint that whenever the customer got trouble on product and looked for help, the staffs in the accessory division always **point out** that software division should be the one in charge, or **vice versa**. And finally, none will be taking care of it. Then, you tell me, what we got to do?"

恩雅：「兩位安靜一下，先別急著搶地盤，這裡有幾個客戶抱怨著說，當他們採購的東西有些問題需要協助時，找耗材部門的人，就說是軟體部門負責，找到部門的人，卻又說這歸耗材部門管，最後就是都沒有人處理；你們說這該怎麼辦？」

After hearing this, both guys suddenly are speechless and **sulking**. Then, Robert speaks out finally.

聽到這一番話後，兩人頓時啞口無言的生著悶氣。這時羅柏終於開口了。

Robert: "It's not **evildoing** if we're very **engrossed in** the performance. But, hopefully, we're also enthusiastic about service and problem solving. Obviously, there're some **phenomena** of **overlapping** and confusion in the dividing of business scope. Maybe we need to re-adjust in the **architecture** of the organization and terms of reference. We need a detailed discussion in next meeting."

經理：「大家很積極的爭取業績，這並非壞事，但希望我們在服務和解決問題方面，也能同樣充滿熱誠；很明顯得，我們在業務範圍的劃分上，出現了重疊不清的現象，或許我們在組織和職掌的架構上，需要再重新調整，下次會議我們需要好好的討論。」

Vocabulary 字彙解析

- **duplicate** *vt., adj., n.* 複製、重複、副本

〔同義詞：**repeat, similar, counterpart**〕

A duplicate license is issued to replace a valid license which has been lost.

Books may be disposed of if they are duplicates.

- **dodger** *n.* 閃躲、欺騙者

〔同義詞：**cheater, coward, thief**〕

These sunglasses are perfect for all reader, magnifier, or dodger wearers.

Our power is wielded by dodgers, and our honor is false in all its points'.

- **opportune** *adj.* 適當的、及時的、順利

〔同義詞：**apposite, timely, fluky**〕

He couldn't have arrived at a less opportune moment.

This is a measure opportune to a wartime economy.

- **collocation** *adj.* 搭配、並置

〔同義詞：**mix, concatenation**〕

The words have a similar range of collocation.

The decor is a collocation of antique and modern.

- **outdone** *vt.* 不甘示弱、超越

〔同義詞：**exceed, outdo, outshine**〕

The men tried to outdone each other in their generosity.

An enormous oak tree stood outdone the cottage.

- **sulk** *vt., n.* 生悶氣、憂鬱

〔同義詞：**stuffiness, depression, sentiment**〕

He was sulking over the breakup of his band.

She was in a fit of the sulks.

Phrase in sentence 片語和句型解析

- **hand out** 傳單、手冊、補貼

〔同義詞：leaflet, pamphlet, subsidies〕

She was shocked when she saw a one-page handout condemning her campaign.

Thousands of refugees subsist on international handouts.

- **out of bound** 撈過界、出界

〔同義詞：out of range, transboundary〕

The cost is thought to be out of bound.

The build is almost out of bound into the eastern wilderness.

- **point out** 指出、通知、提示

〔同義詞：notice, call attention, remonstrate〕

He pointed out the youths behave suspiciously.

She had failed to point out the consequences of this project.

- **vice versa** 反之亦然

〔同義詞：conversely, contrariwise, the other way around〕

Science must be at the service of man, and not vice versa.

We can't really understand the animals, or vice versa.

- **engrossed in** 醉心於、全神貫注

〔同義詞：obsessed, concentrate on〕

They seemed to be engrossed in conversation.

He was engrossed in the theme of death.

∞ Practice in Management

Enterprise organization is a team with respective duties and division of labor. Each position and unit has a specific role and the particular portfolio of responsibility. There's a clear link between each other in the hierarchy management and membership. Most large companies will usually plan out both the organizational structure for the enterprise as whole and individual units, partitions in responsibilities and authority among divisions. And even break out the contents of each individual job duties, clearly stated in **"Statement of Work"**.

In business management, these complete plans are very important basic tools. Not all of the rules and conditions, of course, can be described tremendously by sentences, but should be institutionalized as possible. When there are still outstanding issues encountered, and the enterprise use the ways of coordination and discussion to clarify gradually. Thus the operation of the system can be more completely and smoothly. However, some enterprises, especially those small businesses, weren't or didn't willing to clearly setup the managerial system and became people ruling management. When the work authorities and responsibilities are not clear among peers or divisions, sometimes this will result in cases of business duplication, work conflicts or shirk of responsibility. there might be some omissions or things that are not regulated, only adding the cruelty to misfortune.

經驗與分享

企業組織是一個各司其職、分工合作的團隊，每一個職位、每一個團隊和單位，都有其要扮演的角色，有特定的職掌和責任範圍，彼此之間在管理的層級和隸屬上面，有著明確的連結關係；絕多數較具規模的公司，都會針對整體企業、與個別單位的組織架構，部門的責任劃分與權責等，詳細的規劃出來；甚至也將每個個別職位的職務內容，明確的載明於『**工作說明書**』之中。

這些完整的規劃，對於企業經營管理而言，很重要的基礎工具。當然，並非所有的規定和狀況，都能夠鉅細靡遺的用文字描述出來，但仍應盡可能的將之制度化；當遇到有未盡事宜，再透過協調和討論的方式逐步釐清，讓制度的運行更加完善。有些公司，尤其是中小型企業，無法或不願意好好的規劃制度，流於人治的管理，當同儕間或部門間遇到工作權責不清的時候，有時會造成業務重疊、工作衝突或是互相推諉責任的情況，或者也會有遺漏、事情三不管的情況發生，只使得管理上的問題更為雪上加霜。

Section 3
Processing Management

Tips in Management

Job Description Management

Job Description Management is the creation and maintenance of job descriptions within an organization. A job description is a document listing the tasks, duties, and responsibilities of a specific job. Having up-to-date, accurate, and professionally-written job descriptions is critical to an organization's ability to attract qualified candidates, orient & train employees, establish job performance standards, develop compensation programs, conduct performance reviews, set goals, and meet legal requirements.

Prior to the development of the job description, a job analysis must be conducted. Job analysis, an integral part of HR management, is the gathering, analysis and documentation of the important facets of a job including what the employee should do, the context of the job, and the requirements of the job.

Once the job analysis is completed, the job description such as the job specification can be initiated. A job description describes which activities will be performed and a job specification lists the knowledge, skills and abilities required to perform the job. A job description contains several sections including an identification section, a general summary, essential functions and duties, job specifications, and disclaimers and approvals.

Job descriptions are then used to develop effective HR planning, recruiting, and selection initiatives; to maintain clear continuity between compensation planning, training efforts, and performance management; and to identify job factors that may contribute to workplace safety and health and employee/labor relations.

管理小偏方

工作說明書管理

工作説明書管理，是一種在組織內建立和維護工作説明的管理方法。而工作説明書則是一種針對特定職位，所詳細列舉出其工作任務、職責和具體工作責任的文件。一份即時、準確和專業的書面工作説明，對於公司在吸引優秀的人才，員工培訓，建立工作績效標準，制定福利方案，開展績效評估，設定目標，以及符合法律規定等方面的能力，至關重要。

在進行工作説明之前，必須先進行工作分析。工作分析是人力資源管理極重要組成部分，乃針對該工作許多重要的面向，進行搜集，分析和文字化等工作，包括員工該做些什麼、工作範圍及該職位的條件需求等。

一旦這項工作完成了分析，這項工作的説明，包括工作規範就可開始進行。工作説明書裡闡明了該工作應執行的活動，及執行該項工作所需的知識、技術和能力。工作説明書裡應包括了：職位稱謂，一般説明，基本目標與職掌，工作規範，免責聲明和核准等部份。

工作説明的功能，是用來發展有效的人力資源規劃，招聘和選拔活動；維繫著明確永續的員工福利計劃，培訓成果和績效管理；並載明對於維護工作場所安全與健康、員工／勞動關係，有所助益的因素。

Section 4

Leadership

4-1 Can't Go on
快做不下去了

 Conversation 情境對話

Just after 9 o'clock at night, the light in the manager's room was still on.

晚上剛過了九點，經理室裡燈還亮著。

"Boom, boom, boom!" Someone **knocked** on the door of the manager's office.

『咚、咚、咚！』經理辦公室外有人敲了門。

Jeffrey: "Robert, you free now?"	傑夫瑞：「羅柏，有空嗎？」
Robert: "Oh, Jeff! You seem very tired, and look not so good; Come in, let's sit down and have a **chat** here."	經理：「喔！是傑夫啊！你看起來似乎很累，氣色不太好；來，咱們這邊坐著聊。」
Jeffrey: "Yap. There's something I want to report. For the past few weeks, my team partners and I had been overtimes very late everyday, even till the mid-night sometimes. Now, we're all tired!"	傑夫瑞：「嗯，我是有些事情想跟您報告。這幾個星期以來，我和幾個夥伴們，每天都加班到了很晚，甚至要到半夜才回家。我們都覺得累了！」

Robert: "I know! It's about the project of **data-communication** software designed for the customer in Los Angeles, right? It's really **toilsome** for you all."

經理：「我知道，是關於那個洛杉磯客戶所要的數據通信軟體設計專案吧！你們辛苦了！」

Jeffrey: "Yes! The schedule request by the company is really too tight, and the working time is simply not enough. If so, then we might not be able to do it anymore!!!"

傑夫瑞：「是啊！公司要求的進度太緊迫了，時間根本就不夠！如果這樣，我們可能沒辦法再做下去了！」

Robert: "Relax Jeff, just **take it easy**. Let's **work** it **out** together, and find a way to make things solved more **smoothly**."

經理：「別急，傑夫，先放輕鬆一點，我們一起來想想辦法，看如何讓事情更圓滿的解決。」

Jeffrey: "We had better find the solution **ASAP**, otherwise we all cannot **go on**!"

傑夫瑞：「最好是趕快有個解決方案，否則大家都做不下去了！」

Section 4
Leadership

Robert: "Don't worry, I'm also one of your teams, and this is the challenge we have to face together. How about this! In nine o'clock tomorrow morning, let's **set up** a meeting together to discuss in details about the job content of this project. We'll check through the operation **processing**, manpower planning, resource **allocation**, or even the goal setting in the whole. Then, try to **figure out** if there is anything we can do to improve the efficiency, okay?"

經理：「別擔心，我和你們都是一個團隊，這是我們共同要面對的挑戰。這樣好了，明天早上九點，我們和夥伴們一起開個會，就這個專案作業的執行內容，詳細討論一下，看看我們在整個軟體設計的作業流程、人力規劃、資源分配或是在設定的目標上，是否還有什麼可以改善工作效率的空間，好嗎？」

Jeffrey: "Well, Wish we could find a better way to improve, because everyone is really tired!!"

傑夫瑞：「好吧！希望能找到有效的改善方法，大家都累了！」

Robert: "I know everyone is tired. So, I'll ask you and partners just go home and rest now, and no more discussion before tomorrow, okay? This is a **command**!"

經理：「我知道大家都累了，所以我要求你和夥伴們，現在就趕快回家休息，有什麼事明天再說，好嗎？這是命令！」

Jeffrey: "Ok, **I've got it**! Thanks, Robert. And you need to take a break earlier, too."

傑夫瑞：「我知道了！謝謝您，羅柏；您也早點休息囉！」

📖 Vocabulary 字彙解析

- **knock** *vt.* 敲打、磕碰

〔同義詞：**bang, strike, hit, beat**〕

I knocked on the kitchen door.

She deliberately ran into him, knocking his shoulder.

- **chat** *vi.* 閒聊、交談

〔同義詞：**talk, gossip, chatter, speak**〕

He dropped in for a chat.

She chatted to her mother on the phone every day.

- **data-communication** *n.* 數據通信

The Data-communication technology creates a better understanding among people.

What's the different between data-communication and tele-communication?

- **toilsome** *adj.* 辛苦的、賣力的

〔同義詞：**hard, exhausting, laborious**〕

The specialized work is toilsome to outsiders.

It's a long and toilsome assignment.

- **smoothly** *adv.* 順利、順手

〔同義詞：**evenly, level, flat, flush**〕

Everything seemed to be going smoothly.

The bust is smoothly carved in white marble.

- **ASAP** *as soon as possible* 越快越好

This letter needs to be mailed out as soon as possible.

或者說

This letter needs to be mailed out immediately.

Section 4
Leadership

■ **processing** *n.* 流程、處理

〔同義詞：**finishing, obedience**〕

There're various stages in processing the wool.

The police are now reviewing the processing and procedures.

■ **allocation** *n.* 分配

〔同義詞：**distribution, assignment, dealing**〕

We need to find a way in more efficient allocation of resources.

She had it printed for allocation among her friends.

■ **command** *vt., n.* 命令、指揮

〔同義詞：**order, direction, require**〕

It's unlikely they'll obey your commands.

No party commanded a majority.

Phrase in sentence 片語和句型解析

▪ go on 繼續

〔同義詞：**Continue, hold on**〕

He was unable to go on with his job.

We go on the story from the point reached in last class.

▪ take it easy 放心、別緊張、慢慢來

〔同義詞：**Rest assured, relax**〕

Don't worry, just take it easy!

或者說

Don't worry, just relax!

▪ work out 解決、鍛鍊、將會做得更好

〔同義詞：**solve, exercise, turn out effective**〕

Can you work this puzzle out？

They work out in the gymnasium every week.

We will work out well in that kind of job.

▪ set up 建立、豎立、設置

〔同義詞：**build, establish, develop**〕

Two bridges have been set up over the river.

It seems necessary to set up special schools for talented children.

▪ figure out 弄清楚、找出

〔同義詞：**work out, solve**〕

The doctors finally figure out that Esther had suffered a stroke.

The aim is to figure out the effects of macroeconomic policy on the economy.

▪ I've got it 知道了、得到了

〔同義詞：**get it, catch on, get onto**〕

I've got it! All the chaos comes from me!

Section 4
Leadership

🔖 Practice in Management

Management is a science of problem-solving. In the practical work field, managers eagerly not only try to solve the questions in "things", but also the issues of "people". In most cases, these two factors need to be solved simultaneously, because they're often mutually causality and influence to each other. As a result, the managerial problem has become more and more complicated. Therefore, as a manager, he or she should impress on some series of scientific methods, such as: management by objectives (MBO), organizational behavior..., in managerial efforts, but also need to act the role play as "shepherd" to care, manage and lead subordinates, to achieve the progress in organization, and work efforts smoothly.

In a practical work environment, managers usual deal with problems that is faced with or created by subordinates (like competition from the work or surrounding environment, inadequate in work capacity or resources, or mental and emotional problem... etc). No matter what the problem is big or small, tangible, or intangible, transactional, or interpersonal issues, managers always need to play well in many different roles:

1.As a leader: In the team, the manager is always the most stable at the helm. Their direction is always clear without any panic, and always tries to show the stability and strength, even if they use not fully understood or feel uncertain.

2.As a working partner: When the subordinates encounter problems, managers should encourage the team members to feel that the manager is also part of the team, and willing to face together with the challenges and solve problems.

3. <u>An Arbiter</u>: In many cases, managers, just like the judges, must evaluate the task effectiveness soberly, judge the interpersonal disputes transcendently, and provide the effective incentives and rewards approach.

 經驗與分享

管理是一門解決問題的科學；在實務的工作領域中，管理者同時要解決『事』的問題，更要解決『人』的問題，而且兩者不僅要同時解決，兩者也經常是互為因果、互相影響，讓問題更加複雜；因此，管理者不僅要透過一些有系列的科學方法，例如：目標管理(MBO)、組織學…等，更要以（牧羊人）的角色，關心、管理和領導部屬，讓組織和工作能順利的推動。

實務的工作環境中，管理者經常會碰到部屬所面臨的、或所產生的種種難題（來自工作環境與競爭、工作能力與資源不足、或是心理與情緒上的問題），無論問題是大或小、有形或無形、人際的或事務的，管理者永遠需要同時扮演好許多不同的角色：

1. <u>領航者</u>：在團隊中，管理者永遠是最穩定的掌舵者，方向明確、不會慌亂，即使自己完全不懂、或沒有把握，仍要努力表現出安定的力量。

2. <u>工作夥伴</u>：部屬遇到問題時，管理者應該讓團隊成員感受到，他也是團隊的一份子，大家一起來面對挑戰、解決問題。

3. <u>仲裁者</u>：許多時候，管理者像個法官一樣，必須冷靜的評估工作的成效好壞，超然的判斷人際間紛爭與對錯，提供有效的運用激勵與獎懲方法。

Tips in Management

Management by objects (MBO)

Management by objectives (MBO), also known as management by results (MBR), is a management system started in the mid 2050's of U.S., based on the Scientific Management and Behavior Scientific Theory (especially Participation Management) of Peter Drucker. Basically, it's a process of defining objectives within an organization so that management and employees agree to the objectives and understand what they need to do in the organization in order to achieve them.

The essence of MBO is to participate goal setting, chooses courses of actions and decision making. An important part of the MBO is the measurement and the comparison of the employee's actual performance with the standards set. Ideally, when employees themselves have been involved with the goal setting and choosing the course of action to be followed by them, they are more likely to fulfill their responsibilities.

The system of management by objectives can be described as a process whereby the superior and subordinate jointly identify its common goals, define each individual's major areas of responsibility in terms of the results expected of him, and use these measures as guides for operating the unit and assessing the contribution of each of its members.

管理小偏方

目標管理(MBO)

目標管理(MBO)，或稱之為績效管理，是20世紀50年代中期出現於美國，以泰羅的科學管理和行為科學理論（特別是其中的參與管理）為基礎形成的一套管理制度。主要概念是透過在組織當中，建立起管理階層和員工都可認同的目標，並清楚了解在這組織中，他們要如何做才能達成這些目標。

目標管理的基本精神在於目標設定、選擇行動方法與決策執行的參與；這其中一項很重要的指標，就是評估和比較員工實際表現、與標準值之間的差異；理想上，當員工既已參與了目標的設定與將採行的行動方案，他們就應該可以實踐其應盡的職責。

整個目標管理的系統，可以簡單的定義為一種管理的流程；這流程包括了管理者與部屬聯手所制定的共同目標，也訂定了每個個人其主要的工作範圍及目標責任；並且運用這些評估的標準，來做為營運和管理上的指標，及評定個別成員的貢獻程度。

Section 4
Leadership

4-2 A Warning to Others
殺雞儆猴

 Conversation 情境對話

11 A.M. When Elmer walked toward the warehouse, then some workers just threw away the cigarette reluctantly, then spread out slowly and **nonchalantly**. At the same time, the warehouse keeper hurriedly reported some problems of destroyed equipment and stolen materials to him.

早上十一點，當艾默正走向倉庫時，幾個工人這才不情願的丟掉香菸，慢條斯理又嬉謔的散開來；這時倉管員急忙跟他回報了一些機具被破壞，及材料失竊的問題。

After that two new workers joined in this team, the management of whole job site had appeared subsequently some situation and the morale of workers became more and more **undisciplined**. Elmer feels worried and then reports to Robert.

自從組內來了兩個外地的新工人後，整個工地的管理陸續出現狀況，工人的工作情緒也越來越散漫；艾默憂心忡忡的，趕緊向羅柏報告。

Elmer: "It seems to have some changing status among workers and the entire working mood is so bad. I'm very worried about that."

艾默說：「這陣子工人裡頭似乎有些變化和狀況，整個工作氛圍很差，讓我很擔心。」

Robert: "I had noticed that, too. What's going on there?"

經理說：「我也注意到這些現象了，到底是怎麼回事？」

Elmer: "The workers in our group have always been very **self-motivated**, and you don't really need to worry about their work or schedule. Yet, since those two new workers join in our group, I always saw them chatting with some others in the corner. Then, after a period of time, the other workers are starting to be lazy, too."

艾默說：「過去我們的組內的夥伴們一直都是很自動自發的，工作和進度都不太需要擔心；但自從組內新來了兩個外地工人後，常常就看到他們和其他工人躲在角落嘰嘰喳喳，一段時間之後，慢慢的其他工人也就開始跟著懶散了。」

Robert: "Did you ever talk about it with them?"

經理說：「那你有沒有跟大家好好談一談？」

Elmer: "I did try several times for everyone to calm down and talk. But those two guys always **refute** intentionally with some ridiculous questions, or **exaggerate** the problems raised by others."

艾默說：「我幾次試著讓大家靜心地坐下來會談，但每次那兩人總有意無意的提出一些荒謬的問題來反駁，或是對其他人提出的問題添油加醋的。」

Robert: "Well, it's really a trouble. Did you ever try to understand background?"

經理說：「嗯，這的確是個麻煩！你有沒有特別去了解那兩人的背景呢？」

Elmer: "As I know, those two guys were **laid off** by other construction firm. Maybe we need more manpower, so our personnel ask them to get on board here. The warehouse keeper Nook always complains to me this time around that some machinery in the warehouse was inexplicably destroyed for no reason, while some stolen materials result in a short supply.

艾默説：「據我所知，那兩人是被另一工程公司所解雇的；或許是因為我們需要人手，人事單位才會找他們過來。這陣子，倉管員諾克也常跟我抱怨著，倉庫裡一些機具莫名的就被破壞，另外有些被偷竊的材料導致短缺。」

Robert: "It's not a **trivial** matter. We got to make the whole thing comes to light and be decisively handling it ASAP."

經理説：「這事可非同小可，務必要查個水落石出，趕緊做個果斷的處理。」

Elmer: "In fact, Nook has grasp some clues and figure out all these links with those two guys. I had unannounced several material suppliers and then confirmed indirectly that they did privately bring some materials to **peddle** in there."

艾默説：「其實諾克也掌握了些蛛絲馬跡，發現這事跟那兩人脱不了關係；我暗訪了幾家材料供應商，也間接證實了，這兩人經常私下拿些材料來兜售。」

Robert: "This issue should not be hesitated. We got to take some action to **exterminate** quickly as a warning to others. Or our administration will thereupon become **collapsed**."

經理説:「這事不宜再遲疑了,我們得採取一些行動,趕緊的斬草除根,也藉此來個殺雞儆猴,否則我們的管理會就此潰爛下去了。」

With the assistance of personnel, Robert had an in-depth interview with these two workers. In the morning of the coming Monday, the personnel posts two **dismissal** orders and convenes the review meetings immediately."

羅柏在人事單位的協助下,與那兩工人當面深談了一番;隔週一的上午,人事單位就貼出了兩人的革職令,並立刻召開檢討會議。

Vocabulary 字彙解析

■ **nonchalantly** *adv.* 若無其事的、滿不在乎的

〔同義詞：**indifferently, casually, coolly**〕

She gave a nonchalant shrug.

She had been nonchalantly and had left the window unlocked.

■ **refute** *vt.* 反駁、駁斥

〔同義詞：**retort, confute, contradict**〕

These claims have not been convincingly refuted.

It was now his time to refute the humiliation.

■ **self-motivated** *adj.* 有上進心、自動自發

〔同義詞：**motivated, spontaneous**〕

She's a very independent, self-motivated individual.

The audience broke into a self-motivated applause.

■ **inexplicable** *vt., vi.* 莫名的、費解的

〔同義詞：**baffling, incomprehensible, catchy**〕

For some inexplicable reason her mind went completely blank.

His language is inexplicable to anyone inside the office.

■ **trivial** *adj.* 瑣碎的、細微的

〔同義詞：**fameless, inessential, tiny**〕

Huge fines were imposed for trivial offenses.

The amount required was trivial compared with military spending.

■ **peddle** *vt.* 兜售、叫賣

〔同義詞：**hawk, sell, deal with**〕

He peddled art and printing materials around the country.

He spent the whole afternoon to peddle.

■ **exterminate** *vt.* 殲滅、根絕

〔同義詞：**wipe out, eradicate, out root**〕

After exterminating the entire population, the soldiers set fire to the buildings.

This disease has been exterminated from the world.

■ **collapse** *vt., vi.* 崩潰、瓦解

〔同義詞：**crumble, landslide, fall apart**〕

The roof collapsed on top of me.

The plaster started to collapse.

■ **dismissal** *n.* 解雇、革職

〔同義詞：**fire, dismiss, discharge**〕

His dismissal from the company had surprised everyone.

The only way to solve his arbitrary behavior is dismissal.

 # Phrase in sentence 片語和句型解析

■ **spread out** 散開、攤開

〔同義詞：**open up, disperse, unfold**〕

She stood at the window looking at the town spread out below.

He spreads out the map and laid it out on the table.

■ **lay off** 遣散、解雇

〔同義詞：**disband, dismiss, send away**〕

They needed to rehabilitate injuries or just brush up after lay off.

The war hasn't ended and the organization shall not be laid off.

Section 4
Leadership

🔤 Practice in Management

The interaction between managers and subordinates is very multivariate and subtle. The relationship between both is usually the boss and subordinate, but sometimes they become friends and partners and, on the contrary, they are the opposite. The manager stands in the position of order authority, while the subordinate is in the side of acceptance and execution. It's a very important issue for managers to maintain the balance between pushing the goal of execution and also maintaining the proper distance and interactive relationship in group. **Loose management style** may lead to subordinates to behave casually and carelessly, and then, or course, the task is difficult to complete. **Harsh management style**, on the contrary, may lead to emotional tension and fear, remote distance, and mutual trust, and the task is to be resisted.

It will be a challenge to a manager when the subordinates has questioned and resisted to the command of superiors, especially the gathering or even agitation against to managers: a challenge for the profession, leadership, even the style of managers, even his acting style. The managers should calm down and make the whole thing clear to figure out the insight of situation. Timely and adequate communication is still the most important and easy way to resolve differences between each other. If the situation is roughly under a specific circumstance, managers may, focus on a key person and a key point, adopt the necessary sanctions to prevent the expansion of the event and deterioration.

經驗與分享

管理者與部屬之間的互動，是很多元和微妙的；兩者通常是上司與下屬的關係，有時成了朋友和合作夥伴，但也有時候，兩者的關係卻是對立的，管理者站在命令的角度要求部屬，而部屬則是接受命令與執行的一方。如何在貫徹任務的執行，同時又要維繫兩者間適當的距離和互動關係，一直是管理者很重要的課題，過於**寬鬆的管理模式**，可能導致部屬變得隨便、對工作的執行無所謂，任務當然難以推動；相反的，過於**嚴苛的管理**，不僅讓部屬的工作情緒處於緊張和懼怕，拉開彼此的距離和信任感，對於任務的推動反而是抗拒的。

當部屬對上司的命令有所質疑和抗拒，尤其在部屬中有人集結、甚至是鼓動反對時，對管理者而言，無疑是一種挑戰：挑戰管理者的專業和領導能力、甚至是他的行事風格。管理者應冷靜的去了解整件事情的來龍去脈，對事情的進行方向也有了適當的見解，此時適時與充分的溝通仍是最重要的方式，來化解彼此的歧見，若是情勢所需要，應針對關鍵的人物和重點，採行必要的處分，以防止事件的擴大和惡化。

Section 4
Leadership

Tips in Management

Punishment for warning to others

This is an ancient story from China, and also one of the oldest approaches in management. The proverb **"warning to others"** is a metaphor of managerial method, in which warning other people not to make mistakes by severely punishing to the chosen one, that is, deterrent through threats and intimidation. In the practical management psychology, it is a trickery of the last resort to the public as a means of reconciliation. When the manager encounter some diverse views or revolt from subordinates, especially when the task was disrupted deliberately, then he or she got to deal with severe artifice. It's the punishing approach so that the team can go forward consistently and the commands can be implemented.

This method is adopted sometimes in practical management.

From the studies of organizational behavior; however, after the adoption of such a punishment-style management approach, it might generate several different psychological effects in the mind of other subordinates or even become counterproductive. That's another issue that needs to be deliberate by managers:

1. Trusting to luck: some subordinates might think that this punishment is just a single case, and he should be lucky enough to be away.

2. Psychology of adventure: some subordinates would think that this punishment is just a single case should not happen again. Why not try it again?

3. Psychology of dependence: still some subordinates might consider that only those pushovers will be punished. But he is too important to be punished, and should be more powerful without any fear.

管理小偏方

殺雞儆猴

這是個源自中國的典故，也是古老的管理方法之一；所謂『殺雞儆猴』，比喻用懲罰一個人的辦法，來警告別的人不能犯錯，此即是 "殺一儆百" 的意思，有威脅、恫嚇之意。在實務管理心理學上，這是不得已的權術運用，以做為馭眾的手段；當管理者遇到部屬意見紛紜、反抗，尤其是任務受到刻意阻撓的時候，為使得團隊的步驟能一致前進，讓命令能貫徹執行，而非以嚴厲手段對付不可時，所採用的懲罰式管理方法。

雖然在管理實務上，這個方法常會被採用，但在組織行為學上，當採行這種懲罰式管理方法之後，其他部屬有時反而會產生下幾種不同的心理作用，甚至成為反效果，值得管理者的慎思：

1. 僥倖心理：有些部屬認為，這個懲罰只是個案，應該自己不至於那麼倒楣被扯上。

2. 冒險心理：也有些部屬會認為，這個懲罰只是個案，應該不會再發生，自己不妨再試一試機會。

3. 依賴心理：也有部屬自認為，那些被懲罰的都只是泛泛之輩，自己在團隊裡的重要性，深信再如何也應該不會發生到自己身上，也就更加有恃無恐。

Section 4
Leadership

4-3 Serious Mistake Made by Subordinates
部屬的嚴重錯誤

 Conversation 情境對話

The ground pipeline in a corner of jobsite suddenly exploded. Steam inside the pipe had mixed with mud and sprayed all around. Site security urgently notified Elmer. After Elmer and team members rushed to the spot, they immediately **cut off** the pipeline and temporarily used the sealing valve to control the leaking. The next day, the owner issued a deletion note of site safety which required the identification of accident and the improvement within the deadline. So, Elmer asked for a safety meeting immediately with all workers, with the attendence of Robert.

工地一角的接地管線突然爆開來了，裡頭的蒸汽和著泥水，就到處的噴灑著。工安員趕緊通知艾默，一行人到了現場，立刻剪斷管線，暫時用止水閥控制住外漏的地方。隔天，業主發出了工安缺失單，要求查明原因並限期改善。於是，艾默立刻召集所有工人，舉行工安會議，也邀請了羅柏列席。

Elmer: "Johnson, you're the first witness of the accident. Can you explain to us what's going on?"

Johnson: "It's around 1 pm. I heard a sound of steam **eruption** in the corner when I patrolled to the **turbine** area. Then I found out the steel pipe was cracked in the turning, a strong steam mixed with mud and sprayed out everywhere."

Rudolph: "I had roughly checked the **rupture**. It might not be **caused by** external impact, but the excess of steam pressure inside. But, **according to** the calculation of initial design, a carbon steel pipe should be able to withstand under such pressure."

Elmer: "Didn't you make a testing before the welding? What kind of carbon steel pipe it is? Can't you see it's simply a tube of cast iron with plated surface! Who used these cast iron pipes to execute, anyway?"

艾默：「強生，你是第一個發現事件的人，可否跟大家說明一下發生的經過？」

強生：「下午一點左右，當我巡邏到汽機區時，就聽到轉角處有蒸汽噴發的聲音，結果發現鋼管在轉彎處裂開了，強力的蒸氣和著泥濘，噴得到處都是。」

魯道夫：「我大致檢視了一下這個破裂的地方，這應該不是因外力撞擊所造成的，而是因裡面的蒸汽壓力過大所致。但就當初在設計時的計算，碳鋼管應該是可以承受這樣的壓力才對。」

艾默：「當時技工在焊裝之前，你沒做事先的檢測嗎？這是什麼樣的碳鋼管？難道你看不出來這管子根本就是表層鍍過的鑄鐵罷了！到底是誰拿這些鑄鐵管來施工的？」

Section 4
Leadership

Stalin: "The technician Barton asked me to apply these iron pipes from warehouse. I did mention to him that the quality of pipes doesn't seem right. But he said that it's no problem and easier to construct if using the cast iron. He's my boss, any way, and I got to follow what he said."

史達林：「這些鐵管是技師巴頓要我去倉庫申請的。原本我有跟他反映，這些管子的材質好像不太對，但他說：這些沒問題的啦，且鑄鐵比較好施工啊！畢竟，他是我的老闆，我也只好照辦了。」

Elmer: "Oh, my god! The whole line with more than 20 pipes is all wrong. They need to be **demolished** and revised all **over again**."

艾默：「天啊！這整排二、三十組的鐵管全都不對了，勢必要整個拆掉、再重新修改過了。」

Robert: "It seems to be a tricky trouble, and happens because of our own **negligence** and errors. All right, what the most urgent thing we need to do is to **modify from** the wrong project as soon as possible. We got to finish within the shortest time, anyway. I like to request Elmer for the follow-up schedule and come to me directly if you need any support or coordinating matter."

羅柏：「看來這可是個棘手的麻煩事，而且是因為我們自己的疏忽和錯誤所造成的。好了，現在我們最迫切要做的，就是盡速的將錯誤的工程部分修改回來；無論如何，都要在最短時間內完成。這件事就拜託艾默去規劃了，如果有甚麼需要協助、或協調的，就直接來找我。」

Elmer: "I'd got it. We're still fortunately for just using steam in testing. Otherwise, the consequences will be **disastrous** while using the chemical gas in the actual application."

艾默：「我知道了。幸好現在還是用蒸汽在做測試，否則如果等到實際用的化學氣體時，那後果就不堪設想了。」

Robert: "Elmer. Please transfer Barton from currently technician work, and ask him come to me tomorrow morning."

羅柏：「艾默！請立即將巴頓調離目前技師的工作，並請他明天早上來找我。」

Elmer: "The owner had issued a 'deletion note of site safety' to us. I'm afraid that we might be unavoidably suffered from varying degrees of punishment."

艾默：「業主已經對我們發出『工安缺失』的通知了，我想我們遭受到一些不同程度的懲罰，恐怕是避免不了的了。」

Robert: "It's a warning for us. It might result in the unexpected damage with only a small negligence of errors. After this negligence is completely recovered, we need to review this matter properly, and issue some necessary punishment to the relevant person."

羅柏：「這件事是給我們一些警訊，即使是一個小小的疏忽或錯誤，都可能造成不可預期的傷害。等這個疏失復原完成之後，我們在好好的檢討此事，也要針對相關的人，做必要的處置。」

Section 4
Leadership

 **Vocabulary 字彙解析**

- **eruption** *v.* 爆發、噴出、蹦出

〔同義詞：discharge, ejection, emission〕

All of a sudden an eruption of movement rocks the ground

She couldn't understand the sudden eruption of tension between them.

- **turbine** *n.* 渦輪、汽輪〔機〕

〔同義詞：turbo〕

There was enough hot air in it to power a turbine.

General Electric is already the biggest maker of turbines for power plants.

- **rupture** *v., n.* 破裂、決裂、斷裂

〔同義詞：fracture, crack, estrangement〕

The patient died after rupture of an aneurysm.

The rupture with his father would never be healed.

- **demolish** *v.* 拆除、搗毀

〔同義詞：remove, dismantle, demolish〕

He used the figure to demolish one of the arguments against expansion.

Church authorities decided to demolish the building.

- **negligence** *n.* 疏忽、過失、忽視

〔同義詞：disregard, neglect, oversight〕

Death due to negligence occurred in one per cent of this group.

some of these accidents are due to negligence.

- **disastrous** *adj.* 慘重、災難、不得了

〔同義詞：tragic, devastating, ruinous〕

Such a war can only have the most disastrous consequences.

Our motivations may be pure, but the results are just as disastrous.

Phrase in sentence 片語和句型解析

- **cut off**　切斷、隔除、斷絕

〔同義詞：chop off, interrupt, amputate〕
The caves were cut off from the outside world by a landslide.
The cutoff date to register is July 2.

- **caused by**　造成、引起

〔同義詞：bring about, create, conformation〕
The blindness was caused by this disease.
It pointed out the soil erosion was caused by the rising of sea level.

- **according to**　根據、按照、比照

〔同義詞：under, in the light of, in line with〕
Cook the rice according to the instructions.
The outlook for investors is not bright, according to financial experts.

- **all over again**　從頭再來、重新來過

〔同義詞：all over, over again〕
He'd love to work with you all over again.
She rose, tidied the bed, and sat down all over again.

- **modify from**　修改、更正、改變

〔同義詞：amend, alter, revise〕
Two of the characteristics are modified from human preferences.
Her views were modified from her research.

Practice in Management

In the practical workplace, the errors in work is a subject that is almost impossible to completely avoid. Most of the errors or defects might just reduce the quality or speed of works, or take times to correct or repair. These might cause significant damage for the enterprise. But some errors; however, might be resulted in great distress or even a crisis to enterprise. If an error were able to be forecasted, then the error, basically, might be not happen at all. However, some errors, which may seem to be very trivial, sometimes can turn into a fatal wound on the operation. That's what the managers need to be vigilant in all times.

An error may occur in any level, and in any situation. The reasons of errors be mainly due to the negligence, lack of expertise or technology, or the insufficiently in judgment. Managers can reduce the probability and extent of errors through enhancing the staff training, strengthening the stringency of processing (particularly for those processing regulated by the SOP system), and increase the frequency of reviewing and assessment.

The managers need to pay close attention for the errors are happen on purpose, and solve them carefully and promptly. For these errors, or called sabotages, usually have some hidden intentions and to be more complex and difficult. It's an ordeal of the wisdom and resilience to managers. Managers might need the assistance of executives, if necessary, to stop any further derivative crisis.

經驗與分享

在實務的工作職場上，工作的錯誤幾乎是無法完全避免的課題；絕大多數的錯誤或瑕疵，可能只是降低了一些工作品質或速度、或者要花些時間來改正或修補，對於企業而言，並不會造成很大的傷害；但有些錯誤的發生，可能導致了整個營運上很大的困擾，甚至是產生危機。如果錯誤造成的傷害是能預估的，那基本上錯誤就不會發生了；但是，那些可能看來很微不足道的錯誤，有些卻演變成營運上的致命傷，這是管理人必須隨時提高警覺的地方。

錯誤可能發生會出現在各種層級、和各種情況之下；通常錯誤的發生，主要是人為的疏忽、專業知識或技術的不足、及對於問題的判斷不夠周延所致。管理者可以藉由加強員工訓練、強化作業流程的嚴謹度（特別是一些可以透過SOP制度來規範的）、及增加檢視和考核的頻率，來降低錯誤發生的機率和程度。

值得管理人特別留意的是，若有些錯誤的發生，其實是有人蓄意造成的，必須要很小心且迅速的處理；因為這類的錯誤，或者稱之為破壞，通常背後所隱藏的企圖較為複雜和棘手，管理人必須要能通盤的掌握情勢，必要時需透過高層的協助，以免衍生出更大的危機。

Section 4
Leadership

 **Tips in Management**

Error management (EM)

Error management (EM) starts after an error has occurred; it attempts to block negative error consequences, to reduce their negative impact, or to deal quickly with error consequences once they occur. It further involves "controlling damage quickly, and reducing the occurrence of particular errors in the future, as well as optimizing the positive consequences of errors, such as long-term learning, performance, and innovations."

Errors are traditionally regarded as negative events that should be avoided. However, a pure error prevention approach cannot deal adequately with the fact that errors are ubiquitous. The EM approach assumes that human errors per se can never be completely prevented, and, therefore, it is necessary to ask the question of what can be done after an error has occurred.

EM distinguishes between errors and their consequences. Whereas error prevention aims at avoiding negative error consequences by avoiding the error altogether, error management focuses on reducing negative error consequences and on increasing potentially positive consequences through design or training.

管理小偏方

錯誤管理(EM)

錯誤管理（EM）是指當錯誤發生了之後，試圖防止後續負面後果的發生，降低負面的影響，或快速的處理發生了錯誤的善後。進一步地，錯誤管理也涉及到快速控制損害，並減少了將來特定錯誤的再發生，並將錯誤轉向正面的發展，例如長期學習，績效和創新的發展。

在傳統上，錯誤被視為應該避免的負面事件。然而，純粹的錯誤防制方法，對於錯誤是無所不在的事實，並不能充分地應對。因此，在錯誤管理的方法中，乃假設錯誤的本身是不能完全防止的，因此必須要知道在發生了錯誤後，我們能做什麼的問題。

錯誤管理區分了錯誤及其後果之間的關係。當一般錯誤預防的目標，在於避免產生錯誤，及錯誤所引發的負面後果時，錯誤管理的重點則是在於減少錯誤的負面後果，並經由規劃或訓練，以增加潛在的正面影響。

Section 4
Leadership

4-4 Promote the Subordinate
拔擢部屬

 Conversation 情境對話

The company will undertake another large **electromechanical** engineering center by the end of next year. But in Robert's mind, he's very worried about the case because in the whole construction division, not any one of them is able to manage the whole construction project besides Elmer. Therefore, Robert looks for Elmer to discuss this issue.

公司將於明年底承接另一個大型的機電中心工程，但這事卻讓羅柏的心中非常擔憂，因為目前工程部門當中，除了艾默之外，沒有其他任何人具有管理整個工程的經驗。於是羅柏就找來了艾默，一起討論此事。

Robert: "Elmer, I'd just like to know more about the progress of piping works, and the current status of the overall manpower."

羅柏：「今天找你過來，是想多了解一下配管工程的進度，和目前整體人力的狀況。」

Elmer: "We had worked hard a while ago. The schedule has been caught up gradually, so the manpower is relatively stable now."

艾默：「前一陣子大家都很辛苦的趕工，但目前進度已慢慢追上了，所以人力的運用上也比較穩定了。」

Robert: "I'm quite satisfied with all fellows, except you."

羅柏：「我對夥伴們的表現很滿意，除了你之外。」

Elmer: "Why? What happened?"

艾默：「為什麼？發生什麼事了嗎？」

Robert: "Calm down! I do believe in your professional engineering skills are superb and the dedication in overall construction processing and quality control is perfectly handled. However, **in terms of** management, it should have some rooms for improvement."

羅柏：「別緊張！我相信你在工程的專業技術上無話可說，在整體施工流程和品質的掌控上，也都很盡心盡力，但是在人員的管理方面，應該還有些進步空間。」

Elmer: "Maybe I'm **stringent** sometimes. But I do try my best and share all my skills and experiences with the subordinates. I just don't know if it's enough."

艾默：「或許有些時候我是比較嚴格，但我總是盡己所能，將全部的技術和經驗教導部屬；不知道還有什麼地方做得不夠呢？」

Section 4
Leadership

Robert: "You didn't **bring up** any management person who can do what you do to control the entire project. There's a conclusion in the meeting today that our company might undertake another project of large electromechanical engineering center. When the project is confirmed, then it will be a big challenge for our manpower allocation, especially for the one who can manage the entire project. That's the knotty problem for me."

羅柏：「你沒有培養出一個像你一樣，可以管控整個工程的管理人才出來。今天公司的會議中已經決議，明年我們可能會增加一個大型的機電中心工程案。如果這案子確定了，我們在人力的調配上將會是個挑戰，尤其是要能管理整個工程的人；這也是我現在最傷腦筋的事了。」

Elmer: "Now I know what you mean. It's indeed a big problem. You got any suggestion?"

艾默：「我明白你的意思了，這的確是個大問題，你有什麼建議嗎？」

Robert: "According to my **observations**, Allen and Andrew are good candidates. Through gradual training of the management **trainees**, they could be **future engineering management talents**."

羅柏：「依我的觀察，艾倫和安德烈都是不錯的人選，或許可以逐漸的管理學徒培訓他們成為未來工程管理的人才。」

Elmer: "Both of them have specific engineering **competence**. I can try to divide one field of the sub-project for each of them. But it's still hard to say if they're able to handle the whole project."

Robert: "That's why I remind you not to **mention about** the new project now. It's still uncertain whether the new project will be undertaken by our company, or who will be in charge of it. For the impracticable expectations beforehand, it might only result in distress for everyone. But I like to emphasize again: Fully disciplines and bring up for the potential talents is not only **conductive** to the development of company as a whole, but also helpful to the managers themselves. In many cases, the managers have more chance to be a **corresponding rise** when their sub-ordinates were upgraded. Then in the course of counseling subordinates, managers can also increase the capability and experience in leadership and management."

艾默:「他們兩人的專業能力都有一定的水準,我可以試著各別規劃一個領域的工程分案,讓他們來主導和帶領看看;但他們是否能夠承擔整個工程,目前還很難說。」

羅柏:「所以我認為先不要提及新工程案的事,因為無論未來是否承接、或是由誰負責,目前都是未知數,不要讓大家有個不切實際的期待,以免反而造成困擾。不過我仍要強調:培養和拔擢好人才,不僅可以幫助公司發展,對經理人本身也有許多助益;一方面培養幹部往上提昇,很多時候管理人也更有擢升的機會,正所謂的水漲船高;另一方面,在輔導部屬的過程中,自然也增加了管理人在領導和管理方面的能力與經驗。」

Section 4
Leadership

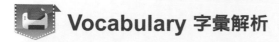

Vocabulary 字彙解析

- **electromechanical** *adj.* 機電的、電動、機電式

〔同義詞：electronic machinery〕

Electromechanical and computerized devices have given the piano a new lease of life.

It's a leading partner in the mechanical engineering and electromechanical industries.

- **stringent** *adj.* 嚴格、困難、嚴厲

〔同義詞：strict, firm, rigid〕

He also argues that more stringent requirements need to be laid down.

There are very stringent rules and conditions in the event of a loss or claim.

- **observations** *n.* 觀察、注目、意見

〔同義詞：monitoring, watching, scrutiny〕

Units kept enemy forces under observation for days.

She was brought into the hospital for observation.

- **trainee** *n.* 實習生、學員、學徒

〔同義詞：apprentice, beginner, learner〕

The trainees have only an hour of theory class a day.

It is understood none of the trainees or managers are under suspicion.

- **competence** *n.* 權限、能力、範圍

〔同義詞：capability, competency, proficiency〕

He found himself with an ample competence and no obligations.

The players displayed varying degrees of competence.

- **conductive** *adj.* 導電、傳導

〔同義詞：conduct, guide〕

The recess is filled with an electrically conductive material.

A displacement material is deposited over the recessed conductive material.

Phrase in sentence 片語和句型解析

■ **in terms of**　就…而言、論　來講

〔同義詞：in the following area, term〕

In terms of speech, he is the best.

We're all rich men in terms of African residents.

■ **bring up**　調出、培養、造就

〔同義詞：feed, breed, rear〕

The leftovers are composted, helping to bring up a new cycle of growth.

Support is what is needed to bring up Canadian cinema.

■ **mention about**　提及、提過、再提一下

〔同義詞：say what, mentioned〕

Somehow Mr Walker forgot to mention about the film's award.

I'm not going to mention about any names.

■ **corresponding rise**　水漲船高

〔同義詞：gone〕

This effect comes with a corresponding rise in water level.

The boat had a corresponding rise with the wave.

Section 4
Leadership

Practice in Management

Nurturing and developing of talent manpower is a very important strategy for companies, especially for those fast-growing companies. The executives usually have a high expectation in this subject. But, when look at many middle managers or supervisors, we can find out that there is a considerable difference. This dilemma happens mainly due to lack of ability, and above all, lack of willingness for these middle managers. One of the aspect is these managers are usually lacking of experiences or knowledge to train their subordinates as the future managers.

But the major obstacle comes from the trepidation of the managers. Those well-trained subordinates might just be the ones to replace the position of current managers, or even become their supervisors. Therefore, many managers are really not interested in the cultivation of successors, or even suppress in some ways. It did happen in some real cases that when a higher position opens, the one who will eventually be promoted could be his subordinate, rather than the manager himself.

It's a common but intractable problem in organizational behavior and managerial problem when try to create a healthy competitive environment in the office, and also try to avoid the grudges among peers. To solve this dilemma, the executives need to establish clear goals and comprehensive promotion system, and then continuously communicate, discuss and assist to the managers for a more effective employees' training.

經驗與分享

人才的培育和養成，對於企業、尤其是正在快速成長的企業而言，是非常重要的策略；對此，公司高層有著很大的期望；但若觀察許多中階管理者的行為，卻會發現這當中存在著很大的落差。這個現象，主要來自於這些中間管理者的能力問題，以及其心態和意願的問題；在一方面，中階管理者對於如何培養未來的管理者，並沒有太多的經驗或知識。

但最主要的障礙，是中階管理者的擔心：這些被培養出來的未來人才，或許就是取代自己職位的人，甚至有可能成為自己的主管；因此許多管理者對於培養接班人，心中都有所顧忌或是興趣缺缺，甚至在某些程度上會有所的打壓。實務上也有不少的例子，當公司有個較高層的職位出缺時，被擢升的人可能是部屬，而非管理者本身。

要創造一個員工良性競爭的環境，同時又避免同儕間的芥蒂，這是組織行為和管理學上，很普遍又難解的問題。面對這樣兩難的問題時，公司需要建立一套明確的營運目標、和完整的升遷制度，並不斷的和中階管理者溝通和討論，以協助他們在培訓部屬的部分，能更有效而積極的進行。

Section 4
Leadership

Tips in Management

Reward management

Reward management is concerned with the formulation and implementation of strategies and policies that aim to reward people fairly, equitably and consistently in accordance with their value to the organization. Reward management consists of analyzing and controlling employee remuneration, compensation and all of the other benefits for the employees. Reward management aims to create and efficiently operate a reward structure for an organization. Reward structure usually consists of pay policy and practices, salary and payroll administration, total reward, minimum wage, executive pay and team reward.

Reward management deals with processes, policies, and strategies which are required to guarantee that the contribution of employees to the business is recognized by all means. Objective of reward management is to reward employees fairly, equitably, and consistently in correlation to the value of these individuals to the organization. The existence of the reward system is to motivate employees to work towards achieving strategic goals which are set by entities. Reward management is not only concerned with pay and employee benefits. It is equally concerned with non-financial rewards such as recognition, training, development and increased job responsibility. There are two kinds of rewards:

Extrinsic rewards: concrete rewards that employee receive.

1.Bonuses

2.Salary raise

3.Gifts

4.Promotion

5.Other kinds of tangible rewards

Intrinsic rewards: tend to give personal satisfaction to individual
1.Information / feedback
2.Recognition
3.Trust/empowerment

 管理小偏方

獎勵管理

獎勵管理是基於公正地獎勵員工的政策之下，如何採行公平而一致的核算與實現其對組織的價值為何。獎勵管理的範疇，包括分析和控制員工的報酬、補償和其他給予員工的福利。因此，薪酬管理乃是在組織內，建立和有效運作的報酬結構。員工獎勵的架構，通常包括了薪酬核付政策和實施方法、薪資與福利的行政作業、總計報酬、最低工資標準、執行付款和團隊獎勵。

獎勵管理的處理流程、政策和策略，應從各個方面，來確保員工對企業的貢獻是確實無誤的。而薪酬管理的目標，就是要以公平、公正和一致性的原則來獎勵員工，以符合這些個人對於組織所代表的價值。因此獎勵制度的存在，是要激勵員工去努力實現其由整體所設定的策略目標。獎勵制度不只關乎薪水和員工福利，還有非金錢上的獎勵，例如認可，培訓，發展和增加工作責任等，也應以同樣的原則來處理。一般而言，獎勵可區分為兩大類：

外在的獎勵：即員工收取實質的獎賞獎金

1.加薪

2.禮物

3.升遷

4.其它可觸及的獎勵

內在的獎勵：即給予員工個人滿足的意念

1.資訊的回饋

2.認可

3.信任 / 授權

4-5 You're the Leader This Time
這次你當家

 ## Conversation 情境對話

With the progress of the pipeline area being far behind the schedule, Elmer pushed the workers on many requirements in order to catch up the deadlines. After a period of time, some workers had started **disgruntled** and complained, and also reflect their ideas to the engineer Allen sometimes. Robert and Elmer, actually, had known all these and also got a **tacit** understanding in both minds. Then, Robert alone looked for Allen and some workers to talk.

由於配管區的工程進度已然嚴重落後，為了趕工，艾默給予工人許多施工上的要求；經過一段時間之後，有些工人開始心生不滿和抱怨，有時也會跟工程師艾倫反映他們的想法。其實羅柏和艾默都知道了這些事，兩人心中也有了默契，於是羅柏就獨自去找艾倫和一些工人，想藉此和大家詳談。

Robert: "I know you guys worked very hard and endured high pressure in order to catch the progress of that **plumbing** construction. I also believe that, of course, you got something your mind regarding the leadership of Elmer. Why don't we just speak out and discuss today?"

羅柏：「我知道各位為了追趕那配管工程的進度，工作的壓力很大、很辛苦，當然我相信你們心中對於艾默的帶領，並定是有些想說的話，是否趁今天的機會說出來看看？」

Bryant: "Working hard is inevitable and that we can still afford. But sometimes, Elmer might push us very tightly with **rude** tone, and never take into account our physical loading."

布萊恩：「工作辛苦是免不了的，這我們都可以承受；只是有時候艾默真的逼得很緊、口氣也不好，都沒考慮到我們體力上的負荷。」

Allen: "Indeed. Even I can't really understand the idea of Elmer. Sometimes he urgently required the workers to work through the night, but after the meeting next day, he wants the workers to be paused from work."

艾倫：「的確，就連我也無法真的理解艾默的想法！有時候要工人徹夜趕工，但等隔天開完會後，卻又要工人暫停下來。」

Robert: "I think the reason of conflict here should be that we can not really understand the difficulty and consideration of the role in each other."

羅柏：「這應該是大家都無法體會，彼此在角色上的難為處和考量點吧！」

Section 4
Leadership

Bryant: "Ya! Elmer doesn't need to actually operate the construction like us. So, he couldn't understand our toilsome and difficulty."

布萊恩：「對啊！艾默又不需要像我們工人一樣實際去操作施工，當然無法了解我們的辛苦和困難啦！」

Robert: "Maybe we need some changes. **There it goes**! I will ask Elmer to go off for two weeks vocation. Allen will be temporally in charge of his position during this period of time. And, of course, you can find some assistants to support you."

羅柏：「或許我們需要做一點改變。不如這樣吧！我會要求艾默先回去休兩個星期的假，這段期間，就由艾倫暫時代理他的位置；當然，你也可以找個副手來協助你。」

Allen: "How about after his vocation break?"

艾倫：「那等艾默休假回來之後呢？」

Robert: "I will arrange him to take care of the pipeline welding works in section A first. He's the expert in this area and I don't need to worry about him at all. That's our arrangement now, and then we can discuss again one month later."

羅柏：「我會安排他先負責A段管線焊接的施工部分，他在這方面是老經驗了，一點也不需要我擔心；我們就先這麼安排吧，等一個月之後，我們再來討論看看。」

About 5 weeks later, Robert called up Elmer, Allen and others.

經過了約五個星期後，羅柏又把艾默、艾倫、和其他人一起召集了過來。

Robert: "The attempt of adjustment in organizational roles this time, in a moment, had lasted over a month. I don't know if you're all satisfying with the new role?"

罗柏：「我们这次尝试性的组织角色调整，一转眼也过了一个多月了，不知道大家是否还满意目前所扮演的角色？」

Allen: "The work in this position is much complicated than my prior expectation. I have to watch out the progress of project and, in the same time, to coordinate with the different opinions from the owner and other engineering units. And, there's always unexpected issue needs to be solved immediately."

艾伦：「这个位置的工作，比我想像的还要复杂；我不但要顾及到工程得进行，同时还要协调业主和其他不同工程单位的意见；而且，总是会有些意想不到状况必须要马上的解决。」

Bryant: "Never mind, Allen. In fact, you did try the best and gave us lots of help. What you need most is the practical experience to confront and deal with problems. After all, Elmer had been our leader for some time, and his command might be quite **handy** to us."

布莱恩：「艾伦，你也别太在意了，其实你也很尽心尽力地、给了我们很多的协助，或许比较欠缺的，就是需要有实际面对和应变的经验罢了；毕竟艾默当我们的头头，也有段时间了，指挥起来当然还是比较顺手一些。」

Elmer: "I got a lot of **acquisition** this time, too. I always thought that with the expertise and experience I did, and then, naturally, I could copy these standards to request my subordinates. However, to teach others is one thing, but to practice by oneself is something else. There's still a big difference. Maybe that's what I need to modify by myself."

艾默：「其實這段期間，我也有不少的收穫；過去我總以為自己擁有不少的專業技術和實務經驗，自然而然就會用這一套標準來要求部屬。但實際上，教導別人是一回事，自己親自操作又是另外一回事，這當中是有段差距的；或許這是我必須要再修正的地方。」

Robert: "I'm glad that we had learned some new experiences from this adjustment. If we can be really open-minded, and then try our best to experience the **standpoint** and view of different roles, I believe that it would be much easier to get along with mutual-communication among people. Maybe, it's the biggest harvest from the experiment of 'role play' this time."

羅柏：「很高興我們都從這次調整當中，得到了許多新的體驗；如果我們能將心門打開，多試著去體會不同角色的立場和想法，相信在人與人之間的相處和溝通，就變得更加容易了；或許，這就是這次『角色扮演』的實驗中最大的收穫了。」

Vocabulary 字彙解析

■ **disgruntled** *adj.* 不滿、滿腹牢騷、怨憤

〔同義詞：**dissatisfied, discontented, aggrieved**〕

I am so disgruntled with my work.

Many small investors were disgruntled with the return on investment.

■ **tacit** *adj.* 默契、默認的、隱性

〔同義詞：**implicit, implied, hinted**〕

Your silence may be taken to mean tacit agreement.

She was aware of his tacit criticism.

■ **plumbing** *n.* 管路、管道、水管

〔同義詞：**pipeline, tube, assembly line**〕

There was no plumbing or central heating in the kitchen and bathroom.

The plumbing system will convey gas from gas fields to factories.

■ **rude** *adj.* 粗暴、無禮、不遜

〔同義詞：**rough, brusque, impolite**〕

She had been rude to her boss.

It would have been rude to refuse.

■ **handy** *adj.* 便利的、靈巧的、合宜的

〔同義詞：**convenient, skillful, appropriate**〕

It's a handy desktop encyclopedia.

He was handy enough to overcome the limited budget.

■ **acquisition** *n.* 獲取、收購、採集

〔同義詞：**purchase, gain, collection**〕

I was alone with no money or acquisition.

He passes this on to his acquisition.

- **standpoint** *n.* 立場、觀點、態度

〔同義詞：attitude, stance, view〕

She writes on religion from the standpoint of a believer.

She took a tough standpoint toward other people's indulgences.

 ## Phrase in sentence 片語和句型解析

- **far behind** 遠遠落後、趕不上

〔同義詞：draggle, backward, drop behind〕

He had far behind in following written instructions.

We are far behind from our initial promise.

- **speak out** 說出來、表明、出聲

〔同義詞：speak up, indicate, aloud〕

She tried to speak out to her father about his drinking.

He spoke out that he never revises his prose.

- **each other** 彼此、互相、交互

〔同義詞：mutual, reciprocal, joint〕

A partnership is based on the respect and understanding to each other.

We were introduced to each other by a mutual friend.

- **go off** 熄滅、離開、賣掉

〔同義詞：extinguish, leave, trade off〕

She had gone off New York for two months.

The firemen were soaking everything to go off the blaze.

- **in a moment** 剎那、一會兒、瞬間

〔同義詞：instantly, awhile, immediately〕

This will be examined in more detail in a moment.

I called for an ambulance in a moment.

■ **open-minded**　開明、豁達、開通

〔同義詞：**enlightened, cheerful, open attitude**〕

They are open-minded to consider anything without any prejudice.

The court needs to be open-minded, unbiased and fair in the hearing.

■ **get along**　相處、共處、生活

〔同義詞：**coexist, get on, live together**〕

The traditional value has been gotten along with modern life in South Africa.

He's very open-minded to get along with others.

Practice in Management

A company is mainly a collection of people with frequent interactions. In the daily interaction with peers, we are naturally all playing with different roles. The manager's role is not only about leading and guiding, but also about listening and learning. Some subordinates under some special situations, have to be a team leader to complete to task. Due to the fixed position set from the organization or hierarchy, the individual role had not only been clarified, but also limited. This might be resulted in the distance between the hierarchy and alienation of the individual roles.

Therefore, managers have a very important mission in regarding the organizational behavior and group interaction. Managers have to narrow the distance among the team members for a more trustful and mutual understanding. Sometimes, managers can offer the subordinates with fully authority and trust to dominate and manage some specific situations or assignments. What managers need to do is to just give reminders when necessary and attributes the outcome to the subordinates. This is the most practical managerial mode, and also a test of judgment and wisdom to managers.

經驗與分享

企業的構成是以一群人的集合為主，人與人之間的互動頻繁，其實在我們每天和同儕互動的過程中，都自然而然的扮演著不同的角色；管理者不單單只是團隊的領導和指揮，有時也是聽從者、或學習者，相反的，有些部屬則在某些特殊狀況時，卻是扮演著領導團隊、或完成任務的功能。只是因著組織對職位或層級的設定，雖然釐清了、但也設限了每個人所應扮演的角色，這也造成了層級間的距離、及對個別角色的疏離感。

因此，在團體的組織行為和互動中，管理者有個很重要的任務，就是拉近團隊的距離，讓彼此更加互信與了解；有時候，可以透過一些狀況或任務的執行，用完全授權和信任的態度，放手讓部屬去主導，只是必要時給予提醒，並將成果歸功給部屬。這是最務實的管理模式，也是考驗管理者的成熟判斷與智慧。

Section 4
Leadership

Tips in Management

Role Playing

One of the most effective training methods for organizational behavior management is role playing. Not just for sales or the customer service training, this technique is an excellent way to achieve a number of benefits for employees, management and supporter. Role playing is not just "practicing working with an imaginary customer out loud." Role playing allows a group of employees to act out work scenarios. It opens communications, and for the amount of time when it puts a player 'on-the-spot,' it also gives a great deal of confidence and develops camaraderie among those participating in (doing) the role play situations.

Role playing can be used in every department by management and employees to practice business situations. Role playing is the systematic building of correct habits while learning the acceptable system and the best way to communicate your ideas to the customer. Role playing should be done in a low-stress environment, which makes it easier to learn. The trainer can critique the role play situation and corrections can be made immediately by more rehearsal. Assimilation of the training material and implementation of a key element of the system can occur quickly in business.

Role playing should be performed where the job will take place. This means at the work desk, on the phone, at the checkout counter, delivery or warehouse area. This setting should provide all necessary notes or equipment the employee may have, and should be performed with the person playing the part of the customer.

管理小偏方

角色扮演

在組織行為管理中最有效的訓練方法之一就是角色扮演。不只在銷售或客戶服務培訓方面，這種技術也是提供員工、管理和支持者無數利益的絕佳途徑。角色扮演的不僅僅是"面對一個假想的顧客大聲說出來"的練習，角色扮演是讓一群員工在工作場景中表演。當它將一個參與者置於現場情境當中，經過一定的時間量之後，就開啟了溝通；同時也給其他參與角色扮演的人很大的信心和情誼。

角色扮演可以用在每一個部門的管理階層和員工，來練習實務的業務情況。角色扮演是系統化的建立正確的習慣，藉以學習到可被接受的系統、及傳達想法給客戶的最佳途徑。角色扮演應該在沒有壓力的情況下進行，使其易於學習。訓練者可以評論角色扮演的情況，立即給予更正和更多的練習。培訓教材的吸收、及系統中關鍵要件的實施，將可以在實務工作中迅速的實現。

角色扮演應該就在工作的場合中進行；亦即是在辦公桌上、在電話中、在收銀櫃台、在運送或倉庫區域上。在配置上，應該提供所有員工原本已有的筆記或設備，並應與扮演客戶的人來練習。

Section 4
Leadership

Section 5

Special Issues in Management

5-1 New Technology System
新科技系統

 Conversation 情境對話

In response to the ever-changing Internet technology and improved efficiency in the global market and competitiveness, this trading company was introduced a new **cloud computing** management system this year. But this new technology system seems to have encountered many obstacles and **bottlenecks** on the way of internal practice.

為了因應網路科技的日新月異，並提高在全球市場的效率和競爭力，這家貿易公司在今年引進了全新的雲端技術管理系統；但這項嶄新科技系統，在公司內部的推動上，似乎遇到了許多阻礙和瓶頸。

This issue was **ardently** discussed at the meeting of all executives.

就在集團所有高階主管的會議上，這個問題被熱烈討論著。

President: "The global trading market is severely competitive, and there's more and more emphasis on speed and efficiency. I believe, just like myself, you had all felt the pressure from competition. In order to improve our efficiency and advantages in operation, we have **commissioned** a team of experts to help our company planning a set of cloud management system. But, unfortunately, there're many obstacles for our internal practice. I like to hear your thoughts."

Linda, the Finance Manager, reflects first: "This system is totally different from our original one, which had been operated smoothly. It's very risky if it was overtaken by the place of the new system immediately."

William of Accessory division then says: "Ya! Who can promise the new system is better?"

總裁：「現在全球貿易市場的競爭日益嚴峻，也越來越講求快速和效率，我相信大家和我一樣，都感受到這股競爭壓力了；為了提升經營的效率和優勢，我們委託一群專家團隊，幫公司規劃了這套雲端管理系統，但是在公司內的推動上，似乎有著許多的阻礙，我想聽聽各位的看法。」

財務部的經理琳達第一個就反映說：「這套系統和我們原來的完全不一樣，過去的系統已經運作得很順暢，如果馬上就用新的系統來取代，這會冒很大的風險。」

來自耗材部的威廉接著說：「對啊，誰能保證新的系統會更好呢？」

Marketing VP, Paul also says: "I'm not sure whether the new system is better or not because we are not familiar with the operation and need to **start over** again. It's very cumbersome and time- consuming."

行銷部協理保羅也説：「新的系統好不好，我還不知道，但是在操作上讓人感覺很陌生，需要全部重新學習，這很麻煩又耗費時間的。」

Newman of Customer Service reflects **feverishly**: "Our colleagues are still not familiar in the translation of customer's data. Then it's always resulting in misplaced date, and many complaints came from customers. They do **suffer from** the adaptation to this system."

而客服部的紐曼更是激動的反映著：「同仁在處理客戶資料的轉換上，對這套系統還不熟悉，經常是張冠李戴，反而讓客戶有所抱怨；為了適應這套系統，可讓我們同仁吃盡了苦頭。」

The scene at the meeting fills with clamors and arguments.

這時會議的現場開始有些鬧哄哄的，大家議論紛紛的討論著。

President: "Calms down! I recognized that we must face some difficulties to **push forward** this new system, and take time to learn and adopt it. But we can never exclude it because we had **confronted with** great challenges in the operation and do need a better computerized system to upgrade our competition advantage. For all the practical problems you encountered, I believe that our staffs in IT division will provide the best support."

Randall from IT division then says: "This new management system, in fact, is very **comprehensive**, convenient, and easy to operate. We are just not quite familiar with it in the very beginning, and need time to learn and adopt. We are glad to conduct several **demonstrations,** and all of you are welcomed to ask questions for our colleagues to answer."

總裁：「大家先安靜下來！我知道推動這新的管理系統，大家必定會遇到一些困難，也需要花些時間學習和適應，但絕對不能排斥它，因為我們在營運上，面臨著很大的挑戰，的確需要一套更好的資訊系統，真正提升我們的競爭優勢。至於各位所遇到實務上的問題，相信資訊部會提供各位最佳的協助。」

資訊部的藍道也接著說：「這套新的管理系統，其實非常的完備和便捷，操作上也非常簡單，只是大家剛開始還不熟悉，需要花點時間來學習和適應它；我們很樂意為各部門多舉辦幾場的教學觀摩會，也歡迎大家多提出問題來，讓我的同仁為各位解答。」

Section 5 Special Issues in Management

President: "Thanks Randall for the support. World is constantly in progress and the environment is constantly changing, no matter we like it or not, the stone keeps rolling. Just like in the initial invention of automobile, for example, it certainly had doubts and exclusion. But now, who will not drive it and exclude its convenience?"

總裁：「謝謝藍道的協助；世界不斷在進步，環境也不斷在改變，不管我們喜不喜歡，石頭還是要繼續向前滾的；就像汽車剛發明初期，人們必定會有所懷疑和排斥，但現在有誰不會開車，會去排斥它帶來的便利呢？」

Linda: "Since it is necessary to push the system, we will just try the best to learn it. But during the **interim period**, we need some **cushioning** and **ancillary** measures to avoid the **chaotic** pace."

琳達：「既然是必須要推動的系統，我們就盡力得去學習如何使用它，但希望在這段過度時期，能有一些緩衝和配套的措施，免得讓大家亂了方寸。」

President: "Thanks Linda for the valuable suggestion. It's very important, and I consigned the mission to our staffs in IT division. No matter what, to push this system is **imperative**, because we can't **stand still** any longer."

總裁：「謝謝琳達的寶貴意見，這是很重要的步驟，就麻煩資訊部的同仁多費心了；但無論如何，推動這個系統是勢在必行的，因為我們不能再原地踏步了。」

Vocabulary 字彙解析

▪ **cloud computing**　*n.*　雲端運算

The practice of using a network of remote servers hosted on the Internet to store, manage, and process data, rather than a local server or a personal computer.

▪ **bottleneck**　*vi., n.*　使⋯為難、瓶頸

〔同義詞：**fickle, stump**〕

Education chiefs were bottlenecked by some of the exam questions.

I reached here through the biggest bottleneck in my life.

▪ **ardently**　*adv.*　熱烈地、殷切地

〔同義詞：**warm, earnest**〕

They offer their thanks ardently to Paul.

The doctor looked ardently at him.

▪ **commission**　*vt., n.*　定制、委任、佣金

〔同義詞：**customize, authority, breakage**〕

A new production line was commissioned at the facility.

He got none commission to redesign the building.

▪ **feverish**　*adj.*　搖擺的、激動的、熱性的

〔同義詞：**fevered, fanatic**〕

He suffered from feverish colds.

Weeds can become a feverish nuisance.

▪ **comprehensive**　*adj.*　全方位、廣泛的、週詳的

〔同義詞：**overall, broad, thorough**〕

Planners need a comprehensive understanding of the subject.

We need a comprehensive list of sources for this study.

▪ demonstration *n.* 示範、表明、遊行

〔同義詞：declaration, parade〕

It is not capable of mathematical demonstration.

It can be used to any form of political dissent, including demonstrations, pickets, and protests.

▪ cushioning *n.* 緩衝、襯墊

〔同義詞：padding, buffer, liner〕

Family and friends can provide a cushioning against stress.

All wrapped plates are fitted snugly into boxes with plenty of extra cushioning.

▪ ancillary *n., adj.* 附屬品、輔助的

〔同義詞：accompaniment, accessorial, adjective〕

The libretto proved a perfect ancillary to the music.

Women with breast cancer may benefit from ancillary chemotherapy.

▪ chaotic *adj.* 混亂的、渾沌的

〔同義詞：random, confusion, chaos〕

It's a chaotic jumble of spools, tapes, and books in classroom.

She was utterly chaotic about what had just happened.

▪ imperative *adj.* 迫切的、勢在必行

〔同義詞：urgent, pressing, eager〕

The bell pealed again and the final imperative called.

The situation is far more imperative than politicians are admitting.

Phrase in sentence 片語和句型解析

▪ start over 重新來過、重頭再來

〔同義詞：**all over again, start from scratch**〕

His revival continued after starting over another brace of tries.

A day later normal service was started over.

▪ suffer from 苦於、苦難

〔同義詞：**suffer, pain, be in distress**〕

He'd suffered from intensive pain.

France will no longer suffer from the existing government.

▪ push forward 推動、推向前進

〔同義詞：**promote, advance, gives impetus to**〕

She pushed her glass toward him.

The troops pushed forward to the capital.

▪ confront with 面對、對抗、應對

〔同義詞：**response, face, cope**〕

The policemen confronted with equal number of union supporters.

He is capable of confronting with stress.

▪ interim period 過渡期、間歇期

〔同義詞：**transition, intermittent**〕

In the interim period, I'll just keep my fingers crossed.

Students were transferred from one program to another while in interim period.

▪ stand still 停滯不前、故步自封

〔同義詞：**laurels, pause, nowhere**〕

The traffic came to a standstill.

She stands still, at a loss for words.

Practice in Management

In recent decades, with the rapid application of information technology, consumer habits change and severe market competition, the modern enterprise management mode employed on its operations and related information systems is bound to change in accordance with the updated demand. The financial accounting system, for example, has passed through from the initial pure artificial bookkeeping, then simplified single software package, then a network of internal accounting system, and then integrated into the overall corporate information systems. In recent years, system has changed once again because of the development of cloud computing, POS systems, or the internet and mobile phone APP application software.

The **development of new systems** is expected to inject some energy and help for the enterprise management efficiency and competitive advantage. In the process of developing; however, the company sometimes might encounter with a lot of resistance, or even be forced to give up. The reasons of failure might be attributed to the system of not fitting the needs of enterprise or inadequate, or, in other case, the resistance from employees and users. The factors of resistance might be the strangeness to the new system, the learning process does not adapt, or supplement tools and schedule arrangement are not comprehensive.

Therefore, when promoting the new information management system, the enterprise should be step by step and very careful, so that each operator can easily use and the new system exert the goals more effectively.

經驗與分享

近數十年來，隨著資訊應用科技的日新月異、消費習慣的改變及市場競爭的日趨嚴峻，現代企業，在其營運上所採用的管理模式、和相關的資訊設備，也勢必要隨著時代的需求而跟著汰舊換新。以財務會計管理為例，從最初的純人工記帳，接著有了單機簡易型的帳務套裝軟體，慢慢演變成內部網路的帳務系統，再整合至整體企業的整合資訊系統當中，甚至在近年來，這些系統因著雲端計算、**POS**系統、或是各項網路和手機**APP**應用軟體等的發展而截然不同。

這些**新系統的開發**，對於企業的經營效率和競爭優勢而言，期待是能注入一些能量和幫助，但在推動的過程中，有些時後仍會遇到許多的阻力，甚至被迫放棄；推究其中的原因，可能是新系統的功能，不符合企業的需求、或者不夠完善，另一種情況就是企業員工與使用者的抗拒；會產生抗拒的原因，通常是對新系統操作的陌生感、學習過程中的不適應、或者是輔助工具和推動時程安排的不周全所致。

因此，當企業要推動新的資訊管理系統時，應該是小心而循序漸進的，讓每個操作者都能順利上手，發揮新系統事半功倍的目標。

Tips in Management

Cloud Technology

Cloud Technology is an Internet-based computing approach. Through this way, the hardware and software resources and information sharing can be provided to computers and other devices on demand. Users no longer need to know the detailed infrastructure of the "cloud", to have the appropriate expertise and to control directly. Cloud computing describes a new Internet-based increase in IT services, use and delivery models usually involve easy extension to provide dynamic and often virtualized resources through the Internet.

Users access to the cloud services via a browser, desktop application, or mobile application. Promoters believe that cloud computing allows companies to deploy applications more quickly and reduce the complexity of management and maintenance costs, and allowed to reallocate IT resources quickly in response to rapidly changing business needs.

Cloud computing relies on the sharing resources to achieve economies of scale, which is similar to the power grid infrastructure. Service providers integrate a lot of resources for multiple users, and users can hire more resources easily and use at any time to adjust the amount of unwanted resources released back into the whole structure. Therefore, users do not need to purchase large number of spikes resources only because of the short-term demand for the purchase of a large number of spikes resources; they just need to enhance the loan amount when needed and surrender to reduce demand. Service providers will be able to hire the resources currently no re-leased to other users, and even adjust the rental in accordance with the overall demand.

管理小偏方

雲端運算

雲端運算，是一種基於網際網路的運算方式，透過這種方式，共享的軟硬體資源和資訊可以按需求提供給電腦和其他裝置。用戶不再需要了解「雲端」中基礎設施的細節，不必具有相應的專業知識，也無需直接進行控制。雲端運算描述了一種基於網際網路的新的IT服務增加、使用和交付模式，通常涉及透過網際網路來提供動態易擴充功能而且經常是虛擬化的資源。

使用者透過瀏覽器、桌面應用程式或是行動應用程式來存取雲端的服務。推廣者認 雲端運算使得企業能夠更迅速的部署應用程式，並降低管理的複雜度及維護成本，及允許IT資源的迅速重新分配以因應企業需求的快速改變。

雲端運算依賴資源的共享以達成規模經濟，類似電力網的基礎設施。服務提供者整合大量的資源供多個用戶使用，用戶可以輕易的租借更多資源，並隨時調整使用量，將不需要的資源釋放回整個架構，因此用戶不需要因 短暫尖峰的需求就購買大量的資源，僅需提升租借量，需求降低時便退租。服務提供者得以將目前無人租用的資源重新租給其他用戶，甚至依照整體的需求量調整租金。

5-2 New Overseas Division
新的海外部門

 Conversation 情境對話

Because of the successful development in new mobile application software, the company has decided to follow up the victory and establish the new service center in Chicago for the North America market. The executives would like to select several candidates within the sales division to assign to the new overseas branch.

由於新的手機應用軟體成功開發與推廣，公司決定乘勝追擊，即將在美國芝加哥成立新的銷售服務中心，希望能藉以打開北美的市場。公司想在業務部門內，遴選幾位適當的人選，外派到海外新部門工作。

For this **seemingly enviable** opportunity, it's not only expected, but also hesitated within the mind of all employees in the sales division.

面對這看似人人稱羨的機會，但在業務部人員的心中，是有所期待，卻也有著猶豫不安。

Annie: "I heard that our company will set up a branch office in Chicago, and then select some candidates from our division to work there. It sounds like a very enviable chance."

安妮：「聽說我們公司要再美國芝加哥成立分公司，而且會從我們部門裡頭選出適當的人來，然後外派到那邊工作。這機會聽起來好令人羨慕啊！」

George: "Ya! It's great to work at such an advanced country, with attractive benefits, allowances, and good potential opportunity to be promoted. And, besides, you can also take the opportunity to **travel around**. It will be wonderful if I could be there."

喬治：「是啊！能到那麼先進的國家工作，不僅福利和津貼都很好，升遷的機會也高，還可以趁這機會到處去旅遊，要是我能去就太棒了。」

Annie: "**By the way**, Mary! You and Peter were just back from the training in Japan, and I think you have the chance to go to Chicago."

安妮：「對了，瑪莉！妳和彼得剛從日本受訓回來，應該有很大的機會被派到芝加哥去喔！」

Mary: "Robert did mention to me about this. But it's **contradictory** in my mind, not only with expectation but also disturbs. I'm worried that my language capacity is still not good enough, and also afraid of adaptability to the overseas living."

瑪莉：「這件事羅柏是有跟我提起過，但是我的心裡卻是很矛盾，既期待卻也不安。一方面擔心自己的語言能力不夠好，另一方面也害怕無法適應那邊的生活環境。」

Section 5
Special Issues in Management

George: "But, **after all**, you're still young and single, not like Peter, who has a wife and a two- year-old daughter. With the implication from family like him, there's always much **misgiving** and **trepidation**."

喬治：「但再怎麼樣，妳畢竟還年輕又是單身。不像是彼得的情況，有個老婆和一個兩歲的小女兒；像他這樣有個家庭的拖累，心中總是有著更多的顧忌和不安。」

At the same time, Robert and Peter come forward and join their conversation.

這時羅柏和彼得走了過來，也加入了他們的談話。

Robert: "The Chicago office will be established soon. It's a very rare and important for both the company and the individual employee. There are many companies, either for marketing or production, have **branched out** into overseas markets now. Therefore, the enterprises go for **internationalization** has long been a common and inevitable trend. As in our own personal aspect, we need to give ourselves more chance to learn and adapt, in order to become a truly successful international talent."

羅柏：「這次將要成立的芝加哥分公司，對我們整個公司、或是員工個人而言，都是非常難得而重要的發展契機。現在有許許多多的企業，無論是針對行銷或生產方面，都已紛紛跨足到海外市場了，所以企業邁向國際化，早已是一種普遍且必然的發展趨勢；至於在我們個人本身方面，是需要給自己更多的學習和調適，才能真正成為成功的國際人才。」

Mary: "It's great to have a trip abroad. But, on the other hand, It's entirely another story to work and live in foreign countries. The problem of language barrier alone might be a challenge to overcome."

瑪莉：「能有機會到國外玩，當然是很棒啦，但要長期在國外工作和生活，那就是完全另外一回事了。光是那語言障礙的問題，就是個有待克服的挑戰了。」

Robert: "I do trust your capacity in language. The language barrier can be overcome just after a period of time to adapt in the foreign country. No matter what, who, or where you contact with, it's totally different in a strange environment. Yet, if you have a cheerful heart, coupled with highly **compressive** strength and patience, and then it will be easier for you to **integrate into** the customs and habits there."

羅柏：「我相信依妳們的語言能力，只要在異鄉適應一段時間之後，語言障礙應該就可以克服了。當然在陌生的環境中，所接觸到的人事地物都截然不同，但最重要的，是要有一顆開朗的心，加上高昂的抗壓性和耐心，自然就更容易地融入當地的風俗民情之中。」

Meanwhile, Peter feels **cheerless**: "But my problem might be more complicated and **tricky**. At present, I cannot **lay aside** my wife and daughter at ease and then go abroad to work alone."

這時，彼得滿臉愁容的說：「但是我的問題，可能就更加棘手了。目前我實在無法安心的拋下妻女在家鄉裡，然後獨自跑到國外去工作。」

Robert: "I can understand how you feel, and this is also the common problems faced by each of **expatriates.** The company may offer regular vocation for the expatriates returning home. After you have been there for some time, and **settled down**, I'll ask the executives to plan out a comprehensive program for the family members go together with colleagues in the work area."

羅柏：「我是可以體會你現在的心情，當然這也是每個外派人員所共同面臨的問題。公司定期的會讓外派人員返鄉休假，等你去那邊一段時間，且生活和工作也較為安定下來之後，我也會請公司規劃出個通盤的計劃，思考看看將家屬也和同仁一併安置在工作地區的可行性。」

Vocabulary 字彙解析

- **seemingly** *adv.* 看似、表面上地、恍惚

〔同義字：quasi, apparently, dimly〕

He looks seemingly to be a competent and well-organized person.

Teaching is a work that seemingly laden with significance.

- **enviable** *adj.* 令人羨慕的、吸引人的

〔同義字：desirable, favored, attractive〕

He had reached an enviable reputation for academic achievement.

It is enviable to exercise some social control over technology.

- **contradictory** *adj., n.* 矛盾、對立、牴觸

〔同義字：conflictive, inimical, opposed〕

He entitles this kind of contradictories analytical.

The attitudes of both parties are contradictory.

- **misgiving** *n.* 顧忌、疑心、疑慮

〔同義字：doubt, hesitation, mistrust〕

They have misgivings about the way the campaign is being run.

Some misgiving has been cast upon the authenticity of this account.

- **trepidation** *n.* 焦慮、不安、擔心

〔同義字：anxiety, alarm, disquiet〕

He had fallen in fear and trepidation.

The drivers are threatening to quit their jobs in trepidation after an accident.

- **internationalization** *n.* 國際化、全球化

〔同義字：international, globalization〕

The internationalization raised solidarity and support for the WTO.

Don't be worry about the increasing internationalization of the world economy.

■ **compressive** *adj.* 壓縮、抗壓、壓力

〔同義字：**press, condense, squeeze**〕

The skirt can be compressive into a small bag.

Compressive data must not be changed even a single bit.

■ **cheerless** *adj.* 憂愁、冷淡、冷清

〔同義字：**gloomy, dreary, desolate**〕

I was sad and cheerless.

They all seemed cheerless rather than angry.

■ **tricky** *adj.* 狡猾、刁鑽、詭異

〔同義字：**cunning, crafty, artful**〕

The operation of applying eyeliner can be a tricky business.

There's a tricky look came into his eyes.

■ **expatriates** *v., n.* 外放，外籍人士、僑民

〔同義字：**exile, diasporas, foreign nationality**〕

They were expatriated to Siberia for political crimes.

There're further incoming expatriates to US from the Southern America.

 # Phrase in sentence 片語和句型解析

■ **travel around** 周遊、環遊、各地旅行

〔同義字：**journey, excursion, wander**〕

Their family outings will travel around many countries.

He decided to travel around the whole France.

■ **by the way** 附帶、順便、取道

〔同義字：**incidentally, apropos, via**〕

Isabel kept smiling by the way of nothing.

They came to Europe by the way of Turkey.

■ **after all** 畢竟、終究、究竟

〔同義字：**eventually, actually, in the end**〕

After all, they arrived at the hotel after midnight.

We must pay attention to what young people are doing after all.

■ **branch out** 跨足、擴充、分支

〔同義字：**expanded, step into, spread**〕

A small side road had branched out the back gardens.

They branched out the fields of business into hotel and property.

■ **integrate into** 融入、整合到、納入

〔同義字：**conform, alloy, merge**〕

The energy planning should be integrated into the whole transportation policy.

They integrate the children with special needs into ordinary schools.

■ **lay aside** 擱置、拋開、放下

〔同義字：**throw down, fling off, set aside**〕

The plans to reopen the school have been laid aside.

The visit had to be laid aside for specific reason.

■ **settle down** 定居、安置、安頓

〔同義字：**set up a home, quiet down, calm down**〕

One day I will settle down and raise a family.

I took him inside and tried to settle him down.

Section 5 Special Issues in Management

Practice in Management

Under the trend of **globalization**, either for personal or for enterprises, the culture shock and adaptation will be the unavoidable subject. When we cross over the boundary of country, it's oncoming the impact of distinct language, culture, laws and environment immediately. As for the individual, they might also encounter many psychological effects, such as strangeness, anxiety, fear, and sometimes even have a feeling that they are treated with discrimination, indifference, or rudeness. This is a challenge for each expatriate, who has to overcome the course of self-refinement.

It has been analyzed as four necessary psychological stages of those expatriates (no matter for expatriate workers or students to foreign countries):

1.Honeymoon: The newcomers will feel very fresh, exciting and interesting to everything around us, just like a tourist.

2.Painful period: Once recognized that they are not tourists, they will start to encounter so many difficulties from languages and obstacles in life, or even some setbacks. They are starting to feel anxious, suspicious, not sure whether they could carry on or not.

3.Adaptation period: They try to adjust their ideas and habits gradually overcome the frustration in language and mental disorders. Then, with the rhythm of the existing environment and life, they have successfully settled down their mind, at least.

4.Home life: When they integrate themselves into this society and country, they might become appreciated of the fun and warmth in here, more or less. They will meet some good friends here. With the process of identification and recognition, they eventually treat this strange land as their home.

 經驗與分享

面對國際化的趨勢，無論個人或企業，文化的衝擊和適應，都將是無可避免的課題；當我們跨到不同國度的領域時，立刻迎面而來的，就是截然不同的語言、文化、法令和環境的衝擊，這同時在個人的心理層面上，他們可能會面臨許許多多的陌生、不安和害怕的心理，有時也會感受到被歧視、冷漠或無禮的對待，這都是對每個旅外人的挑戰，也是自我淬煉的過程。

曾有人對那些異鄉客（無論是海外留學生或外派工作者）來到不同國度時的心理狀態，分析成了四個必經的階段：

1.蜜月期：初來乍到，對周遭所能接觸到的一切，都會感覺到很新鮮、興奮，就像觀光客一樣，對所有的人地物都很有興趣。

2.痛苦期：一旦認知到自己不是觀光客，開始發現到許多語言和生活上的困難和障礙，甚至遇到一些挫折，心中會開始不安、害怕，甚至懷疑自己能不能繼續下去。

3.適應期：跨過心理的挫敗和語言的障礙，一點一滴調適自己想法和生活的習慣，跟隨著現有生活的環境與節奏，至少讓自己的心情能安定下來。

4.居家期：將自己融入新的國度社會當中，也慢慢體會出在這邊的樂趣和溫暖，認識一些知心的當地朋友，逐步的認同過程中，也把這異鄉當成了自己的家。

Tips in Management

Multinational corporations (MNC) and Transnational corporations (TNC)

Multinational corporations (MNC) or multinational enterprises (MNE) are organizations that are owned or controlled productions of goods or services in one or more countries other than the home country. For example, when a corporation is registered in more than one country or has operations in more than one country, it may be attributed as MNC. Usually, a MNC is a large corporation which produces or sells goods or services in various countries. It can also be referred to as an international corporation, or a "transnational corporation", or perhaps best of all, as a stateless corporation.

The problem of moral and legal guiding behaviors of MNC's, given that they are effectively "stateless" actors, is one of the urgent global socioeconomic problems that emerge during the late twentieth century. MNC plays an important role in globalization. The first multinational business organization was the Knights Templar, founded in 1120. After that came the British East India Company in 1600 and then the Dutch East India Company, founded on March 20, 1602, has become the largest company in the world for nearly 200 years.

A transnational corporation (TNC) differs from a traditional MNC in that it does not identify itself with one national home. While traditional MNCs are national companies with foreign subsidiaries, TNCs spread out their operations in many countries sustaining high levels of local responsiveness. An example of a TNC is Nestlé who employs senior executives from many countries and tries to make decisions from a global perspective rather than from one centralized headquarters.

管理小偏方

多國企業與跨國企業

多國公司（MNC）或多國企業（MNE），是指在一個或多個外國地區，擁有或控制商品生產或服務的企業組織。例如，當一家公司的業務設立，登記在一個以上的其他國家、或有一個以上的其他國家營運時，即可稱之為多國公司。通常，多國公司是在不同國家從事生產或銷售商品、或提供服務的大型公司。它也可以被稱為一個國際公司，或者一個「跨國公司」，更佳的解釋，是一個無國界的公司。

多國公司所產生的道德、和法令遵循行為的問題，就因為他們是實質的「無國界」的主角，已然成為二十世紀後期，全球性社會經濟所緊迫解決的問題之一。多國公司全球化的部分具有舉足輕重的作用。歷史上第一個跨國經營的組織，是成立於1120年的聖殿騎士團。後來在1600年有了英國東印度公司；荷蘭東印度公司成立於1602年3月20日，並成為全球最大的公司近200年之久。

跨國公司（TNC）不同於傳統的多國公司，在於它本身無法識別隸屬於任一個母國。傳統的多國公司是本國母公司與國外分公司，而跨國公司則分散其經營在許多國家，並保持高度的在地應變能力。較具代表性的例子是雀巢公司；他們僱用了許多不同國家的高級管理人員，並試圖從全球的角度、而不是從一個集中的總部做出決策。

5-3 Pilferage in the Warehouse
倉庫失竊了

 ## Conversation 情境對話

4:30 A.M. Robert was **awakened** from sleep by the phone ring. After the phone, Robert rushed to the scene of the warehouse. The doors and windows of warehouse hadn't been destroyed, but the area inside near the welding materials and equipment was already a mess. Elmer and Vincent were on the way onto the warehouse, and Johnson still waited at the door.

凌晨4:30。電話鈴聲將熟睡的羅柏吵醒了，聽完電話後，羅柏匆匆忙得也趕到了倉庫現場。倉庫門窗並沒有被破壞，但裡頭的焊接材料和機具附近，已經是一片凌亂，這時艾默和文森正準備進到倉庫內，強生也正在門口。

Robert: "Johnson, you're the night guard. What's going on here?"

羅柏：「強生，你是夜班的保全，這到底怎麼回事？」

Johnson: "Near 4 am, I found out the warning light of warehouse side door had been **lit up**, as I returned to patrol guard post. Then I turned back to the warehouse again. There's nothing abnormal in the surrounding and all the doors and windows were closed, just unlocked in side door. Yet, when I approached to the warehouse, I found out that everything here was in a mess."

強生:「接近四點時,我剛巡邏回到警衛哨,才發現倉庫側門的警示燈亮了起來;我折回倉庫後,四周並沒有任何異狀,門窗也緊閉著,只是側門沒有上鎖,但一進到倉庫裡面,才發現到處亂七八糟的。」

Robert: "That's weird! Did you see any **suspicious** person in the night? Or you had fallen asleep!"

羅柏:「這就有點奇怪了!這整個晚上都沒發現到可疑的人出入嗎?還是你半夜睡著了?」

Johnson: "No, no! I did my duty **earnestly** in the whole night. How's that possible I had fell asleep? But I didn't find out any outsiders throughout the night, except for the access of few workers."

強生:「不,不!我整夜都認真的執勤,怎會睡著了呢?但整個晚上除了幾個工人進出以外,我並沒有發現到任何的外人出現啊!」

Robert: "Okay! Now you **call up** the whole night **surveillance** video, especially for the inside warehouse, and then carefully examine them all over again. Then Elmer and Vincent, you both make an **exhaustive** check to look at the actual situation of loss. But be sure to wear gloves all the time, and keep the original appearance of the site."

羅柏：「好，那你去調出整晚的監視錄影帶，尤其是倉庫的內部，再仔細的檢視一遍；另外艾默和文森，你們也到倉庫內詳細的檢查一次，看看實際損失的情況如何，但記得務必全程要帶著手套，並盡量保持現場的原貌。」

About 30 minutes later, Elmer and Vincent walk out of warehouse.

經過約三十分鐘後，艾默和文森走出了倉庫。

Vincent: "It looks messy inside, but, in fact, there's just something to be **overturned**, and no damage is done to doors and windows. However, there're several boxes of expensive welding rods and tools disappeared. Those worth a lot!"

文森：「倉庫裡看似很亂，但事實上都只是東西被翻倒而已，門窗也沒受到任何的破壞；倒是有好幾箱昂貴的焊條和焊接工具，都被搬走了，那些東西的價值可不低喔！」

Elmer: "The **thieves** might be experts in the welding-related skills. I found that they intentionally picked out some welding materials that are easy to be **sold off**. And, besides, some important **circuits** inside the new welding machine have been destroyed, too. Not everyone is capable of doing that."

艾默：「偷東西的人，應該對焊接相關的技術非常內行。我發現到他們刻意精挑一些容易出脫的焊接材料；此外，好幾部新型焊接機內部重要的迴路，都已經遭到了破壞，這一般人是辦不到的。」

Robert: "This case seems to be more complicated than I expected. The thieves should be very familiar with the internal operation and daily routine of our organization, or even are..."

羅柏：「這事情看來並沒有想像中的單純，竊賊應該很熟悉我們內部的運作和作息，甚至是⋯⋯。」

Johnson: "I have clearly checked with the video but didn't find out any stranger in the whole night. And after Vincent left this place at half past eight p.m., only Jabber and his aides got into the warehouse. But the monitor of side door didn't appear any image after midnight."

強生：「我仔細查閱過了錄影帶，整夜並沒有任何陌生人進入廠區內；而在晚上八點半文森離開之後，就只有賈霸和他的助手進入倉庫，但側門的監視器，在半夜之後就沒有影像了。」

Elmer: "Jabber? Hasn't he been absent for two or three days? Why did he suddenly appear in the warehouse last night? Could it be...? Do we need to call the police?"

艾默：「賈霸？他不是已經兩三天沒來上班了嗎？怎麼又會出現在倉庫裡？難道⋯⋯？你看我們需要報警嗎？」

Robert: "Just **hold on** before further ascertain. This is most likely a **deliberate sabotage** of our staff, and also a warning for our management. Elmer, you inform all workers for a special 'toolbox meeting' and try to clarify the problems among workers these days, and also identify if there's any other suspects to avoid further affecting."

羅柏：「在進一步查明之前，暫時先不要！這極可能是內部員工的蓄意破壞，也是我們在管理上的警訊。艾默，你去通知所有工人來參加特別的『工具箱會議』，一方面了解最近工人間發生的問題，另方面找出其他可疑的人，避免進一步影響其他人。」

Elmer: "How about jabber and those guys?"

艾默：「那關於賈霸他們呢？」

Robert: "Allen, you go to Jabber's house. Once you met him, make sure to bring him back to the company immediately. I'll wait for him at the office. But if he's not at home and doesn't come to the meeting, then we will **call for** the police. We need to find him to clarify the whole situation. This case gives us some warning both in security and personnel management. We have to be more vigilant against any possible anomalies, to take **preventive masseurs**."

羅柏：「艾倫，你先到賈霸的家找他。如果遇到了他，就立刻帶他到公司裡，我在辦公室等他；如果他不在家，也沒來參加會議，那就只好到警局報案，務必將他找出來將事情釐清。這件事也給我們一些警訊，無論在保全或人員管理方面，我們都要更加提高警覺，對任何可能的異常狀況，才能防患於未然。」

Vocabulary 字彙解析

■ **awaken** *v.* 叫醒、覺醒、開悟

〔同義詞：**arouse, comprehend, realize**〕

Anna was awakened by the telephone.

She couldn't awaken her chaos in marriage life.

■ **suspicious** *adj.* 可疑的、懷疑、多心

〔同義詞：**dubious, skeptical, oversensitive**〕

He was suspicious of her motives.

Johnson was suspicious to everyone and everything.

■ **earnestly** *adv.* 切實地、認真地

〔同義詞：**conscientiously, cordially, sincerely**〕

She earnestly believed that she was making life easier for Jack.

He'd come by the money earnestly.

■ **surveillance** *n.* 監控、監視、監督

〔同義詞：**monitor, supervise, reconnaissance**〕

He found himself put under surveillance by military.

Students were under the surveillance of the faculty member at all times.

■ **exhaustive** *adj.* 詳細的、全面的

〔同義詞：**comprehensive, full, thorough**〕

He has undergone exhaustive tests since becoming ill.

We need more exhaustive information for study.

■ **overturned** *adj.* 推翻、掀翻、翻車

〔同義詞：**upturned, overthrow, rollover**〕

The cars were overturned by the crowd.

The chemicals tank was overturned when the truck in accident.

Section 5 Special Issues in Management

■ **thief** *n.* 竊賊、盜賊、小偷

〔同義詞：robber, burglar, housebreaker〕

They had accused her of a stealing thief.

The thieves put down their footmarks in the back yard.

■ **circuit** *n.* 線路、迴路、路線

〔同義詞：line, route, loop〕

I ran a circuit of the village.

The shape of the circuit seems simple but in fact it is not.

■ **deliberate** *v., adj.* 商榷、故意的、蓄意的

〔同義詞：discuss, intentional, calculated〕

She deliberated over the menu.

I have seen your deliberate involved in numerous situations.

■ **sabotage** *v., n.* 蓄意破壞、怠工

〔同義詞：destroy, breaking, vandalism〕

They were prepared to sabotage the machine.

He called on the public to report any instances of criminal sabotage.

Phrase in sentence 片語和句型解析

▪ lit up　點燃、點亮、亮了起來

〔同義詞：**light up, ignite, beam**〕

The lamplight had lit up her pale features.

The room was lit up by a number of small lamps.

▪ call up　調用、使回憶起、打電話

〔同義詞：**induct, recall, hang**〕

Yoga stretches was used to call up compacted joints.

He could not quite call up the reason.

▪ sold off　拋售、變賣

〔同義詞：**undersell, sell-off,**〕

The bankrupt force their family assents to be further sold off.

The thief had sold off everything he got.

▪ hold on　稍等、堅持、抓住

〔同義詞：**hang on, adhere to, clasp**〕

He was held on his fork into the sausage.

She tried to hold on the breath when in danger.

▪ call for　要求、呼籲、呼喚

〔同義詞：**claim, appeal, require**〕

Three patients call for operations.

Police are calling for information about the incident.

▪ preventive masseurs　預防措施、防微杜漸

〔同義詞：**precaution**〕

The gloves are worn to take preventive masseurs for injury.

He had taken the preventive masseurs of seeking legal advice.

Section 5

Special Issues in Management

Practice in Management

Within the business group, we might sometimes encounter some situations of opposition or sabotage, such as theft, undermine, disinformation, differentiation, and so on. These cases might be because that some employees feel resentful to the supervisor, the company, or the bad treatment he suffers. Yet, in many cases, there are just some disgusting and unruly guys. Most of the time, these cases are carried out secretly in private, and not willing to show up, but occasionally under certain circumstances, these employees might gather and openly oppose. There are still few cases of damage came from the competitor, who use the way of poaching or bribing to destroy the harmony of the group.

Whenever the challenge happened, the manager should try to find out the curse decisively, and, with the support of all parties, try to remove or isolate any questionable person under a lawful and decisive way. Then the manager tried to placate all other staffs and subordinates, to recover the group as soon as possible. The manager also needs to setup some protection approaches and pay close attention in order to avoid a recurrence of expanding or resurgence.

These incidents, of course, represent some problem in management. During the time of resolution, managers need a complete discussion openly with the subordinates and the executives in such cases. All members should be fully reviewed and revised the operating system, if necessary.

∞ 經驗與分享

在企業團體當中，有時候我們可能會遇到一些反對、甚至破壞的情況，例如偷竊、暗中破壞、造謠、分化等等；這些情況，或許是一些部屬對其主管、對公司或者對於自己所受待遇的不滿，但很多時候，就是一些本身素行惡劣、難以駕馭的員工；通常，這些情況都是在私底下偷偷的進行，不會讓別人知道，但也可能某些情況下，這些員工會聚眾反對。也有些破壞的情況，是來自於同業的競爭，利用挖角、收買的方式，破壞這團團體的和諧。

面對這樣的挑戰，管理者當機立斷的就是要找出禍源，並尋求各方的支援，以合法而果決的方式，先將有問題的人員清除或隔離；隨即要透過各種方式，安撫其他的員工和部屬，讓團體的運作能盡速恢復正常，並且設定一些防範措施、隨時檢視，以免事件再度擴大、或是死灰復燃。

當然，有這類的事件發生，代表著在管理上必定出現了某些問題，因此在事件的處理過程中，管理者應與公司和部屬，開誠布公的討論整個事件的始末，無論是在制度、維安或是人員管理方面，都能做一番通盤的檢討和修正。

Section 5
Special Issues in Management

Tips in Management

Crisis management

Crisis management is a business process to resolve the criteria threatening that might damage to the organization, shareholders and the public. Crisis means the event or procedure which shutdowns the original system from continuous operation. There are three definitions of crisis: (a) the threat to organization (b) emergency (c) important events required prompted decision making. Crisis management is different from risk management. Risk management is to identify potential threats and find out the coping mechanisms. Crisis management is a response to the threat that has occurred. It involves a broader definition to identify, assess, understand and respond to the serious situation.

In the processing of crisis management, we need to determine the type of crisis. Different kind of crisis requires different management strategies. The crises can be classified as: natural disasters, technological crisis, confrontation, malicious damage, tissue malignant behavior, workplace violence, rumors, and supply by terrorism and artificial barriers. Each crisis might cover three stages:

1. The signal of impending trouble and the emergence of risk.
2. Select a strategy for market counter-attack.
3. Change the firmly implement procedure with close monitoring.

When the company has experienced a crisis, and has properly processed it, corporations will be able to learn the following aspects of leadership in crisis during the follow-up restructuring procedures.

1. Build up the trust environment.
2. Change the philosophy of enterprise.
3. Find out any obvious or hidden corporate weaknesses.

4.Smart and prompted decision making with courageous behavior.
5.Learn and share the experience from crisis.

 管理小偏方

危機管理

危機管理是一種解決對企業組織、股東和公共大眾行為有威脅的流程。而危機，是事件和程序讓原有系統無法持續營運的流程。一般來説，危機有三種定義：(a)對於組織的威脅 (b)突發事件 (c)需要短時間決策的重要事件。危機管理與風險管理不同，風險管理是發現潛在的威脅，找到應對的機制。危機管理是應對已經發生的威脅，涉及更廣泛的定義用以鑒定、評估、理解和應對嚴重的情況。

在危機管理流程中，需要確定危機的種類，不同的危機需要使用不同的危機管理策略。一般可將危機劃分：自然災害、科技危機、對抗、惡意破壞、組織惡性行為、工作地點暴力、 謠言、恐怖主義供給和人為的障礙等。一般而言，每場危機可能會經歷三個階段：

1.即將發生的麻煩和風險出現信號

2.選擇市場的逆襲策略

3.貫徹變革流程，進行監控

當經歷過了危機，並予以適當的處理之後，企業在後續重組過程中，將發現可以學習到下列方面的危機領導力：

1.建立信任環境

2.改革企業思維

3.發現明顯、隱藏的企業脆弱點

4.做出明智、快速的決定，以及有勇氣的行為

5.從危機中學習、分享經驗

5-4 Reception with Special Guest
接待貴賓

 Conversation 情境對話

David Angie, CEO of British GT Group, is about to fly from London to visit the company. He wishes to have a more concrete understanding about the company as for the preparing of potential international investment cooperation between two parties. He might be the most important visitor ever. Robert is responsible for the reception, and asked Jenny to airport for **pick-up**. Near 8 p.m., Robert finally got the phone call from Jenny.

大衛・安吉，英國GT集團的執行長，即將由倫敦飛來拜訪公司，以實地了解公司營運狀況，雙方可能進行的國際投資合作案，這是公司歷來最重要的訪客。羅伯負責全程的接待事宜，並請珍妮先行到機場接機。但到了當晚接近八點時，羅伯終於接到珍妮的電話。

Jenny: "Robert. The flight from Hong Kong had arrived for more than two hours and all passengers had left the airport hall. But we had never met Mr. Angie. What we got to do?"

珍妮：「羅柏，香港飛來的班機早已抵達二個多小時，旅客也都離開航廈了，我們卻一直都沒遇到安吉先生，這下該怎麼辦？」

Robert: "Did you ask for **broadcasting** from the airport hall, or check with the airline counter?"

羅柏：「妳有請航廈大廳廣播，或是到航空公司櫃檯查詢嗎？」

Jenny: "Of course, I did! But he doesn't seem to be on the **boarding** passenger list. I heard that the previous flight from London to Hong Kong had serious delayed due to the mechanical failure of aircraft. So I'm wondering if he missed the **connecting** flight. But the problem is, we don't know where he's now!"

珍妮：「有啊！但他似乎不在登機旅客名單內，聽説前一班倫敦到香港的班機，因飛機機件故障而延誤了很久，我擔心他因此就趕不上轉這班飛機。但問題是，我們不知到現在他在哪裡？」

Robert: "Oh, that's too bad! **No wonder** even I have been **dialing over and over**, his cell phone was always under no boot. Well! Now you go to inquire the hotels around the airport. Leave them a message to contact with us if any information of Mr. Angie's lodging."

羅柏：「這下可糟糕了！難怪我不斷播他的手機，卻都是未開機狀況。這樣吧！妳就到機場附近的飯店詢問一下，並留下訊息，若有看到安吉先生住宿下來，請他們務必跟我們連繫。」

Section 5 Special Issues in Management

Like all others, Robert was very impatient and anxious. No matter how they had tried all the possible approaches, there's just no **whereabouts** of Mr. David Angie. Till that midnight, Robert could finally relax his perturbed mind after received a phone call. In the next early morning, Robert, Jenny and the site guard Johnson appeared together in front of a suburban hotel lobby. Before long, David **happened to** oncoming.

羅柏和所有人一樣，心中像熱鍋螞蟻般的急躁和不安，即使想盡了各種辦法，卻是毫無音訊。一直到午夜時分，羅柏接過了一通電話，忐忑的心情才中於放鬆了下來。隔天清晨，羅柏、珍妮和工地警衛強生，出現在郊區一家飯店的大廳前，過沒多久，大衛正巧迎面而來。

David excited: "Is you, Johnson! I sincerely appreciated for your help last night. Otherwise, I really do not know where I'm **wandering** now."

大衛興奮的説：「強生，是你啊！昨晚真的非常謝謝你的幫忙，否則我現在還不知道要流浪到哪裡呢？」

Johnson: "You're welcome, and glad I can help. These are our manager Robert and Ms. Jenny. Come! Let's talk after we **get on** the car."

強生：「別這麼客氣，很高興我能幫上忙。這兩位是我們的羅柏經理和珍妮小姐；來，上車再聊吧！」

David: "It's really a nightmare yesterday. After the serious delay of flight in London, I really don't know how many connecting flights I had took to be here finally. And, so far, my baggages are still missing. When I walked out the airport building for cab, the driver couldn't speak any English **at all**. He does recognize the logo on your business card. That's why I came to the jobsite gate reluctantly. Fortunately, I met Johnson then."

Johnson: "When I was patrolling, I suddenly saw a foreigner came out of the taxi, without any luggage. Although I didn't know who he is, I just **went forward** to help."

大衛：「昨天真的就像經歷了一場噩夢般，倫敦那班飛機嚴重延誤之後，我也不知輾轉了幾趟飛機，才能來到這裡，但是我的行李至今卻仍不知下落。出到航廈外想叫計程車，偏偏司機又不懂英文，只認得你們名片上有個工程的標誌，勉強才來到那偏僻的工地門口；所幸遇到了強生。」

強生：「我當時正在巡邏，突然看到一個外國人走出計程車，身上沒任何行李，雖然不認識他，總想過去了解和關心一下。」

David: "Johnson's really a guy of enthusiasm. He treated me a cup of hot cocoa so I could be calmly in such a strange and helpless place, and also helped me lodging in this restaurant. He also talked something about his work last night. I could feel his sincerely and **solidarity** to his job, especially the highly expectation to the future of company. It's **touching**. He might not really know me, but that's the most realistic part. I could perceive some corporate spirit of your company."

Robert: "I'm glad to hear that, Mr. Angie. All members in my company just couldn't wait to **greet** you as our special guest. I believe that you will deeply appreciate the quality and culture of our business after your personal visitation."

David: "But, the whereabouts of my two luggages are still unknown now."

大衛：「強生真是個熱心的人，不但讓我能在陌生無助的地方，讓我能平靜的喝一杯熱可可，還幫我安置在這飯店裡安歇；昨晚他也和我聊了一些工作上的事，看他對這份工作和環境，是那麼的熱誠和向心力，尤其對公司的未來充滿著期待，很令人感動；雖然他不太認識我，但這卻是最真實的，我可以感受到一些貴公司的企業精神了。」

羅柏：「安吉先生，很高興聽到你這些話；我們公司上下，正期待著歡迎您這位貴賓呢！相信當您親自到我們公司參觀之後，更能深刻體會我們企業的素質、和經營的文化。」

大衛：「但是，我那兩大箱的行李，目前還不知去向呢？」

Jenny: "Don't worry, Mr. Angie. We had found your luggages this morning, and now they're delivered to the hotel room you're going to stay."

David: "Wow! I have to say that your staffs are not only full of passionate and solidarity, but also highly efficiency in work. I think I can't wait to cooperate with you now. Ha ha ha!"

珍妮：「別擔心，安吉先生！今天凌晨，我們已經想辦法找到您的行李了，目前正由專人送到您要下榻的飯店房間裡呢！」

大衛：「哇！沒想到你們公司的員工，不但充滿熱情和向心力，工作的效率更是迅速得無話可說；我想，我已經迫不及待，想跟你們合作了。哈哈！」

Vocabulary 字彙解析

■ **broadcasting** *n.* 廣播、播放

〔同義詞：transmission, telecast, webcast〕

The television broadcasting here offer programs in Mandarin, English, and Japanese.

He became aware of an attractive reporter on racing broadcasting.

■ **boarding** *n.* 登機、登船、寄宿

All passengers need to present the passport and boarding pass.

The illegal boarding of ships had been considered an act of war.

■ **connecting** *n.* 轉接、連結

〔同義詞：linkage, joint, connection〕

They assess the connecting between unemployment and political attitudes.

He always keeps a close connecting with the university.

■ **whereabouts** *adv., n.* 在何處、下落、行蹤

〔同義詞：track, conduct, place to go〕

Whereabouts do those strangers come from?

His whereabouts always remain secret.

■ **solidarity** *n.* 團結、互助、聲援

〔同義詞：unanimity, unity, accord〕

Those factory workers voiced solidarity with the striking students.

There is almost complete solidarity on this issue.

Phrase in sentence 片語和句型解析

■ **no wonder** 難怪、毫無疑問的

〔同義詞： **no doubt, certainly**〕

I dwelled on the tale to Steve.

She dwelled on the yard, enjoying the warm sunshine.

■ **over and over (again)** 反覆、一遍又一遍

〔同義詞： **repeatedly, alternately, frequently**〕

They have been warned over and over but with no effect

They go swimming in the lake over and over again.

■ **happen to** 剛好、碰巧

〔同義詞： **just, exactly, occur in**〕

He experienced the same thing happened to me.

The accident was happened to be at exactly 12:00 p.m.

■ **get on** 乘車、進行、生活

〔同義詞： **to sit, get along, achieve**〕

We have to get on the bus before too late.

There's less and less opportunity to get on advanced degrees.

■ **at all** 根本、簡直、絲毫

〔同義詞： **simply, stark, in the least**〕

The soldiers searched the house thoroughly but got nothing at all.

The fire destroyed none of the buildings at all.

■ **go forward** 前進、向前、前往

〔同義詞： **advance, forge, go ahead**〕

The rebels went forward to the capital during night time.

We can't go forward our investigation anymore.

Practice in Management

As for the evaluation of a company, the public community and investors are mostly focus on the figures like volume of business, profitability, and return on investment that recorded in those financial statements. Some of the larger investors might study and predict in further to the future to the potential of products and development of this company. All these are tangible factors for definite analysis. However, there're still some invisible factors, such as the solidarity and cohesion of employees, which might influence the company's overall strength. But these factors are less likely to objective assessment, or often easily to be ignored.

The impact of this invisible power will be obviously manifested when the company deals with some emergency challenges. We might be occasionally heard some real stories in our society that when one company had faced with great challenge in business, the employees were willing to sacrifice their own interests, and jointed the survival of company with even more firmly cohesion. Yet, such special and unique organizational behavior is basically brought up from the diligent cultivation of managers daily. With the positive interactive with employees daily, the sense of team identity could be cultivated gradually.

When such invisible power has been brewing constantly, the organization might gradually form a common code of conduct and identity. And then a unique corporate culture was created. Many successful and well-known international companies have their unique corporate culture and values. And the culture will be continually hesitated, follow with the growth and expansion of business. It's a very important intangible asset to all business.

 ## 經驗與分享

對於一個公司營運的評價，一般的社會大眾和投資者所最在意的，可能是其財務報表上所呈現的數字，像營業額、獲利能力、及投資回收之類的，有些較具規模投資者，可能會進一步研究和預測該公司產品與經營的未來發展潛力，這些都是有形的、或可具體分析的因素；但有一些無形的力量，例如員工的向心力、凝聚力等等，是可以左右公司的整體實力，但這些因素較不容易客觀的評估，也往往被忽略了。

這種無形力量的影響，往往在公司遇到特殊的事件、或是緊急的情況時，就會很明顯的彰顯出來；現實社會中，總會聽過一些的例子是，當公司營運碰到極大挑戰時，有些員工願意犧牲自己的利益，和公司共同度過難關，且團結的凝聚力更加堅定。這種很特殊、難得的組織行為方式，卻是要靠管理者平常用心的經營而來的，透過與員工間平日正面積極的互動中，慢慢才培養出了團隊的認同感。

當這種無形的力量不斷的醞釀著，就會逐漸形成大家共同的行為規範和認同感，因而形成了企業的文化；許多成功且知名的國際企業，都有其特有的企業文化和價值觀，隨著企業的成長和擴充，也將企業的文化不斷的傳承著，形成企業很重要的無形資產。

Section 5
Special Issues in Management

✓ Tips in Management

Corporate Culture is gradually formed in the practice of company production and management, and then to be compliance with all employees. It's the mission, vision, purpose spirit, values and philosophy with the organization characteristics, as well as the sum of the management system, employee behavior and corporate external image. Corporate culture is the soul of enterprise. The values here are not refer to a variety of business management in cultural phenomenon, but the values held by an enterprise or business employees who engaged in commodity production and operations. In the modern managerial science, the culture style was built by a series event of enterprise. Once established, this culture will become the criterion to form the internal employee behavior and relationship, and also the common values shared by all members. With the culture, all members can share the common value and congest together. It's a significant role to keep the unity and cohesiveness of the enterprise. Thus, the new managerial theory had got the extensive attention from modern enterprises.

Corporate culture is mainly composed of three levels

The first level is the corporate philosophy, which is the core of corporate culture. Corporate philosophy can also be referred to locate business development and future vision.

The second level is the company's core values. It refers to the principle of doing things clear, that is, the principle that companies treat the employees, the customers and also the work.

The third level is the corporate image and identity, which include the external image of the enterprise, a series of behavioral norms like employee uniforms and vocabulary.

管理小偏方

企業文化（**Corporate Culture**）是企業在生產經營實踐中，逐步形成的，為全體員工所認同並遵守的、帶有本組織特點的使命、願景、宗旨、精神、價值觀和經營理念，以及管理制度、員工行為方式與企業對外形象的總和。企業文化是企業的靈魂，是推動企業發展的不竭動力。它包含著非常豐富的內容，其核心是企業的精神和價值觀。這裡的價值觀不是泛指企業管理中的各種文化現象，而是企業或企業中的員工在從事商品生產與經營中所持有的價值觀念。

在現代管理學裡，這是一種企業主動通過一系列活動，來塑造而成的文化形態；一旦這種文化被建立起來後，會成為塑造內部員工行為和關係的規範，也是企業內部所有人共同遵循的價值觀，所有成員因為共享共同價值觀而聚集在一起，對維繫企業成員的統一性和團體凝聚力起很大的作用。這種新型管理理論，得到了現代企業的廣泛重視。

企業文化主要由三個層次組成：

第一層面是企業理念，它是企業文化最核心的層面，企業理念也可以被稱為企業發展的定位和未來的願景。

第二層面是企業的核心價值觀。它是指明確的做事原則，也就是企業對待員工、對待客戶、對待工作的準則。

第三層次是企業的形象與標識，其主要包括，企業對外的形象，員工工作時著裝/用語等一系列行為形象的規範。

5-5 Serious Delay in Shipping
嚴重的延滯

 ## Conversation 情境對話

Jenny received an urgent email from the southern site. It mentioned five sets of fire system that are **contracted** by the company have exceeded the delivery and installation deadline. The deadline has originally been extended for a month through coordination. However, the executives were highly unsatisfied with this and required the execution must be started within ten days. Or they will **claim** the **extension** fee daily, and may ask for huge **compensation**.

珍妮收到南方工地發來的緊急電子郵件，信中載明公司所承包的五套消防系統，早已過了交貨安裝的期限，原本協調可以展延至一個月內開始安裝，但業主高層很不滿意這次的延宕，要求必須在十天內開工，否則將逐日索賠滯延費，並不排除要求鉅額的賠償。

After reading this, Robert recognized the urgency and seriousness of the matter, and call for related staffs with information ready, to discuss the response approach together immediately.

羅柏看完此信，自然明白此事的急迫和嚴重性，立刻要相關的人準備好資料，一起討論因應辦法。

Robert: "I believe you guys had read this letter and know the urgency. Now, where's the equipment?"

羅柏：「相信各位都看到這封信了，應該知道這件事的急迫性。現在那些設備在哪裡呢？」

Queenie: "They could be still in the departure port, or just being **outset**. But the shipment took at least 20 days by ship to reach the port destination. The time is definitely too late."

昆妮：「可能還在出口港、或是剛出發。但經由船運到南方，最快也要二十天才能到達目地港，這時間上肯定來不及了。」

Robert: "But according to the schedule, shouldn't these equipments be delivered a month ago? What's the key point of these problems?"

羅柏：「但按照行程，這批設備不是在一個多月前就該交貨運送了嗎？這中間是哪個環節出了問題？」

Queenie: "The manufacturing of supplier has encountered some problems beforehand. That's why the delivery has been delayed for more than a month and just arrived to the dock last week. However, the **freighter** still couldn't depart because of terrible weather."

昆妮：「先前供應商的生產現出了些狀況，因此交貨遲了一個多月，直到上週才送到碼頭；但偏偏又遇到了天候不佳，貨輪遲遲無法出海。」

Robert: "No matter what the reason is, we got to accomplish the mission within the deadline. After all, we're the one who signs the contract with owners, and all the installations are our responsibility. I can't imagine how the owners' claims will be if the installation is not in time."

羅柏：「這件事無論造成的原因如何，我們都必須要在期限內達成任務，畢竟和業主簽約的是我們，所有安裝責任也都是我們要承擔的；我無法想像若沒按期安裝，業主對我們的索賠會是如何！」

Elmer: "But we can't install them all at the same time even all of them had arrived. According to the loading of the jobsite, the maximum numbers they can install at once are two sets of equipment. After these two equipments has been roughly positioned, then we can continue the **subsequent** installation. The **interval** takes at least one or two months."

艾默：「但即使設備都送到了，也無法全部同時安裝啊！依現場的負荷量來看，一次最多也只能安裝兩套設備，等兩套大致定位完成後，才能接續後面的安裝，這中間的間隔，至少也要一、二個月時間。」

Robert: "This case is seemingly **fraught with** difficulty. However, there's still some **margin for maneuver** if we'll calmly considerate. First of all, Jenny! You assist in Queenie to contact with supplier, ask them to prepare two sets of new equipment right away. Make sure that they deliver it through **aviation** express to the southern site within a week."

羅柏:「這事看來到處都充滿了困難,但若冷靜思考一下,這其中還是有些轉圜的空間。首先,請珍妮協助昆妮和供應商連繫,要他們立刻準備兩套新的設備,用航空快捷的方式,務必在一週內送達南方工地。」

Elmer: "In one week? We have to **hurry up** for the preparing."

艾默:「一週內送達?那要趕快準備一些安裝前的作業了。」

Robert: "Sure, You and Peter prepare to go to the south immediately. Once arrived, you report to the owners that: due to the consideration of job-site **loading** and engineering safety, we will install the first two sets within ten days. The other equipments will also be followed up subsequently. And then, help the site supervisor there for the cargo pickup and installation preparing."

羅柏:「當然,你和彼得準備一下,就立刻趕到南方的工地。到了那邊,你們先向業主報告,基於現場負荷量和工程安全的考量,我們會在十天內進行前兩套設備的安裝,其餘的設備也將在隨後陸續進行;另方面協助現場工地主任,準備提貨事宜和安裝的前置作業。」

Section 5
Special Issues in Management

Queenie: "How about those equipments with sea transportation?"

昆妮：「但那些走海運的設備怎麼辦？」

Robert: "Now you contact the shipping company to check whether the flight had departed or not. If the freighter's still parking in the **harbor**, be sure to ask the supplier to retain those two equipment, or transfer to the air freight directly."

羅柏：「現在妳先跟船運公司確認一下，那班船是否已經出發了；如果船還沒走，務必請供應商連繫船公司將兩套設備留下來，或者直接轉空運。」

Queenie: "The freighter might be departed **whenever necessary**. I'd better hurry up!"

昆妮：「我想船隨時都可能出發，我得趕緊去了解看看。」

Robert: "Anyway, Jenny. You need to **stare at** them closely for the sent out of air cargo first. Even if the freighter has departed, we still can request a refund of the extra equipments because of the delayed delivery caused by the supplier. However, we'll not start any negotiation with the supplier until the cargo had been determinately sent out."

羅柏：「無論如何，珍妮，你務必緊盯著他們空運的貨物先寄出來。如果船已經出發了，既然這是供應商延遲交貨所造成的，我們就可以要求退回多出來的兩套設備；但有關後續的協調事宜，最好等空運的貨確定寄出了之後，再開始進行。」

Vocabulary 字彙解析

- **claim** *v., n.* 要求、索賠、主張

〔同義詞：**request, claimant, proposition**〕

The court had denied their right to claim.

He claimed that he came from a wealthy, educated family.

- **extension** *n.* 延期、擴張、展延

〔同義詞：**exceeding, expansion, outspread**〕

The rapid extension of MRT system helps the development of suburban Taipei.

There's always some deadline extension for public construction.

- **compensation** *n.* 賠償〔金〕、索賠

〔同義詞：**claimant, reparation, recompense**〕

The labors are seeking compensation for injuries suffered at work.

The courts required the suspicious to make financial compensation to his victim.

- **outset** *n.* 出發、啟航、開始

〔同義詞：**departure, start, originally**〕

His outset left an enormous gap in each of their lives.

The ship departed at the outset of February.

- **freighter** *n.* 貨輪、貨船

〔同義詞：**cargo ship, watercraft, cargo vessel**〕

The bridge opens only for the certificated freighters to pass through.

There're hundreds of containers in this freighter.

- **subsequent** *adj.* 後續、隨後、連串

〔同義詞：**follow-up, thereafter, consecutive**〕

The theory was developed subsequent to the earthquake.

We had suffered by five subsequent years of serious decline.

- **interval** *n.* 間隔、區間、間隙

〔同義詞：**gap, space, interim**〕

There was an interval of many years without any meetings.

In the interval I'll just keep my fingers crossed.

- **aviation** *n.* 航空、飛行

〔同義詞：**flight, air travel, piloting**〕

There's a massive cargo aviations of food, blankets, and medical supplies coming.

Manila Int'l airport is the most crowded aviation base in the world.

- **loading** *n.* 承載、負擔、裝貨

〔同義詞：**dress, shipping, charging**〕

In addition to their own food, they must carry a loading of up to eighty pounds.

The increased heart loading was caused by a raised pressure.

- **harbor** *n.* 海港、港口、避風港

〔同義詞：**port, haven, dock**〕

Over 33 ships are waiting at Kaohsiung harbor to load and unload cargo.

This bay is a natural harbor for wildlife.

Phrase in sentence 片語和句型解析

■ contracted by　簽約、承包、合同

〔同義詞：**agreement, job, charter**〕

The project was contracted by a wide range of agencies.

The employment agreement should be contracted by both parties.

■ fraught with　充滿、充斥

〔同義詞：**full, fill with, full of**〕

Marketing any new product is fraught with danger.

The nature was fraught with evidence to support the theory.

■ margin for maneuver　轉圜空間、迴旋

〔同義詞：**room for maneuver, leeway**〕

The government still has some margin for maneuver to introduce new policy.

We do have some margin for maneuver to choice.

■ hurry up　趕快、抓緊時間

〔同義詞：**make haste, hasten, tear**〕

We'd better hurry up.

He hurried up to refute the assertion.

■ whenever necessary　隨時、必要時

〔同義詞：**at any time, when required, ever**〕

You can ask for help whenever necessary.

Whenever necessary we have to close the window.

■ stare at　盯著、呆望著、瞪著

〔同義詞：**fix one's eyes on, gaze, gape**〕

He stared at her in amazement.

He could only stare at her in astonishment.

∞ **Practice in Management**

In the key moment of emergency, pressures have always been placed on leaders. You, as a leader, will be expected to be calm and firmly eliminate all anxiety of others. Crisis is not definitely a bad one. When faced with the chaos already happening, besides the panic, you should have a positive thinking of how to be profited from the crisis. you have a chance to reclaim some of the loss, and start to repair the prior confusion.

While dealing with the crisis, Warren Buffett has some pertinent and practical advice to us: "do it right, do it quickly, with quickly withdraw, the problem been solved." Try to be calmly with the following four steps:

Step 1: Define the crisis

Crisis exists in every possible way. One of the important steps is to figure out what the immediate crisis is. Clarify two aspects of the crisis, will make people more clearly define the scope of the crisis.

Step 2: Assess the crisis

A deeper analysis in the level of the crisis that will help to decide the subsequent allocation in manpower and resources, and the priority of response. There's one simple way, which uses the affection as the horizontal axis and possibility as vertical, and counted from 1 to 4 as the degree of crisis to analysis the difference. It's the moderate risk when with high possibility but low affection, while the high risk when with low possibility but high affection. The most serious crisis is when with both high possibility and affection.

Step 3: Solve the problem

There are 4 strategies to be followed:

1. Avoid the crisis: when there's a problem from the supplier, for example, then try to look for other suppliers as a replacement to avoid the risk of budget excess.

2. Transfer the crisis: try to find other sector for bearing, when the supplier's in trouble, there may be some able to take responsibility from other channels to transfer the risk.

3. Reduce the crisis: when it's neither avoidable nor transferrable, then try to "stop the bleeding", at least not bled to death.

4. Accept the crisis: when the crisis's not so serious and all the approaches tried are useless. Then, just let it be.

Step 4: Control the crisis

The last step is watching closely the dynamic changes of the crisis, every change of minor element may need some strategy adjustment and maintain a state of alert to avoid the situation out of control.

Section 5
Special Issues in Management

經驗與分享

在緊急的關鍵時刻，大家把沈重的壓力放在領導者的身上，期待身為主管的你表現出權威而有把握的樣子，消除眾人的焦慮。危機不是百分之百的壞事，面對無法逆轉已然發生的狀況，除了恐慌的情緒之外，更進一步的正面思考方向是如何從危機中獲利，讓你有機會回收部份損失，並且開始修補之前的混亂。

對於處理危機，股神巴菲特有一番中肯且務實的建議：「做得正確、做得迅速、快速抽身、解決問題。」依循以下四個步驟沈著處理。

第一步：界定危機

危機以各種可能的方式存在，搞清楚眼前的危機是什麼，是最重要的一步。釐清危機的兩個層面，將讓人更清楚界定危機的範圍。

第二步：評量危機

進一步分析危機的層級，有助於後續人力、資源的調配，以及決定因應的先後順序。一個簡單的方式是，以影響力為橫軸，可能機率為縱軸，試著從一到四，做出危機程度的差異分析。高可能性、低影響力的危機，屬於中度危險；低可能性卻高影響力的危機，則屬於高度危險；最嚴重的，當然就是可能性與影響範圍都高的危機狀態。

第三步：解決危機

解決危機時有四種因應策略，分別是：

1. 避開危機：例如供應商出問題，那麼試著尋找其他的供應商接替，避開預算超支的風險。

2. 轉移危機：試著找出其他環節來承擔，例如出問題的供應商，可能有其他管道能夠負起責任，移轉風險。

3. 減緩危機：如果避不開危險、也沒辦法轉移，那麼就想辦法「停止出血」，至少不要失血過多而死。

4. 接受危機：如果危機所造成的影響不大，努力防堵不見得有效益時，那麼就試著承受這個小風波。

第四步：控制危機

最後一個步驟，就是持續檢視危機的動態變化，每一個要素發生改變，都可能需要重新調整策略與行動，保持戒備狀態，隨時彈性因應，避免情況失控惡化。

Section 5
Special Issues in Management

Tips in Management

Risk Management

Risk Management is a management process, which includes the definition, measurement, assessment and development in response to the risk. The aim here would be to avoid the risk, and minimized the cost and loss. Desirable risk management has been prioritized the risk in advance, the maximum loss and highest probability events can lead to first priority, and then followed by a relatively low risk events. In a practical situation, however, the risk is not consistently with the possibility; it's difficult to be in order.

Risk identification is the first step in risk management. Only with the comprehensive knowledge of the risks, we're able to predict the possible harm caused by risk, and then choose the effective way to deal with the risks. Risk prediction is estimating and measuring to risk. Risk managers use the scientific methods to analysis and research the statistics data, message and character of risk systematically, then confirm the frequency and intensity of risk and select the appropriate risk management methods to provide evidence.

The usual ways to deal with risk are:

1. Avoid the risk: negatively avoid the risk.
2. Prevent the risk: take the necessary measures to eliminate or reduce the risk of negative factors
3. Captive the risk: the enterprises take the risk by themselves.
4. Transfer the risk: transfer out before the risk happen.

管理小偏方

風險管理

風險管理(Risk Management)是一個管理過程,包括對風險的定義、測量、評估和發展因應風險的策略,其目的是將可避免的風險、成本及損失極小化。理想的風險管理,事先已排定優先次序,可以優先處理引發最大損失及發生機率最高的事件,其次再處理風險相對較低的事件。實際狀況中,因為風險與發生機率通常不一致,所以難以決定處理順序。

風險辨識是風險管理的首要步驟。只有全盤了解各種風險,才能夠預測可能造成的危害,進而選擇處理風險的有效方法。風險預測實際上就是估算、衡量風險,由風險管理人運用科學的方法,對其掌握的統計資料、風險信息及風險的性質進行系統分析和研究,進而確定各項風險的頻度和強度,為選擇適當的風險處理方法提供依據。

風險的處理常見的方法有:

1. 避免風險:消極躲避風險。
2. 預防風險:採取必要的措施,以消除或者減少風險發生的因素。
3. 自保風險:企業自己承擔風險。
4. 轉移風險:在危險發生前,將風險轉移出去。

Section 5
Special Issues in Management

好書報報

Learn Smart! 044

管理人英語 4 週養成計劃！

28 項管理精要+全面提升英語力

作　　者　黃啟銘
封面構成　高鍾琪
內頁構成　華漢電腦排版有限公司

發 行 人　周瑞德
企劃編輯　劉俞青
執行編輯　陳韋佑
校　　對　陳欣慧、饒美君
印　　製　大亞彩色印刷製版股份有限公司
初　　版　2015 年 3 月
定　　價　新台幣 360 元
出　　版　倍斯特出版事業有限公司
電　　話　(02) 2351-2007
傳　　真　(02) 2351-0887
地　　址　100 台北市中正區福州街 1 號 10 樓之 2
E - m a i l　best.books.service@gmail.com

港澳地區總經銷　泛華發行代理有限公司
地　　　　址　香港新界將軍澳工業邨駿昌街 7 號 2 樓
電　　　　話　(852) 2798-2323
傳　　　　真　(852) 2796-5471

國家圖書館出版品預行編目(CIP)資料

管理人英語 4 週養成計劃！：28 項管理精要+全面
提升英語力 / 黃啟銘著. -- 初版. -- 臺北市：
倍斯特, 2015.03
　面；　公分. -- (Learn smart! ; 44)
ISBN 978-986-90883-7-4(平裝)

1. 商業英文 2. 讀本

805.18　　　　　　　　　　104003254